W9-BFH-095

DISCARD

Cary Area Public Library
1606 Three Oaks Road
Cary, IL 60013

By Andy Mozina
Contrary Motion

STORIES
Quality Snacks
The Women Were Leaving the Men

CONTRARY MOTION

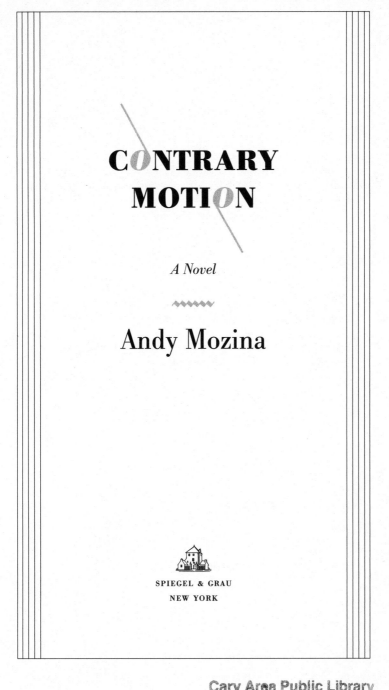

CONTRARY
MOTION

A Novel

Andy Mozina

SPIEGEL & GRAU
NEW YORK

Cary Area Public Library
1606 Three Oaks Road
Cary, IL 60013

Contrary Motion is a work of fiction. Names, characters, places, and incidents are the products of the author's imagination or are used fictitiously. Any resemblance to actual events, locales, or persons, living or dead, is entirely coincidental.

Copyright © 2016 by Andy Mozina

All rights reserved.

Published in the United States by Spiegel & Grau, an imprint of Random House, a division of Penguin Random House LLC, New York.

SPIEGEL & GRAU and the HOUSE colophon are registered trademarks of Penguin Random House LLC.

LIBRARY OF CONGRESS CATALOGING-IN-PUBLICATION DATA
Mozina, Andrew
Contrary motion / Andy Mozina.
pages ; cm
ISBN 978-0-8129-9828-3
ebook ISBN 978-0-8129-9829-0
1. Title.
PS3613.O96C66 2016
813'.6—dc23   2015014573

Printed in the United States of America on acid-free paper

spiegelandgrau.com

246897531

FIRST EDITION

Book design by Simon M. Sullivan

For Lorri and Madeleine

CONTRARY MOTION

1

~~~

I'M A MIDWESTERNER, born and raised in Milwaukee, where they manufacture beer and the heavy machinery you should not operate while drinking it. The youngest son of a civil engineer and a nurse, with four brothers and two sisters, I was a large but inert child in a subdivision crawling with three-sport athletes, Eagle Scouts, and kick-the-can prodigies. I grew to be six feet one, cube-headed, block-shouldered, an average white male with no vowels in my last name, and I fell in love with the harp, of all things. I chose a musician's life, which has proved difficult because at every moment—and for reasons I'm still trying to understand—I go about my business with a deep-seated sense that I am about to fail. This has undermined me both as a harpist and as a person, not to mention as an American.

Nevertheless, for twenty-five years now, I've dedicated myself to winning a principal harp chair in a top-drawer orchestra. I moved to Chicago, got educated, degreed, and married, had a daughter—Audrey—and finally, sixteen months ago, drove my wife, Milena, into divorcing me. Shortly thereafter, the truck that carried me away from my family and our drafty but close-to-the-lake apartment ejected me to the curb on Rockwell Street in Humboldt Park, where rents are low, car windows are occasionally smashed, and, in warm weather, young men hang out on the stoops with live snakes wrapped around their shoulders.

After regrouping for a year, I met a smart and attractive woman and, against all odds, managed to build a relationship with her that is approaching the crucial four-month mark. Cynthia is a lawyer, short and feisty, very like a gymnast, with a fantastic crinkly-eyed smile and somewhat anxious ways. To be honest, I haven't totally hit my stride with her—maybe because I want to please her so badly—but things definitely have the potential to get serious. In fifty-seven days, I have an audition with the St. Louis Symphony. Since my maniacal practice habits were part of my downfall with Milena, I'm on my guard against making the same mistakes. Luckily, Cynthia is somewhat of a work fiend herself and no stranger to crazy, high-pressure deadlines.

Topping all this, with the suddenness of an earthquake that has me feeling around for familiar objects in its aftermath, my father died three days ago. Because he had been battling a stubborn prostate cancer for about eight months, his heart attack has come as a surprise.

In the days since, his death has shifted appearances, making everything sadder, but also clearer, starker. In a sort of post-traumatic stress response to the many harp auditions I've endured over the years, I see even the smallest challenge as a make-or-break audition—from parallel parking to opening the plastic liner in a box of Cheerios without tearing a horrific gash. But this perception has never felt as all-encompassing as it does now. I get the sense that I'm auditioning not only for St. Louis, but for an entirely new life.

. . .

It's the first Wednesday of April, overcast, with the temperature struggling to do a chin-up on the fifty-degree bar. Picking up Audrey to take her to my father's wake, I get buzzed into Near North Montessori and head to the six-to-nine-year-old classroom, where the after-school program has just begun. I spy Audrey potting a tiny plant on a low table. She's got Milena's pale green eyes and straight black hair—cut short because she prefers tomboy to girlie-girl right now—but her nose and mouth echo my own. Milena and I will always be together in our daughter's face, which is comforting and also at times pretty much unbearable. As I approach, I see she's spilled a fair amount of loamy dirt on the table, on the small chair she stands in front of, and on the carpet.

"Stay *up*, you stupid plant!" she says. She presses down too hard near the base of the stem, tilting the plant toward her.

"Hey, sweetie," I say. I feel an aching desire to fold her into myself, to let her step into me, like a violin slipped into its case, to what purpose I do not know.

"This plant won't stay up."

"It's all right," I say.

She growls and pushes the orange plastic pot away from her. The stem leans over a landscape of her violent fingerprints in soil.

Aggravation sets in as I try to clean up before one of the overworked teachers gets involved: finding the broom and dustpan for the dirt Audrey spilled, dampening paper towels for the finer residue, leaving black smudges on the carpet because damp paper towels were a very bad idea, ruing the curious location of this gardening operation, getting a headrush from stooping and standing, directing Audrey's clumsy movements, encouraging her so she doesn't melt down. I can't help thinking about my

5

own father's impatience, which I see in myself, and which I'm desperately trying to escape one instant at a time.

I sign Audrey out, then we go to her locker, which contains her coat, splotchy homeward-bound artwork on crinkled paper, a clay bug with a painted body and pipe-cleaner legs—I can tell that one of its plastic bubble eyes will not adhere for long—and the stuffed unicorn she calls her "guy." There are also two black dresses on a hanger zipped into a see-through dress bag and a backpack full of clothes, courtesy of Milena.

Milena got along surprisingly well with my father, and she had sounded genuinely sad to hear about his passing. "You take care," she said earnestly when our brief conversation ended.

Milena's lack of spirituality coupled with her deep belief in shopping and dance clubs had initially made my parents wary of her. I remember being especially nervous at our rehearsal dinner. It took place at a Nob Hill restaurant in San Francisco, in a private room with sea creature murals. I was afraid my mother might slip Milena a pamphlet on the rhythm method while my father insisted on sending her the household budgeting software he'd written. It was also the first time our parents met each other, and Milena's parents were alarmingly smooth and chic. Shortly after introductions, via a segue known only to him, my father launched into a careful explanation of how the suspension cables transmitted forces on the Golden Gate Bridge. Then he excused himself to get a beer. Near the end of cocktails, Milena found him sitting alone and pulled up a chair. It wasn't long before she had him laughing and smiling his big smile, the one that showed the gold caps on his back teeth.

After we collect Audrey's things, she is quiet, pensive. We're in the hall, heading for the door, so I risk it:

"Sweetie, are you thinking about Grandpa?"

She shakes her head no.

I have no idea how to talk to a six-year-old about death. At least she has almost no sense of what's proper, so no matter what idiotic things I might say—"Grandpa's spirit is in every can of soda we drink!" or "We're all very angry at God for making it so we die"—my child probably won't think less of me.

We get to my ancient red Volvo station wagon, and I open the back door for Audrey. Two-thirds of the split-folding backseat is down to accommodate my harp, on which I'll perform at my father's funeral mass, with one-third reserved for Audrey's car seat.

Audrey's hands strangle her unicorn. Her brow clouds over. She stands stiffly, tormented by something.

"What's wrong? Time to get in the car." I know how I sound: as if I'm intent on beating rush-hour traffic and don't really care what's bothering her.

She starts to cry.

"What's wrong, sweetie?"

"I don't want to."

"Don't want to what?"

"Get in the car!"

"Why not? We'll probably go super fast."

"No!" she shrieks, and starts sobbing.

I crouch, put my hand on her back and rub around, comforting her and searching for her "off" switch—it's the same motion. Her eyes are squinted shut, her cheeks red. Tears run down her face. Her breaths come in huffs and puffs. My patience gets a miraculous second wind, and I bring her to me in a sideways hug.

"Are you upset about Grandpa, sweetie?" I ask with the side of my face against the back of her head.

"No!" she shouts. "I told you I wasn't." I can barely make out these last words, she is crying so intensely, breathing so raggedly.

I release her from the hug, set my hands on her shoulders, and try to understand where all of this is coming from, but she

7

looks down and away. "Okay," I say. "I'm sorry you're so upset, but we need to get in the car. We have to go see Grandma." The freeway is only two blocks away. I can hear traffic getting worse by the second.

"I don't want to go," she says, and she sits cross-legged on the sidewalk, hunched over, with her unicorn pulled into her lap.

"Why not?"

"I don't want to tell you."

"Come on, we have to go. You want me to pick you up and put you in the car?"

"No!" she wails. "You're making it worse!"

Up and down this street of small, closely packed houses, drapes part and stoopsitters finger their phones. I can see them working it out in their minds: *Care or abuse? Parenting or kidnapping?*

"Well, why not?" I say. "Please tell me why not, or we're just stuck here."

She stifles her tears. "What if we get in an accident?" she asks.

"Audrey, we've never been in an accident. I always drive super safe and we're going to go really slow on the freeway." Thousands more cars are filling the northbound lanes as we speak.

"I don't want to have an accident," she says piteously. "I want to stay with Mama!"

My child is not normal. My child does not approach the world in a reasonable way. And it's probably my fault. Audrey has always been on the weepy and high-strung side, but the divorce has made her needier and more babyish. Despair, disbelief, and rage boil together. I sense my eyes beginning to pinwheel.

"Sweetie, we're going to Grandpa's funeral in Milwaukee. Grandpa's *dead,* it's very serious."

"I'm not going!"

Rapidly, with my voice rising, I say, "We have to go, so let's get in the car!"

A large woman in a breast-cancer-awareness hoodie stops on the sidewalk across the street. She's staring, maybe about to say something.

"No," Audrey wails. "We're going to get in an accident!"

I'll give you an accident, I think, but I hear myself saying, "Here, let me give you a hug." I kneel next to her, envelop her in my arms.

She says, "I don't want a hug!"

I stand up, and her body rises with mine.

Audrey starts screaming—"I want Mama! I want Mama!" She kicks my thighs, landing sharp blows.

"Hey, stop kicking me!" I bellow from some place way beyond my control.

She stops everything for a moment, then reverts to crying. This is not her tantrum crying, it's her "I'm hurt" crying, her "I'm very sad" crying, and it breaks my heart but she physically gives up the fight. I strap her into her car seat and close the door.

In the driver's seat, my arms are tingling so intensely that I wonder if the steering wheel is electrified. I begin to steady myself and finally pull away from the curb. The woman in the hoodie has been watching us the whole time and has advanced into the street, her face hung up between consideration and disgust. I nearly brush her as I drive off. She touches the car by Audrey's window—like a blessing, or maybe she's affixed a tracking device.

Audrey cries. Audrey cries for a good ten minutes. Of all the sounds the world makes, two of the most distressing to me are Audrey coughing and Audrey crying. While she cries, the three lanes that will become the Edens toward Wisconsin are crawling even worse than I feared, while the three lanes that will go on to become I-90 cruise at near-freeway speed. I look longingly at those lanes, as if they represent some happy alternative life. Our dysfunctional lane accelerates and stops, accelerates and stops, and I gather myself. In a reasonable voice, I apologize for yelling at her and ask her to please stop crying.

But she doesn't.

"If you don't stop crying, Audrey, you're going to distract me so much that we *will* get in an accident." The words are out before I think of saying them.

"No!"

"Then stop it!"

She stops instantly, like she's been thrown in the water and has to quickly hold her breath. Only a few whimpers are left. She works pathetically hard to control herself.

Though I feel sick to my stomach, I can't make myself apologize again. And once she has stopped crying, I no longer understand why letting her cry wouldn't have been okay. It's suddenly obvious to me how badly I've handled this from the beginning.

Then I hear her tiniest voice: "I'm sorry," she says.

It takes everything I've got to keep from putting my head on the steering wheel and closing my eyes.

"No, sweetie," I finally manage to say, "you're all right. I'm sorry I yelled at you."

"That's okay," she says.

"You're a good kid, Audrey. I don't know if I deserve a kid as good as you."

"I'm glad we're going slow," she says, as if she hasn't heard me.

After we crawl another mile and a half, I rub my face with both hands and change the subject: "How do you like your new house?"

"Pretty good."

"Does Mama like it?"

"Yeah, she likes it, but there are too many airplanes."

"Really."

"They make a lot of noise and Mama's friend can't sleep."

Mama's friend is Steve, a securities analyst, and Milena is now living with him in a new house on the Northwest Side. They must be under some flight path to O'Hare. "Can Mama sleep through the planes?"

"I don't know, but Steve has sensitive hearing."

"Oh," I say. "Well, I'm glad you like the house." I regrip the steering wheel and relax in my seat a bit.

"Steve says Mama has to think sometimes," Audrey adds.

"Think?"

"And he called her a bad name."

"Oh, Audrey," I say, hung up between trying to soothe this turmoil and wanting to see Steve twist in the wind. "Is Steve nice to you?"

"Yeah," she says. "And he said 'sorry' to Mama."

"He needs to be nice to you guys," I say. "That's important."

2

≈≈≈

A S IT TURNS out, there *was* an accident just before the Demp-
ster exit, and once we're past the pulsing sheriffs' cars and
the huge yellow tow trucks—none of which Audrey and I
acknowledge—it's a fairly clear shot to Wisconsin. We turn into
my parents' subdivision and roll down sidewalk-free asphalt
streets that curve and loop as if the suburbs are really just the
expression of a certain taste in geometry. Everywhere you look,
there are well-tended shrubs, meticulously edged walkways,
and savvy uses of pea gravel, but the neighborhood has aged.
No kids are out playing softball in the turnabout, or tackle
football in front yards, or basketball at the hoops that are still
hung over garage doors.

When we walk into the lower level of my parents' tri-level
house, the smell is familiar—a mix of mothballs, used-
bookstore mustiness, and something I can't describe, overlaid
with the aroma of one of my mother's lasagnas, strongly sea-
soned with rosemary. She often makes two or three pans at
once, then freezes the extras for just such an emergency meal. I

can hear people talking upstairs in the kitchen. We are about forty-five minutes late and they may have started eating. In any case, our arrival is going unnoticed, and I pause on the entry mat, which is really just a matching carpet remnant, let go of my suitcase and a suit bag, slip off my coat, and wade into nostalgia and grief, but only up to my knees, as though my father won't have died until I see the faces of my family. Audrey pauses, too, setting down her stuff.

The family room is shadowed with indirect late-afternoon light. Crowding the windows, on sills and stands and hanging in baskets, are all kinds of plants—aloe, ferns, hibiscus, and other green things I don't know the names of—that my mother tends to diligently. On the wall opposite the windows are squat bookcases stacked on low, barge-like dressers. The shelves are filled with classic novels; spirituality, psychology, and philosophy paperbacks; and ten-pound art books, all of which my father snagged from the Goodwill for pennies on the dollar. Sitting on a dresser top, in front of the shelves, is an old food processor.

For as long as I can remember, but more intensively after he retired ten years ago, my father shopped thrift stores and rummage sales, scouting mainly for unloved appliances he could rehabilitate or cannibalize for parts. He couldn't resist making broken things *work,* repairing toasters and microwaves for neighbors and friends, gifting relatives with rehabbed blenders and vacuum cleaners, regardless of need. He tinkered feverishly in the basement, as if he were repairing a crucial solar panel on a dying space station. When he would emerge for meals, his fuse was as short as a firecracker's, his sense of humor sarcastic as hell. Between bouts with the appliances, he chugged hardcore books on psychology and spirituality—everything from James Hillman to the Upanishads—though he remained as tightly wound as a first-octave A string.

"Matthew, is that you?" my mother calls. She appears at the

top of the short flight of steps, wearing an apron over slacks and a blouse.

"Hi, Mom," I say. "I'm sorry," I murmur as I climb the stairs.

"I know, I know," she says. Her eyes are puddles behind her big plastic-rimmed glasses.

We hug. "Why didn't he listen?" she asks the air behind me. "Why didn't he listen?" The sentiment is bitter but she whispers it like an endearment, trying to bond with me over how frustrating he was for her.

She moves on to hug Audrey. "Hi, little honey," she says in a louder voice. "Your grandpa was a good man. Did you know that?"

Audrey nods solemnly.

We head into the kitchen, and I find that of my six siblings, only the two other out-of-towners are stopping in for dinner. Three years older than me, my brother Tim is a portfolio manager in Boston. He's been divorced for a couple of years now, never had kids. Tall and athletic-looking with a sharp crew cut, he has confessed to me that he has an uncontrollable thing for women who tend the cash registers of convenience stores and gas stations, at least one of whom broke up his marriage. He rises for a firm handshake that evolves into a back-patting hug. Emily is a high school social studies teacher in Phoenix with large, strong hands and a black belt in Kobudo. Eyes downcast, she moves in for a quick tight embrace. Her husband, Patrick, a clean-cut, blue-eyed lawyer who drafts legislation in Arizona's statehouse, and their kids, Gretchen and Otto, are also seated at the table. Patrick reaches for a handshake and gives me a tight-lipped nod.

My mother has held off dinner as long as possible, but apparently everyone was just sitting down to eat when we arrived. The visitation starts at the funeral parlor in a little over an hour and everyone still needs to get dressed.

Looking pale, shoulders slumped, Mom leads us in the standard meal blessing, everyone aware that this is Dad's job. No longer observant, I mumble along with my hands together, barely vocalizing at all, but somehow unable to avoid participation.

People start serving themselves in silence, which only brings back more strongly memories of childhood meals with all nine of us passing dishes and slurping and wiping our mouths on our sleeves and yammering and laughing. Bart, George, and Luke, my three oldest brothers, might trade baseball cards, knuckle each other in the ribs, or spoon half-chewed food from their own mouths onto each other's plates. Tim would show me below table a grasshopper he'd trapped in a perforated sandwich baggie, and I'd respond with something I'd found in the ditch, maybe a rusty bolt or a small colored stone that held no interest for him. Our sisters—Mary Ellen and Emily—had their own conversations at the other end of the table, about which I can't remember a thing. Though Dad was usually silent, stirring leftovers on his plate in appalling combinations, when he was in a good mood, he'd retell jokes he heard at work and begin laughing himself during the punch lines.

I can't remember the last time the whole family sat at this table together for supper, an arrangement gradually eroded by my brothers and sisters missing meals for practices, games, and jobs, and then moving out. It now strikes me as a moment that's lost to history.

Finally, Mom says, "Thank you for coming, everyone."

"Sure, Ma," Emily says.

I cut Audrey a small square of lasagna, praying she doesn't complain out loud.

"I warned him about the doughnuts," Mom says, as if someone has asked. "I said, 'You're eating the stress!'"

Lasagna is not one of your leaner foods, even though my mother has always made it with cottage cheese instead of ricotta. I decide against an ironic joke.

"You tried to tell him," I say.

"I just wanted him to *relax*," she says miserably.

Dad had been scheduled on Thursday for what they called cryosurgery—basically, they were going to try to kill the cancer cells in his prostate by freezing them—and he was having trouble sleeping. When I talked to him on the phone about the procedure just a week ago, he said, "It's nothing." Then he added, "This is what I get for living so long." In recent years these two statements, along with "What can you do?" were my father's triumvirate of go-to expressions.

"You did your best, Ma," Emily says.

"Thank God he had his faith back," Mom concludes, as if his legendary "crisis of faith"—when Dad stopped going to church for a few months—happened recently and not over thirty years ago.

"He did, Ma," I say.

"He put his house in order," Tim intones, with a distant look in his eyes.

I have no idea what Tim means by that.

My father had his heart attack while listening to one of the meditation CDs my mother had been begging him to try. When my mother called me with the news, she said, "He was spiting me!"

This seems entirely possible.

Now the conversation stumbles, collapses, struggles to stand—like a drunk in a strange alley. We try to catch up with each other. Tim admits sheepishly that his fund is doing very well and the brokerage as a whole is doing even better. Mom is officially a self-sacrificing, blessed-are-the-poor sort of person, but it's always been plain that she loves it when her kids thrive financially. Tim's comment might seem a little selfish at a time like this, but it's more likely to cheer her up than saying something about Dad.

"How's your business, Matthew?" Mom asks politely, though

she'd just as soon see me pack in the harp and get a real job, one with which I could keep a wife and stabilize a family.

"Never better," I say, which isn't saying much.

I teach a handful of students and play weddings, brunches, and parties in Gold Coast high-rises, plus the occasional orchestra concert. Milena went fifty-fifty in the divorce, but I am slowly burning through my portion of our meager savings.

"Never better," she repeats, almost musing. "That's nice," she decides, as if my harp career and my father's death are somehow parallel lines coming together at the vanishing point of civilization. In fact, my father had encouraged my music in his way, keeping me oversupplied with electronic metronomes. "Is Cynthia coming up?"

"I don't think so."

"Oh."

"Mom, she hasn't met any of you and she's busy," I say a touch too sharply.

"Just asking, honey," she says calmly.

"I know. Sorry," I mutter in a frequency only a dog might hear. I blush violently at the memory of my phone call to Cynthia. "I'd like to have you with me," I had said, "but I know you're buried in filing deadlines right now."

"Whatever you need," Cynthia had replied.

Now Audrey works at her lasagna with her fork, trying to separate the layers. If she doesn't like what she's been served, she often performs a sort of on-the-plate predigestion that involves breaking apart the food and spreading it around without actually taking a bite.

As Tim offers my mother help getting her financial affairs in order, I whisper to Audrey, "It's a lot like spaghetti, sweetie." Emily's ridiculously well-behaved preteens are chewing with their mouths closed, elbows off the table.

Audrey whines in a muted way and paradoxically the memory of our meltdown in the car helps me keep a tenuous grip now. I offer her the basket of bread and she takes a piece and begins munching.

"I shouldn't have said *a word* about the doughnuts," Mom suddenly throws in, rapping the knuckles of her tiny fist on her placemat. "He'd still be here!"

At the wake, my family forms a long receiving line, a bucket brigade of grief, passing mourners toward my father's casket. The queue stretches out the door of the capacious viewing room, which seems to energize my mother, who asks about the people paying respects as much as she accepts condolences.

Afterwards, Tim heads out, ostensibly to return to his hotel room but more likely for a mini-mart tour to indulge his romantic compulsions, while Emily and her family retire to two of the upstairs bedrooms at my mother's house, where Audrey and I are also staying. As everyone else sleeps, I wander the house like a squirrel: moving abruptly to look at a picture on the wall, nibbling on some food, pausing, stepping up to a window, scratching my face with two hands, rising on my toes, listening.

Eventually, because I can't help myself, I approach the converted bedroom where my father died. Someone has pulled the door shut, but I turn the knob and the hollow brown wood door swings open to reveal a sewing table and a very old exercise bike. The post lamp on the front lawn casts upslanting light through the window, like a rising sun, spraying the tops of a few bookcases. The house is so quiet I can hear the dull roar of trucks and cars on I-94, which runs behind the houses across the street, the suburban version of oceanside surf. Across the room, green LED letters on the Goodwill stereo indicate that the CD player is engaged and disc one is still cued up.

I turn on the lamp by the reading chair. On the floor at my feet is the blue exercise mat on which my father had his heart attack. Beneath this is a shag carpet in shades of green. These may have been the last square yards of sincere shag installed in the United States.

At dinner, my mother had gone on to reveal that my father had brought home doughnuts again on his final day. They had stopped for skim milk and ground turkey and bananas at Jewel after church, but with these cheap and healthy items acquired, my father had directed the cart toward the bakery. She had dutifully stood by him, protesting only in a restrained way while he ordered his half-dozen Boston creams. But when they were home and Dad had eaten one and then started on a second, things had flared up, though she could not bear to tell us what had been said. Whatever it was, it made Dad smash the remainder of that doughnut plus the box with the four other offending pastries into the trash can, an act which took the argument to a whole new level.

Yet by the end of the yelling my father had somehow agreed to try meditation instead of doughnuts to manage his fears about the upcoming cancer-on-ice procedure. For all of his anger, the man was never beyond giving in. But there are sacrifices that heal and sacrifices that are more like suicide bombings, designed to hurl shrapnel at loved ones. And it was probably the resentment and anger buried in this agreement that made him try meditating *immediately,* while he was still riled up. My mother, in her busybody way, was curious about whether he had "a nice meditation," so after she heard through the door that the voice on the CD had stopped, she knocked, entered, and found him—right at my feet.

I will not lie on the exercise mat of death, but I can't stop myself from reaching over and pressing Play. A sensitive male voice comes on, soothing but too loud: "Welcome to Part 1 of the stress reduction and relaxation pro—" I turn down the volume, close the door, and turn off the light for good measure.

I settle into the reading chair, and the voice goes on to assure me, as he did my father, "You are assuming an active and powerful role in improving your health." He invites me to think of this meditation as "a nourishing time, a time you deserve to give yourself some positive energy and attention." But even these words could have been an affront to my father because they imply *you need help*.

"In doing work of this kind," the voice continues, "it's important to remember not to *try too hard* to relax. This will just create tension." There: a note of accusation, of judgment. But then the voice rights itself and begins to narrate a meditation exercise. He asks my father to breathe with his toes. Then the bottoms of his feet. The tops of his feet. His ankles.

When he gets all the way up to the thighs, an eerie wind stirs in my head, maybe a ghostly aftershock of my father's passing in this very place, listening to these very words: it suddenly seems clear that by this moment in the CD my father was already gone. He must have known that he *was* trying too hard to relax, that he would always try too hard—even after the voice had warned him not to!—and this in turn would have produced *more tension,* creating an infinitely reinforcing stress loop, until my father had his final paroxysm.

I think I should cry now, and my throat muscles tighten, and I have a strange facial event during which I seem to chew the air, but then the feeling rumbles away like distant dry thunder.

I wish I could sell this version of events to my mother, to convince her that he died battling his demons, not her, but my intuitions rarely persuade others, and I'm reluctant to trespass on her grief. People's emotions are just a series of flooded streets crisscrossed with downed power lines, and I try not to walk there. He was my father, but he was her husband, and she will want to own why he died as much as she wants to preside over the lives of her children.

I sit in the dark for another few minutes, listening to the calm instructions, wondering which of these words were actually the last my father registered. Then I imagine I hear my mother's slippers whispering toward me across the shag. I stop the CD, quickly leave the room, and close the door before she can find me here.

At the funeral mass, I play crushingly sad tunes at prelude time: "Clair de lune," *Gymnopédie* no. 1, "Moonlight Sonata." I should be missing notes through my tears, buzzing strings, eventually tipping over the harp and running from the room with my hands over my face. But no. Like an anorexic who brings rich desserts to the picnic and smiles politely while others foolishly indulge themselves, I play with what feels like an expression of bland concentration, laying it on thick as scattered weeping breaks out in the congregation. Audrey stands in the third row of my siblings and their families. Whenever I catch a glimpse of her, she is looking down but I can't tell if she is moved or bored.

After the mass, there's a buffet lunch in the church basement. I slop some baked beans, potato chips, carrots, and a ham sandwich on my plate and sit on the periphery of my siblings and their spouses, not saying much. My brothers talk about home repair, and my sisters talk about each other's kids. The only apartment dweller in the family, I express sincere amazement at the bathrooms remodeled and the drainage tiles laid. Audrey spends little time eating, and I let her hang out with a handful of cousins who eventually disappear, probably to run the halls of the parish school upstairs. Halfway through my chow, I dump my paper plate in a big trash barrel. Out in the corridor, I run into my brother George, who's about six years older than me, exiting a restroom, self-consciously running a hand over his cue-ball head.

In February, George finished nine months in Felmers Chaney Correctional Center, a minimum-security prison in Milwaukee, for insider trading in the shares of Joy Global, the company where he worked designing electric mining shovels. To make a new start and achieve "total transparency," he shaved off both his beard and his full head of hair.

"Hey, George," I say. "How's it going?"

"Could be worse," he says. "I've got a lead on a job at Briggs and Stratton."

"That's awesome."

"I've learned my lesson, man," he says. "Total transparency from now on."

"Right on," I say. "Nothing to hide."

"Not anymore," he says. "Not like our goddamn family."

"Really."

"Really. Look at the man who just died, our dear old dad. All the secrets."

"Well, they must be pretty well kept, because—"

"The hospitalization, man. The nuthouse."

For a second, I wonder if he's referring to his own incarceration in Felmers. "For Dad?"

"Yes." He nods emphatically. "Yes. Absolutely."

"I don't remember anything like that."

"You were just a little shaver. Actually, it was right after you started playing the piano and Mom thought you were a genius. Anyway. Ancient history, well suppressed by Mom. Don't bring it up with her. She'll freak. The secrets must be maintained or the fragile people crumble."

"Well, what happened?"

"Dad had some kind of nervous breakdown. Locked ward, suicide watch, the whole nine yards. 'Crisis of faith' is Mom's cover story. Was on serious meds for the rest of his life, I'm pretty sure."

"He tried to kill himself?"

"Who knows? That's my point."

I don't know how to respond, so I run my right hand up and

down the inside edge of my open suit jacket as if I'm playing a glissando.

"Look, I'm sorry, brother," George adds. "This is the wrong time. *I chose the wrong time.*" But he says this last with a pinch of irony. "Now is the time to grieve."

He pats me twice, heavily, on my shoulder.

"Our patriarch is dead," he says soberly. "Long live Mom."

3

~~~

Back in Chicago on Saturday, I drop Audrey at Milena's house and hurry home to my Humboldt Park apartment to tidy up for Cynthia, who is stopping by after a typical weekend day at the office.

I scoop up some stuffed animals and Polly Pocket pieces and dump them in Audrey's big plastic toy box. I gather up loose sheets of paper on which she and her best friend, Natalie, have drawn their own board games using the Candy Land model, with places like "The Skunk Pach," "The Secret Jayl," and "Dragin Montin," and I set them on top of the box. I make one pile out of the scattered newspapers, filled with dread-inducing stories about the "surge" in Iraq, and another pile of musical scores. I bag up seven empty Mountain Dew cans, revealing still more square inches of my carpet, which is the dark gray of certain bleach-resistant strains of mold. Around Audrey's bed, I find several balls of her munchkin socks and a Dora the Explorer nightgown with what looks to be an ice cream stain on it. I throw all that into the laundry hamper.

From under a thin layer of fresh junk mail on the dining room table, I uncover the letter from the St. Louis Symphony, with its finely embossed letterhead:

Dear Matthew Grzbc,
   I am pleased to inform you that the Committee has approved your application. You are hereby invited to audition for the Orchestra's Principal Harp Chair. Please prepare the enclosed repertoire.

I tack the letter and the repertoire list to the corkboard above the desk in my bedroom, next to pictures of Cynthia: mugging wide-eyed excitement at our table before a Second City show; wrapped in a navy peacoat with a raspberry ski hat featuring a big pom, set to throw a snowball at the picture taker (me). In my favorite, she's wearing a light blue top and blue dangly earrings, looking right into the camera, tilting her head to the side, her hair swept back behind one ear and straight down on the other side. Her expression is open, eyes pleased, with an undoubtedly natural smile. It's an expression I haven't seen so much from her lately.

We met on the thirty-third floor of the IBM building, where I was playing solo at her firm's holiday party. She requested *any* song by Tony Bennett, which made us laugh, and joked about my upcoming set at Hydrate, a well-known gay bar. When I told her I'd never been to Hydrate, she quickly said, "I didn't mean to stereotype you!" I wasn't bothered or surprised, since almost every other American harpist I know is either a woman or a gay man, and soon we were exchanging numbers.

On our first date we went to the Art Institute. It was on a Thursday evening and the museum was free for locals, which may have been Cynthia's first nod at my relative poverty. She has her BA in art history and answered my questions with joy, confidence, and, sometimes "no idea!" When a picture excited her, she bounced on her toes and leaned into me, which I found extremely affirming. In front of Picasso's *Crazy Woman with Cats,* she said dryly, "Ah, that's me," and then laughed.

Afterwards I suggested we go across the street to check out Orchestra Hall.

"I'll show you mine and you show me yours," Cynthia said with a smile.

Her apparent penchant for awkward sexual innuendo relaxed me by seeming to preempt any awkwardness of my own. But what really lifted the moment was that we both understood what she meant and were proud of the interests we were bringing to each other.

Then when we reached the entrance, the gold handle on one of the front doors wouldn't give.

"Orchestra Hall!" I said loudly, with a flourish of my hand. "They keep it locked when not in use."

Still, we had enough momentum to make it through dinner at a steak house on Jackson. Things were going so well, I had to fight the impulse to flee before something went horribly wrong.

Pushing our luck, we went for a nightcap at a State Street dive frequented by Chicago Symphony players. We became drunk and swapped fragmented personal histories. Cynthia described her difficult decision to give up art history grad school for a more practical legal career, and I commiserated from the starving-musician perspective. Then about fifteen feet from our booth, a fight broke out between a woman and one of the two men with whom she was standing at the bar. Her hands flew at this guy's face and they tussled and slapped and grabbed each other until she pulled him onto the floor. The other man had to break them up.

I was unsettled, but Cynthia took it in stride. After the troubled trio left, she pounded a fist on the tabletop and said, "We won't have full equality until men and women engage in bar fights at the same rate!"

At the end of the night, I kissed her cheek with aplomb. Not perfect by any means, but given that Milena and I met in college and didn't really "date," it's the greatest pure date I have ever been on.

Now, before I can finish tidying up, there's a rapping at my door. She's here. Cynthia.

I let her in, a big smile on my face.

"Cynthia," I say. "It's you!"

"Hey," she says, a bit subdued. Her eyes are tired and slip quickly from mine. She's wearing jeans and a turtleneck sweater; her shoulder-length hair is pulled back into a short ponytail. She hugs me. "How are you?" she says.

"Good, good," I say.

She pulls out of our embrace.

This is the first time I've seen her since my father died, and I realize how odd my cheeriness must sound. I'm taken aback myself by how thoroughly my father's death was out of my mind the moment I opened the door. My desire to please her has pushed away everything else.

She walks toward the harp and absently touches the column.

"I'm okay," I add. "Okay as can be expected. How was work?"

She gives me a searching glance. "Oh, you know," she says. "Hey, can I use your bathroom?"

I bow stiffly and extend a welcoming hand.

"Thanks, sailor," she says.

Parsing Cynthia's moods is something I still don't have the hang of. "Sailor" is actually a curious remnant of our first date. The fight we witnessed morphed surprisingly in our couple lore until Cynthia started referring to my propensity for drunken brawls while on shore leave. This was soon followed by the occasional "Hey there, sailor" before she moved in for a kiss. I read on the Internet that couples with pet names for each other have stronger relationships, so overall I take it as affectionate, though it doesn't sound especially so today.

Propped against the wall next to the harp is a large square mirror, five feet tall, which I use with my students to work on hand position. Looking through the harp, into the mirror, I see myself in jeans and a black T-shirt. My neck and shoulders are tense like I'm trying to balance an egg on my cube-shaped head. My expression suggests I am a worried robot.

I turn away and discover Audrey's plastic, eight-seater Barbie "adventure van," stuffed with a few plastic mermaids in sea-shell brassieres, emerging from beneath the coffee table. The mermaids are built on a larger scale and protrude out of the van's sunroof. I wonder if Cynthia has already noticed the plastic van and if my putting it away now will read as unremarkable or as fussy. Actually, Cynthia doesn't seem to care how clean things are, has never commented on my sketchy neighborhood, and is apparently unfazed by the existence of my daughter, yet when her mood slips I sometimes start to wonder what she's not saying. Is she offended that I didn't invite her to the funeral?

Now she walks out of the bathroom and, on her way to the kitchen, she takes in the fact that I'm still standing exactly where she left me. I hear her opening cupboard doors and know she'll have to drink from my last clean glass—the "Call Before You Dig" hotline coffee mug I picked up at the Salvation Army on Milwaukee Avenue. She runs tap water into it and, still drinking, wanders into the dining room. Then she sets the mug on the Formica-topped table, and assesses me as the man who is still where he was.

"You are a strange person, Matt," she says, not unkindly.

"And you're beautiful," I say.

"No, I'm not."

"Oh, yes, you are."

"Are you hungry?" she says.

"For what?"

"*Food*. Do they have such a thing on your planet?"

"I don't know. It's after five, isn't it?"

"Let's go to Arturo's," she says. "I feel like I haven't eaten for days."

"All right, sure."

She's definitely not happy. Maybe she wants to break up with me, but she can't right now because my father just died.

I put on my brown hoodie, and we hop in Cynthia's green Mini Cooper and tool over to Arturo's, a Mexican diner, and get an imitation-wood booth by a window with a tiny cactus on the sill. Behind the long counter, an impassive man with a shiny face tongs up the meat that's sizzling on a huge griddle. We're the only gringos present. I bobble my head inanely for a few measures to the Mexican Top 40 playing on the jukebox. Something about *mujeres encantadas* and *no puedo nada*. A dark-haired waitress takes our orders—a relationship-death burrito for me, a get-me-away-from-this-guy *torta milanesa* for Cynthia.

Cynthia's been quiet since we left the apartment. So after the waitress puts a sangria in front of each of us, I decide to put us out of our misery. "What's up?" I ask. "You seem worried about something."

She sips her drink, sets it down, and smears the condensation on the glass with her forefinger. Without looking up at me, she says, "Work is bad."

"Busy?"

"You know the main partner in my group—Dan Whitaker?"

"The guy who says, 'It's not about the lawyer, it's about the client'?"

She snorts a rueful laugh and rubs the center of her forehead. "Yeah." She pulls a napkin out of the dispenser and starts folding it like she's making a paper football. Without looking up, she says, "He made a pass at me."

"Really?" I say.

"Tuesday night he came by my office, late." She folds the napkin, turns it, folds. "Nine o'clock. Pushes my door closed.

Tells me what a great job I'm doing. I thank him for being supportive, blah, blah." Her voice is steady but strained. She finishes what does turn out to be a napkin football and wedges it under her drink. Big exhale. Her eyes look up but seem to bounce off my head like I'm wearing a space helmet.

"He did some stuff," she finally goes on. "Kissed me, grabbed my breasts like a twelve-year-old. It was so *stupid*. I told him to get away. I tried to get out of my chair, but he was pinning the armrests to my desk."

"Scum," I say.

"I finally shoved his head away from me. He said he was sorry. Can you believe that?" She laughs in disgust. She removes her napkin football, lifts her glass, then puts it down without drinking. She rotates her glass with her hands.

"The prick," I say. "I'll annihilate him. Where does he even fucking live? Does he even have a house? I'll go there and fucking—"

"I *hate* being small," Cynthia says, ignoring my nutty outburst. She sets her mouth grimly, on her own track of thought.

"Cynthia, I'm really sorry," I say. "This is horrible. Are you going to press charges?"

"In a perfect world, I would do nothing but press charges." This apparently allows her to finally look me in the eye. "But I'm coming up for partner in the fall, and guess who writes my main review?"

"So then don't you *have* to say something?"

"I don't know yet. There's a compliance committee in the firm that's supposed to handle harassment things confidentially, but it's no panacea. I've got to figure out what to do."

She puts her head in her hands. She holds tensely still for seconds, then she lifts her face again.

"I just wanted you to know," she says, "so it's not another thing coming between us, okay?"

"Sure," I say.

"I'm done talking about it now."

"Okay."

"Thanks, sailor," she says, and lets herself sip sangria.

I look down at my menu and pretend to consider it. I'd love to noodle out exactly what she needs right now, but I'm consumed by decoding her reference to *another* thing coming between us.

One possible referent is our less-than-outstanding sex life. For most of my romantic life, I've been a bit self-conscious in the sack, a bad recipe as everyone knows, and these days, I have to admit, I can barely get hard. The first few times with Cynthia actually weren't bad. I was so deprived and Cynthia was so attractive that I was pretty close to normal, though sometimes Cynthia got chafed and red. After that she started bringing fruit-flavored lubricants into our bedroom and I started reverting to form. And though now my wambly erections take a noticeable amount of work, neither of us has said anything about them. We just put our heads down and keep going at it.

I realize that we've already ordered, so I put my menu behind the napkin dispenser.

"All right," I say. "Okay, then. Well, speaking of stuff not coming between us, I've got the St. Louis repertoire, so I might have to—"

"That's all right," she says, waving a hand. "I'm swamped with depositions."

Our food shows up and she dives in, which I trust is a good sign.

"But, yeah," I say. "I was going to say, I still want to make time for you."

"You don't have to *make time* for me," she says sharply, despite a mouthful of food. "Sorry—that came out wrong."

I laugh. "No, what I said was totally wrong—I mean, I meant it, but it was one of those dumb things to say, wasn't it? Like saying 'I'll be there for you.'"

"What's wrong with saying 'I'll be there for you'?"

"Nothing. I mean there's nothing wrong with *meaning* it."

She sets down her utensils and splays her fingers: "Look, I know how important your music is. I'm rooting for you. You deserve something like this." Her voice is charged with tension.

"Well, thanks, but I feel weird about wanting St. Louis in the first place."

"You don't have to say that."

As much as I want to win the audition, I periodically glimpse the havoc this would wreak on my relationships. We've talked about a firm in St. Louis that does her sort of work, and she seemed game though not thrilled at the prospect. And then there's moving away from Audrey, a possibility I repress more thoroughly. I fork up refried beans. They're like pureed lead.

"We both have to do what we have to do," she adds, "and it's going to be fucking okay."

4

~~~

Trying to pose as Cynthia's knight and protector, I get the tab, though I'm making a direct withdrawal from my grocery money.

We pull up to my two-flat apartment building, which displays a blue "For Peace" sign in the tiny front yard, duly tagged by the Latin Kings, possibly not as a way of endorsing peace in Iraq and Afghanistan. My landlord, T.R., lives upstairs and is a tireless (and fearless) political yard-sign poster. Just over a month ago, Greg Harris, our state representative and a friend of T.R.'s, introduced a bill that would recognize same-sex marriage in Illinois. The sign promoting that bill has been stolen twice and is currently unreplaced.

T.R. sits outside in a camp chair on the small porch at the top of a wooden staircase that runs up the front of the house to his second-floor apartment. He's a retired commodities broker whose "buy low, sell high" ethos has put him on gentrification's bleeding edge. Next to him is a small table strewn with dishes.

Charles, his much younger friend, stands at the railing with his shoulders slumped and his arms crossed, smoking a cigarette.

In a theatrical voice, Cynthia calls, "Hi, T.R.! Is that you, Charles?" Her good cheer seems to have come from nowhere, and I admire her ability to conjure it.

"Hello," T.R. drawls in his soft, hoarse, old guy's voice, like Winnie the Pooh gone to seed.

Cynthia grins and doesn't seem to notice that Charles hasn't responded. His tag for me is "the breeder below." He might resent that I've taken his place in T.R.'s two-flat, the consequence of a temporary falling-out he had with T.R. They may have been lovers at one point, and could still be lovers, but T.R. seems more of a father figure to Charles, who now has his own apartment a few blocks away.

T.R. often lets young men crash for days or weeks in the house's attic—Charles calls this place "T.R.'s Home for Wayward Boys." Lately, it's been Max, a tall, thin aspiring actor with short spiked blond hair. Before Max it was Seth, a UIC student whose parents had cut him off, and before Seth it was Rich. One night Rich wandered down to my apartment, told me he was unsure about whether he should have been embodied in this world, asked for a shot of hard liquor "for the road," and went back upstairs. T.R. always asks me if it's okay when he brings in someone new, and I always say that it's his house. Cynthia thinks I'm naïve for imagining T.R.'s motives are paternal rather than sexual, though of course we could both be right. I was just happy to find a cheap place with a harp-tolerant landlord, plus no stairs between my back door and the alley, a rare harp-moving convenience.

"What's for dinner?" Cynthia calls up to T.R.

"Thai, my dear," T.R. responds.

"Don't get your hopes up," Charles says. "He's eaten it all."

"Hey, I got the list for St. Louis," I say. "I'm going all out until the end of May, so let me know if it gets to be too much."

"Are you going to play tonight?" T.R. asks without excitement. "Charles and I would love to hear something."

"No, we wouldn't," Charles says. But he does laugh afterwards.

"Sounds like someone has had too much coconut milk," Cynthia says.

Seeing how happy she is to talk to Charles and T.R., I look at her as if to ask, *Should we invite them down for a drink?*

"Don't invite us down for a drink," Charles says, as he ashes over the railing. He's looking over the tops of the two-flats across the street.

Cynthia laughs. "You're the best, Charles," she says, and she takes my hand and squeezes it as we head into my apartment.

Just inside the door, she turns to me, and we hug. We hold each other. Seconds go by. Each second represents a degree of emotional intensity and support. *She's perfect,* I say to myself. *She's perfect.* And she is.

With her cheek against my chest, she says, "Thanks for what you said in the restaurant—about that fucking asshole." Her words are harsh but her tone is quiet, almost tearful: "I get so mad that I'm on edge with everyone, even sweet guys like you."

I kiss the top of her head. I often look down at her like this from my height, and it occurs to me that the top of her head has almost become her second face to me, the part in her hair a crooked smile, and it makes me realize that maybe I, too, have a second face of some kind, to someone else.

She finally looks up at me, with caring and closeness in her eyes, and I smile, so grateful to be brought back toward her, so eager to be as positive as possible about us, united against

Whitaker, and when she smiles, too, I kiss her on the lips. She kisses back.

And I think, *Good. But won't it be horrible if we keep going and I can't get hard?*

Then it's like when the weight of the roller coaster tips downward: our kissing and caressing and undressing gather speed.

As she unzips my jeans, I brace for her touch, for her seeing me. As I've been doing more and more lately at these critical moments, I imagine, of all people, my ex-wife, though not as I've come to know her, but as I first experienced her in undergrad, when we'd go jogging together around Northwestern's Lakefill. Milena'd wear silky running shorts without underwear and midriff-baring T-shirts. Reveling in the anticipation that built during our cool-down stretches in the living room of her apartment on Maple Street was the happiest I've ever been. But today using her memory to build excitement strikes me as more wrong than usual.

Cynthia pulls my pants to my knees to reveal my ambivalent unit. My face heats up like a radiator.

She expertly addresses my lame erection. A silence descends. We continue to touch and finish undressing. Then it's as if she's giving me a fireman's carry out of a burning building: there's a sense of mortal danger that leads to quick but controlled acts of lifting, positioning, moving. I break a hot sweat, as if I'm in that burning building; my breaths get short. I'm suddenly aware that this scene is also playing itself out in the mirror on the other side of the harp, then I remember my father expressing his judgment on his prostate cancer: "It's nothing." I am on the futon couch poised over her body—which is heartbreakingly attractive and good, though it seems odd that it's *hers* or that it's *her*—when we both realize that her rescue attempt has been unsuccessful.

This is different from the other times. No hope. None. Game over.

When the going gets tough, the tough give head, I think, kissing my way down her torso. It occurs to me that Whitaker, the perv, was probably hard as a coat hook when he was molesting her.

She grabs my ears and pulls me up to her.

"You don't have to," she says.

"I want to."

"We should talk."

"About what?"

"About what's going on."

Still hovering over her, propped up on my arms, I don't say anything. We're both naked, and this is suddenly an excruciating condition. I squeeze myself next to her on the couch, lying on my side to give my arms a rest.

"Look, I really like you, Matt. I do. And I shouldn't even say anything right now, I know." She moves toward the edge of the couch and turns to face me. The endless need to arrange our bodies with respect to each other, on this couch, in this room, in all spaces, for all time, suddenly seems like a death sentence. "It's just that you've been so on your guard—or just kind of weird."

"Really?"

"Yeah. About sex, but also in general. And I don't want you to feel uncomfortable with me. And I guess I don't know how to make you feel more comfortable."

"I feel comfortable with you," I say, though I know that in certain important ways this isn't true. The fact that she's not just dismissing this particular failure as a consequence of my grief is a shattering reminder of just how lame I've been the last few times. "I'll get over this," I assert, but in my chest I sense that something irrevocable has happened. "It'll just go away by itself."

"By *itself*?" she asks, a little too loudly. Then she lets her shoulders sag. "Oh, Matt, I shouldn't have said anything.

Everything's been a bit too much lately. I just need you to—"
She stops herself.

"What?"

"Just be okay. I just want you to feel okay."

She stands and follows the trail of her clothing back to where we began what feels like the final sex act of my life. I find her so attractive—something in my engine is revving—but I no longer have a transmission to gear my desire into action. I don't understand why I can't just transmit my feelings to her directly, without having to do or say anything.

"I really care for you," I say.

"Oh, I know," she says quietly. She straightens up, holding her clothes against her bare chest, and we make eye contact. She closes her eyes and smiles wanly, as if she's remembering some catastrophe that turned funny over time. "It's fine," she adds, from another vocal register, something, unfortunately, in the resigned-mother range.

Once we're both dressed, she looks through my apartment window toward her car. I brace myself again.

"I've got something to draft," she finally says.

"Why don't you work on it here?" I say. "I can do some practicing."

She nods, though her eyes are still focused outside.

Then she leaves the apartment to get her laptop from her car, and I walk into the kitchen so I won't be standing in the same spot if and when she returns. I rest my head against a cupboard, telepathically begging her not to drive away. A breeze of dizziness blows through my head.

Finally, I hear the front doorknob turn. I spring into the dining room and quickly clear a place for her at the table, smiling and gesturing like a QVC product model. She avoids looking at me as she sets up.

Then I go to the harp. I pick up a tuning fork, rap it against the wooden underside of my seat, place the base of the vibrating fork on the soundboard, and a resonating A blooms forth. The robot in me knows there's something to be said for such mechanical responsiveness.

I tune to that, while, upstairs, Charles bursts into loud, easy laughter.

5

~~~

I NOW HAVE FIFTY-FOUR days to perfect the twenty-five audition pieces for St. Louis, which range from a twenty-three-
second cadenza in Ravel's *Tzigane*—arguably the most exciting
twenty-three seconds in all of harping—to a six-minute excerpt
from Strauss's *Ein Heldenleben*. But size isn't everything: when
I first took on the *Tzigane* just after undergrad, I worked on it
for three years before I could play it without a mistake. I've long
since figured out happy fingerings and propitious pedal moves
for ninety-five percent of the concertos and orchestra excerpts
on the list, but as with most auditions, St. Louis is also throwing in one obscure piece, Moncayo's *Huapango*. I'll have to
write them for a copy of the music and reserve extra practice
time to work that number up from scratch.

I finish tuning and consider where to start. The score for
Symphonie fantastique is still on my music stand. It's got a
speedy tempo and several thorny spots of contrary motion:
tricky sequences of notes that trend either up or down the
scale but that involve some notes that move in the opposite

direction—a "two steps forward, one step back" arrangement that requires acrobatic right-hand fingerings. In rehearsal 22, I've got to play seventeen notes of contrary motion in about three seconds—and they're kicking my ass. One thing I've been working on is getting the volume perfectly even when using each finger. Harpists count our thumbs as our number one fingers and our ring fingers as number fours; we never use our pinkies. Despite a fierce exercise regimen, my four has never developed the same strength as the others, making it harder to play notes with the four as loud, and the contortions required by *SF* threaten to expose that.

What I really need to do is set the metronome at a slower tempo and achieve total uniformity first, then gradually increase my pace. But I'm not in the mood to work anything out in front of Cynthia, so I'm tempted to practice the significantly easier *Nutcracker* cadenza.

I fiddle with the height of my stand and flatten the pages of *Fantastique,* which are open to the place where I left off this morning. I've already practiced for several hours today, so I pop two Tylenol from a bottle I keep on my windowsill to mitigate shoulder soreness and a post-sangria headache. I futz with my finger hygiene kit, but since this morning's trim and buff my nails haven't grown, my calluses haven't changed; I'm just steeling myself for the plunge. Then I hear someone coming down the back stairs.

It's Charles. When he's visible through the screen door to my kitchen, Cynthia calls, "You're not driving after all that coconut milk, are you?"

"I've always wanted to be in a car accident," he says. "But I'm walking, sister."

"Bye, Charles," I say.

"Ciao," he says in an amiable tone, and he steps out the back door.

His departure makes me feel marginally less scrutinized, and there's no use trying to avoid embarrassment in front of Cynthia now. With my electronic metronome at a less frantic pace than the score demands—though it is still clacking maniacally—I lean the harp on my right shoulder and take a run at the *SF* passage.

Even at the slower tempo, two mistakes obtrude in twelve measures. "Fuck," I say under my breath. Biting a pencil like it's a bridle bit, Cynthia ticks away on her laptop, seemingly lost in her work, which involves defending corporations against the claims of injured people—sort of the opposite of *Erin Brockovich*. Maybe she does her pro bono work in the dating realm?

One of the two overhead bulbs in the dining room light fixture is burned out, so she sits in dim light. I've got a goose-necked lamp clamped to my music stand in the otherwise dark living room. On the floor near my feet, at the edge of the spray of light, is the front end of the plastic Barbie adventure van. It's motionless yet seems to speed out of the darkness toward me.

"*Fuck,*" I mutter, and I take another run at it.

Just how *did* a half-man/half-robot like me ever come to play the harp?

I have a heart murmur, apparently benign, and ever since its discovery minutes after I exited the womb, my mother has been plagued by the idea that she gave birth to a fragile child. So I spent most of my early days in a playpen, segregated from my six older siblings. My brothers loved to punch each other, hurl pillows like missiles, and play football in the living room with the couch as the end zone. Meanwhile, mute and staring, I'd gum a plastic hammer or slump with my drooling mouth against the mesh wall of my enclosure. I don't remember the first time I sat down at the old and neglected upright piano that we inherited from my father's aunt, whom I never met and no one ever talked about. Though I was disturbingly late to the wonders of speech, cruising past the thirty-month mark with about two dozen words and an aversion to sentences, I'm told that I began playing piano in earnest at age three. I imagine this was a great relief to my mother because it kept me out of harm's way and also served as an indirect argument against expensive speech therapy.

Just as I turned thirteen, my first piano teacher retired. Mrs. Kauss was not a very good pianist but she was crazy for proper technique. When she discovered that I was eager to execute her instructions to the smallest detail, she drove me hard and took credit for my playing as if it were her own. Just as I was beginning to consider rebellion, Mrs. Kauss took down her faded shingle and passed me to a new teacher. Ms. Beckwith lived in an off-white, two-story clapboard house in Elm Grove. She had gray hair, cut short like a monk's, and generally wore jumpers or one of seemingly hundreds of pairs of corduroy pants. Her house had a citrus smell that I loved and which almost masked her occasional cigarette. The lessons took place at the baby grand in her living room, but in her sunroom she had a Lyon & Healy concert grand pedal harp. Harp was her first instrument. She taught piano because Milwaukee didn't produce enough aspiring harpists to pay her mortgage.

Around this time seventh grade was ending, most of the girls and some of the boys at school, including myself, were well into puberty, and inklings of unrestricted freestyle humping infused the air like the scent of lilacs. This mass sexual awakening had no practical application for me—I was scared to death of the girls in my class—yet I was starting to dream. One day, Ms. Beckwith demonstrated something for me on her harp. The music was beautiful, but what struck me was the posture of her body, the way the harp nestled between her legs, the way her arms wrapped around it. When she was done, I asked her if I could play her harp, blushing as if I had asked to try on her underpants.

"Let's have you try it," she said.

She explained that a harp was essentially a piano turned on its side. When I sat down to the instrument, I immediately noticed the four large holes in the back of the rounded sound box. The bottom of the soundboard was broad and slightly curved like a woman's hips. When I leaned the harp back on my right shoulder to pull the chord as Ms. Beckwith had instructed me, it felt like I was drawing a girl toward me in an intimate embrace. In my thirteen-year-old mind, the instrument was clearly a sex-training apparatus.

After that, we agreed to tack on fifteen minutes of harp instruction to the end of every lesson.

Your chest is a soundboard, your mouth is a sound hole, your nerves string you from tip to toe. It's this way with all of us. I floated through my days with this new knowledge, at least half-erect at all times, and if not fingering notes, then imagining myself fingering notes. At night, I had wet dreams involving Ms. Beckwith's niece, Claire Houghton, a harpist herself. She was a beautiful Black Irish lass with a beguiling taste for cowboy boots and untucked shirts with pearl buttons. I was completely obsessed and needed my own harp to practice on, though I doubted my parents would approve. Any household expense had to be rigorously justified, and it wasn't *efficient* to like two instruments when one was enough for my mother to prove that she could produce a cultured child.

Luckily, there was a harp at the high school where Ms. Beckwith taught part-time, and when school let out in June, she made arrangements for me to practice there. I still played piano an hour a day, but then I would hop on my bike, a copy of Ms. Beckwith's key to the music room in my pocket, and practice harp for hours. Word was, Ms. Beckwith was a lesbian, and for my mother, this justified her anxiety about my shifting musical interests. My mother's way of addressing this was to mention that Ms. Beckwith was "a smoker," which made her "worried for" me. But in a weird way, Ms. Beckwith's sexual orientation confirmed my own. We both played the harp. We both loved ladies. She was a bit mannish and I was almost a bit mannish. We were a special team.

Ms. Beckwith never seemed to over- or underpraise me. Her explanations were always clear, and at the time, I trusted her more than my parents, who disturbingly seemed to have no expertise in the area I now cared about most.

"Do boys play the harp?" I asked her one afternoon.

"Yes," she said, sounding extra casual.

After I finished the next piece, something shifted in her and she said, "My teacher at Indiana was a man. And the principal harpist of the Chicago Symphony is a man. Would you like to see him play?"

My mother was dubious until she learned that Ms. Beckwith's sixteen-year-old niece was also going on my CSO outing. Somehow she believed that Claire would keep Ms. Beckwith from probing me with a dildo—or whatever it was lesbians did when they took straight boys across state lines.

By the time Ms. Beckwith's station wagon had merged onto I-94 en route to Chicago, Claire had one slender arm stretched across the front bench seat, her face turned over her shoulder, and she was talking to me.

The topic of conversation was Claire, her interests, dreams, and accomplishments. And these were manifold.

Eventually, out of the blue, she said, "Aunt Kathy tells me you're an amazing player."

Ms. Beckwith shot Claire a look.

"What?" Claire said. "You said he was good." Turning back to me, she added, "Which means you're amazing."

"She's an amazing teacher," I said, instantly embarrassed by daring to comment on my teacher when she was within earshot.

"Which do you like better—harp or piano?" Claire asked.

"Harp," I said impulsively, trying to please Claire and at the same time realizing it was true.

"That's cool," she said. "I don't know any guys at my school who would dare to be harpists."

A future of wedgies, swirlies, and titty twisters unfurled before my mind's eye, but no one would touch me, I thought, if I were going out with a girl like Claire.

Now I saw Ms. Beckwith spying me in the rearview mirror, and I said, "Yeah, I definitely want to keep playing the harp." Ms. Beckwith's eyes returned to the road—and I relaxed and looked out the window. Cheese shops lined the frontage roads, the roof of one supporting a huge blue fiberglass mouse with a wedge of cheddar in its paws. I was feeling so in my element that I blurted, "Hey, look at that big rat!"

Claire responded by withdrawing her arm from the back of the bench seat and facing forward.

I didn't begin to recover from that arm removal until after the lights went down in Chicago's Orchestra Hall, Claire to my left, Ms. Beckwith to my right, *Also sprach Zarathustra* on the program. The CSO's principal harpist was Eddie Patrinski, who looked like an aging Eddie Munster—saggy-faced with jet-black hair oiled back from his widow's peak. His harp was black and gold with a blue tassel in the center of the column. I haven't seen a tassel like that on a harp since. Ms. Beckwith had told us that his harp was nicknamed the Dragon, and I noticed that when he leaned it back just before he began to play, the tassel swayed like a mane and the instrument looked alive and rampant.

After he tore through his glissandos near the end of *Zarathustra,* I had to resist the urge to run down the aisle and leap onto the stage with arms spread. I was dead set on being a harpist, one as kick-ass as Eddie, thereby winning Claire as my wedded wife.

Only later did it dawn on me that Eddie and Arnold Reynolds—Ms. Beckwith's teacher at Indiana—were old-timers, guys who started out when orchestras were almost entirely male and straight men ruled the harp world. They broke into the biz before the seventies, when judges started using screens during auditions to hide the identity of players. The screens led to a boom of women winning seats without the discrimination transparent auditions enabled—though, sadly, too late for Katherine Beckwith.

But at the time, I didn't know these things about the world. I knew only that something had happened to me. In the span of those few hours in Orchestra Hall, my musical ambitions and my sexual awakening fused in a transformative rush. To this day I can't hear the opening fanfare from *Zarathustra*—which Kubrick famously used to begin *2001: A Space Odyssey*— without feeling some tingling remnants of horniness, aesthetic inspiration, and joy.

With only one more step-up in tempo to go in my practice session, I have the passage more or less evened out. I lean the harp forward to rest on its base, and Cynthia awakens from her laptop-induced trance. "All done?" she asks.

"Are you?"

She stands and stretches her arms over her head, grunting with released tension. "For now," she finally says.

This has always been a problem for me: making the transition from instrument to people.

Still sitting at the harp, I say, "Sorry I played like crap."

"It was fine, you were fine."

"Was I making a strange face while I played?"

"I wasn't checking," she says, getting annoyed.

I twist on my stool from side to side.

She starts packing up her stuff with increasing speed, as if she has finally realized that in fact she *is* in a burning building,

I'm beyond help, and she must save herself. Should I accept her cues or push against them, toward something that I wish were true but isn't?

"Do you want to stay over?" I ask.

"No," she says, and sighs. "No, I can't." She zips her laptop bag closed, and I get the feeling she's restraining herself from saying something worse. "I just need to go, actually." She looks up and studies some part of my face away from my eyes. "I'm really tired, Matt."

"I don't blame you," I say. "Here, let me send you off with a hug."

She has her laptop strap on her shoulder. She doesn't drop it, but sidesteps toward me, like a teenager suffering a good-bye kiss from her mother. I've got to be careful not to make the strap slip off of her, so it turns out to be one of the more awkward of all the hugs humans have ever shared.

"Good luck out there," I say. "If you're having a bad day at work, just call me, okay? Say the word and I'll end his life."

"Thanks," she says quietly, without smiling, and she kisses me on the lips, quickly but softly, and then she leaves.

6

~~~

AFTER CYNTHIA'S MINI Cooper pulls out onto the street at a rate halfway between normal and burning rubber, I turn off the lights and throw myself onto the futon couch, the better to dwell on the history of my sexual failures. I note an unsurprising pattern: the more I admire a woman, the more I want to impress her, the worse I'll be in the sack.

Milena was a special case. She came to Northwestern from Chico, California, on a soccer scholarship. A torn ACL her first year ended up costing her a spot on the team, and she settled into campus life as a party-first econ major with vague career goals. I met her at a dorm party after my sexual ineptitude had torpedoed a flotilla of short-lived relationships. Strangely, she pursued me, and I found the ease and openness of her pursuit wildly appealing. She was unneurotic and non-catty and laughed easily. There was simply nothing in the way, no gap to bridge. Her eyes are somewhat misaligned—her right eye is a bit lazy—and maybe to obscure this, she has always let her bangs grow long so they sheepdog her eyes. I'd heard people say she looked somewhat dopey, but to me it looked like she was suggesting that vision is overrated, a stance I found to be an enormous relief. Sex struck first, early, and often, with a naturalness that bordered on the impersonal. Our bodies began to feel like communal property, like a kitchen table or a shared bank account. And then they weren't. "I'm sick of you always trying to fuck me!" she said near the end of our marriage. It was a bad sign.

I'm having so much trouble with Cynthia because she's too smart and can see too clearly the type of nervous schlub I am. She grew up in White Plains, New York, and went to Swarthmore, then the University of Chicago for law school, and she's well versed in all the subjects that I blew off to fit in extra harp practice. Things in the bedroom have become consistently, depressingly disappointing, but thus far I've considered taking the little blue pill to be cheating, a flimsy mask on deeper psychological issues. Now I also wonder, given tonight's performance, whether Cynthia would get suspicious if I suddenly turned stud. She could see dosing as an admission of defeat or bad faith.

Lying on the futon couch, I feel like a fly injected with spider venom: paralyzed, my body slowly liquefying—but somehow still acutely conscious. I have a brunch to play tomorrow morning and need to go to sleep, but I can't make myself get up and go to my bed, which is not really a bed but a mattress and a box spring on the floor. Though this futon is the site of tonight's debacle, the sheer volume of struggles I've experienced in my bedroom makes the living room an oasis by comparison. Moreover, the streetlight casts a comforting glow on these walls, whereas my bedroom is a cave, with one small square window that stares at the building next door. I will try to sleep here.

But whenever I get close to sleep, I remember how Cynthia drove away—the upsurge of frustration and sadness, barely in check in my apartment, that I'm theorizing finally found expression in a poorly calibrated flexing of her foot on the gas pedal—and I resurface into horrific, agitated thoughts.

I muster enough energy to grab my last two beers from the fridge and return to the couch. At some point, an especially powerful wave of alcohol sweeps in, lifts me, and then takes me under.

I awake to a distant buzzing sound that had been part of a dream where I was stuck in Michigan Avenue traffic, late for a gig, and somehow without my harp. In the dream, the buzzing had seemed to be the faraway siren of an emergency vehicle navigating the gridlock. In real life, the buzzing is my bedside alarm, which at this distance sounds more like white noise than a jarring call to consciousness.

I bolt upright. It's Sunday morning. Audrey's Hello Kitty clock confirms: I'm late for brunch.

You can practice audition excerpts till the cows come home, do your chamber concerts and recitals, sub for the principal harp in the Chicago Symphony, make recordings, and lord it over neophytes at music camps throughout the Great Lakes region; you can shape all these things into a sense of yourself as a rising musician—all of which I've done—but if you want to pay rent and put gas in your car, you must, whenever possible, play brunch.

I anticipate the rage of Vikram, the food and beverage manager at the Marriott's Green Terrace Restaurant, as I shower, shave, and throw on my ash gray suit. I brush my teeth and gulp a glass of water, but have no coffee, no cereal, no food whatsoever. I'll be chowing down on every conceivable form of breakfast entree during my first break, and again after I'm done playing. But first I have to get there.

I have some ten hours of pop tunes in two enormous black binders, each page of sheet music preserved in plastic like a

Kraft single, and I hurl these binders into my black shoulder bag, along with a book-shaped holder of replacement strings coiled in pouches, a tuning key, a tuning fork, and nail clippers for cutting strings. I throw the old mustard-colored cloth mitten over my Aphrodite grand concert harp, an action that feels like shrouding an innocent man on his way to a hanging. In a corner of the dining room await the harp dolly, a collapsible music stand, and a padded stool that matches the harp. I stuff the collapsible stand into the inner pouch of my backpack, and into the customized outer pouch I snap the seat of the harp stool, letting the legs stick out behind me. I grab the dolly, nestle the harp onto it, strap the harp in place, then roll it through the kitchen and into the junk-strewn back stairwell. Then I wedge the screen door open by sliding a nut along a rod, roll the harp over the threshold, and find myself alive in the world, skirting T.R.'s dormant garden along a brick path to the alley.

Way past late, I forgo backing my Volvo out of the cramped garage; instead, I leave the car where it is and open the tailgate against one edge of the garage door. This is precarious, so I quickly reach inside the cover and grab the harp with both hands, use my thigh to help lift, and balance the ninety-pound contraption on the edge of the flatbed. Just before I slide the harp up and in, the tailgate starts to close, and I reach out to stop it with my right hand—and drop the harp. The base hits the concrete, the top of the column swings over and up. I clutch a handful of the harp's cover to steady the instrument itself, and the tailgate closes softly on my arm.

I feel the harp's shock: it's like having all my nerve ends yanked. Sweat bursts out on my forehead.

"Shit!" I say, imitating my father, who championed that word while trying to bring our white Pontiac station wagon back from the dead for the umpteenth time.

I extract the harp from the car's jaw and set it up in the alley. There's no time to check for damage, only to do what I should have done before: pull the fucking car out of the garage. After finally getting the harp onto its bed of pillows, I load the dolly, the shoulder bag, and the laden backpack. Then I slam the tailgate and lock up again.

I'm sweating into my suit, though the temperature is in the forties. I should have started playing "What a Wonderful World" ten minutes ago.

Taking advantage of the relatively light Sunday morning traffic, I scream through the alley and haul ass toward the Mag Mile, trying to convince myself the harp is fine. I bang down Western to Chicago, then take LaSalle to Ohio, entering the building-shaded land where tourists roam among the ritzy franchise shops and flagship stores the jet-setting bastards demand near every big city's cluster of convention-friendly hotels. Instead of turning on Rush Street and getting unloaded and valet-parked at the Marriott's entry, I must trek across Michigan Avenue, cut over on St. Clair, and then come back one-way on Grand, all because Vikram is a "service entrance for the help" kind of manager. I pull up to the shipping entrance and wave to a security slouch in his glass-enclosed office. He fingers something on his desk and the garage door opens, thereby earning him an annual income doubtless higher than mine. I beach my car at one end of the loading dock.

A young man in work boots and a navy blue uniform comes through a broad doorway and onto the platform. "Yo, harp man," he says, and he presses a button and disappears again. A huge metal lift slowly descends from the loading dock, making a rust-grinding screech.

I work everything onto the lift, which is slimy and black with decades of unknown spills, and stand stupidly until the guy finally comes back and hits the button for the lift to rise. Then it's a long trip from the loading dock down various corridors to an elevator to the fourth floor, wearing my backpack and shoulder bag and pushing the harp.

As soon as I finally wheel my harp into the restaurant, Vikram is on me. "Come on," he hisses before I can offer an explanation. "Let's go!"

Vikram is always busting my balls, but I don't mind him that much. He has standards for food and beverage management, which is honorable. Though he's clearly pissed, he brings a small round table and an enormous brandy snifter with a house five-dollar bill in it to start the flow of tips. I hate having a tip jar, but Vikram insists on it. It's part of my "compensation," part of why he sleeps at night paying me $275 for a four-hour gig.

Ignoring my apologies, he sighs as I remove the worn cover from the harp, but maybe there are too many customers nearby for him to chastise me further; he finally hurries away. I run my eyes over the wood but can't find any cracks; somewhat relieved, I set out my business cards and begin tuning. With each string I tune, I'm prepared to hear the effects of freaking dropping the thing. When I'm down in the metal bass strings, Vikram busies by, tapping two fingers on his suit cuff. All the bending and lifting has pulled out my shirttail. A bead of sweat stings my left eye. I slyly tuck in my shirt, sit, ease back the harp, and begin "What a Wonderful World."

The eggs Benedict eaters probably can't hear the sarcasm. The smell of all the food is driving me bonkers, as Milena would say, but I'm stuck here for two hours. Unable to risk Vikram's further displeasure, I'll have to play through my first break.

After "Wonderful World," I flow onward with "I Will Be Here," reminding myself I won't hit the chow line any time soon. For reminiscing about last night with Cynthia, I plink out "Can You Feel the Love Tonight?" More upbeat numbers pass forty minutes before I bring the room to my level with "Love Story," "Send in the Clowns," "Scarborough Fair," "Suicide Is

Painless," "Do You Know Where You're Going To?" and my personal arrangement of Pink Floyd's "Us and Them."

Finally, I pull the room out of its nosedive by firing up "The Muppet Show Theme"—which sounds fantastic on the harp, by the way—just as a couple with two young kids, a boy and a girl, walk by. I wink at the girl, who looks about Audrey's age, and she stops to listen, which makes the whole family stop. They all smile, even the boy, who looks about eight. Well warmed up, I truly gambol through this Muppet theme. When I finish, the girl claps, looking a little too cute for her own good. The dad slips a bill into my snifter. "Good songs!" the mother says brightly. The four of them walk away happy.

I take care of business straight until twelve-thirty, then hop up from my stool to imaginary applause, sprint toward the chafing dishes, and load up on scrambled eggs, spicy breakfast potatoes, bacon, a waffle, a banana, and orange juice. I make sure Vikram is busy prowling the floor, then take my plate down a back hallway to his office. He doesn't want me eating in front of the guests, and something tells me he's never shown me the employees' break room because he fears some unpredictable outcome to that fraternization. Instead he offers up his own quarters.

After I close the door, things are whisper-quiet. I take a chair on the visitor side of his desk and use my plate to nudge aside a stack of catalogs featuring Hobart kitchen machines and forty-gallon drums of ranch salad dressing. I hunch there and eat, making sounds like a hyena over a zebra. When I finish, I stand up to swig my orange juice—no reason to sit now, when I've got another 105 minutes of sitting ahead of me.

As I drink, I circle the room, taking in the westward-looking vista, which is dominated by the Hilton at State and Grand. In the West Loop and Near North neighborhoods, new thirty-story apartment towers have sprung up with tiny, open balconies on which I can see gas grills and stacked plastic chairs. The railings seem only waist high, and I wonder about the wisdom of creating so many suicide perches throughout the city. On the other hand, it's always been my dream to live in an expensive Loop or lakefront high-rise, so I imagine those tenants are less suicidal than the average Chicago resident, who has only lived in the vast three-story brown brick neighborhoods that make up most of the city. I sometimes feel guilty bringing Audrey to my not entirely safe street (a factor in my having her only two days a week), but the snake handlers up the block also gave my ancient Volvo a jump one frigid day and much more normal life than not goes on there. In any case, this is where I'm at right now.

Then I step to Vikram's side of the desk.

There's a picture of his family: a portly unsmiling wife in a brilliant green sari; three kids, two boys and a girl. Vikram himself stands stiffly in an undertaker's suit, eyes harried by something he can't solve just then. The oldest boy's eyes seem hooded with gloom. The youngest is smiling too much, and the girl is studying to be her mother in expression. That Vikram chose to put this image on his desk attests to how we all might suddenly take a very wrong turn somewhere in our lives and never even realize it.

I force my eyes away from the family portrait. Maybe Vikram's family is perfectly normal and happy and I'm seeing things negatively on account of my bad attitude. Did Milena *have* to kick me out? I wonder. As if to get an immediate answer to this question, I pick up Vikram's phone and dial her. While her phone rings, I try to account for why I'm calling her. People go wrong incrementally. They touch an elbow, take another sip of Chardonnay, mail-order a chain saw, and then, eventually, someone is dead and they're in prison. What am I going to say?

"Hello?" Milena says, with something vulnerable in her voice.

"It's me."

"Hey, Matt," she says warmly. "How are you? How was Milwaukee?"

"All right."

"Did you give your mother my best?"

"I did."

"I sent her a card."

"She loves cards, she really does." This makes me laugh.

"So what's up?" she says, shifting to sound more businessy.

"Well," I say, winging it. "About Tuesday. My student wants to come late for her lesson, so I might not be able to get Audrey until six."

"I can't get her, Matt. I work late when you have her."

Milena is a benefits manager at Smith Barney, where she acquired the deep knowledge of health care costs, 401(k) saving goals, life insurance, and salaries that made me look inadequate as a financial partner.

"I know. You don't have to do anything. Just, if they call you, you'll know that I'm on my way."

"Why don't *you* call *them*?" she asks.

I just don't remember this irritability as any part of her character when I fell in love with her. She was so damn sweet and ready to laugh and hump. When she was pissed, she used to narrow her eyes and give me the finger, so this strikes me as something her therapist has coached her to say, which is another surprising development. What's a totally psychologically normal and healthy gal like Milena doing in therapy?

"You're right," I say. "I should just call. God, why can't I think of these things?"

"They're going to charge extra for time after five-thirty." Education and child-care-related costs have always been a flashpoint in our relationship, ever since Milena's parents, frightened of Chicago's public schools, talked us into enrolling Audrey in Near North Montessori as a three-year-old and offered to pay most of her tuition—an offer that we accepted, resulting, I suspect, in my everlasting emasculation in Milena's eyes. "And don't forget she has to be at the Y for swimming lessons at seven."

"How is Audrey?" I ask.

"Fine."

"That's good."

Milena sighs. "She had another bad playdate yesterday."

"Oh, no."

"She threw a toy at Natalie and hit her in the face. Her lip was bleeding."

They're only six, but their relationship is alarmingly fraught. They'll play together great for hours, but often, at a certain point, Natalie will withdraw, and Audrey can't stand that and will plead with and badger her to no avail and then break down crying. Lately, they sometimes don't make it through sleepovers, and an unlucky one of us parents ends up shuttling one kid or the other home in the middle of the night.

"My God, what did she throw?"

"I don't know, I think it was a plastic zebra."

"I mean, why?"

"Because I was paying too much attention to Natalie." Milena's disgust is at a perfect smolder. "Audrey got jealous, she just lost it. And Natalie said she would never talk to Audrey again in her whole life. And I have to explain this to her mother?"

"Did Audrey apologize?"

"Yeah, but Natalie wouldn't accept it. So when Marilyn came to pick up Natalie, Audrey was the one crying and Natalie was looking daggers at the wall."

Silence overtakes the line. And beneath the silence are the unspoken accusations: if you were a normal man, we would have had a second child and Audrey would have worked out her jealousy issues in the privacy of her own family; if you didn't make me divorce you, Audrey wouldn't have been traumatized into becoming a controlling little pest from whom I have to protect her own friends. And so on.

"Dang, I don't know what to say," I murmur.

She sighs, as if this is par for my course. "Look, her last day of swimming lessons is Wednesday night and parents are invited. She's excited about it." Another sigh. "She wants you to be there."

"She actually said that?"

"Yeah."

"Does that mean you won't be there?"

"I'll be there."

"Wow," I say. "Never thought I'd see you in a swimsuit again."

There's another pause. I squinch my eyes shut, bracing for a verbal cuff upside the head.

Finally, she breathes into the line: "What am I going to do with you, Matthew?"

The intimacy of her tone catches me off guard and my body starts to respond.

"So Wednesday, then, we'll swim with Audrey," I stammer, swiveling Vikram's leather executive chair. "What about Steve?" I add, an ill-advised afterthought.

"What *about* Steve?" she says.

Just then Vikram opens the door and finds me turning in his chair.

"Gotta go, Milena, thanks," I say, and I hang up.

Only his respect for the rule of law keeps Vikram from choking me with both hands. All he allows himself is "Get out there," spoken with withering contempt.

I stand up. "I'm going," I say moronically. I grab my plate and glass.

"Stop," Vikram says. Once he has me frozen there, he fixes me with his eyes and says, "I can fire you."

"That makes sense," I say.

He also sighs. "Please, Matthew. It is very, very important to start on time, and the cover for your harp—we want things looking nice around here."

"I'm not against a new cover for the harp—"

"And we need *up*beat music. Why do I have to repeat these things?" He clenches his fist and brandishes it. *"Celebration!"* he says.

"Okay," I say, making a break for it.

I scoot down the hall and into the restaurant. My harp stands like a friend who'll wait in a crowded corridor while you use the restroom. I hand my dishes to a waitress, hop on the stool, shift the pedals into gear for "Stardust," and keep the music coming.

My final number is a reprise of "Wonderful World," my signature. I hold my head perfectly still, staring into space, playing from memory, as the lyrics course through my mind. Then I notice out of the corner of my eye two women—one about forty, one pushing sixty—standing by a table, observing me as if I'm performing a concert. The younger woman wears a blouse and skirt, the thin strap of a small purse hanging from her shoulder. The older woman is heavy, in a green pantsuit, with a clunky green plastic bracelet on her wrist and green hemisphere earrings; her red-brown hair, no doubt colored, sprouts in different directions like the fronds of a palm tree.

When I finish playing and close my music binder, the younger woman approaches. There's something weathered about the pallor of her skin and the way her bodiless dishwater-blonde hair clings to her head and drops to her shoulders, but her eyes are bright. I fall in love with her, a little bit, right then.

"It *is* a wonderful world, isn't it?" she says, smiling. "You're pretty good with that thing."

I can't stop staring at her, or smiling sheepishly.

"Do you mind if I introduce myself?" she continues. "I'm Marcia Marquardt. I'm the director of a hospice in Elmhurst."

She puts out her hand.

"Matt Grzbc," I say.

"Ger-bik" is how we pronounce it, though most people want to say "Grizz-beck." I wonder if it's significant that my name is spelled like something an infant would randomly type at a keyboard. I can hear my founding ancestor, faced with choosing our surname, saying in Slovenian: "I don't care what it is! Christ! Just pick five letters!" He sounds like my father.

Marcia and I shake. Her grip is matter-of-fact.

"Are you familiar with hospice care?"

"Sort of," I say.

"When treatment is over, we make people comfortable. We've just had a harpist leave us—she moved to Florida."

"Lot of dying people down there, I bet," I say.

"Yes," she says, eyeing me a bit more closely. "Well, how'd you like to come out and play for us sometime?"

"I don't know," I say as politely as I can. I shouldn't add commitments with the audition looming. "Probably not."

"Probably not?" she repeats incredulously. She turns to her older companion: "Eleanor, he says, 'Probably not.' "

Of course, Marcia has no idea that my father has just died or that her request puts pressure on my fundamental life conflict: practice time versus time I can spend with people. I desperately need to accomplish something musically in order to feel I deserve to exist, and I desperately need to be with people to make existing at all tolerable.

Eleanor shakes her head. She's seen it all before. You can't supervise death on a daily basis without getting a wry outlook on the human condition.

"Eleanor's our volunteer coordinator, by the way. Eleanor, come on over here and help me strong-arm this gentleman." Marcia adds, "We've just had brunch with some donors and we're on a roll." She laughs and her eyes sparkle at me.

Eleanor approaches and puts out her hand. "How do you do?"

"Good to meet you," I say, my shoulder muscles tightening.

Marcia leans in and touches my upper arm. "In the past, we've had musicians on a volunteer basis," she says confidentially. "But maybe we can do something for you."

It's the hospice Mafia with an offer I can't refuse. "Well," I say, "I don't want to sound mercenary . . ."

Her touch melts me, and having disappointed Cynthia, Vikram, and Milena in a sixteen-hour span leaves me highly disposed to please and connect, no matter the cost. And I may have shaken off belief in my parents' religion, but they succeeded in pounding in the value of sacrificing for the good of others, so even though I am often a selfish bastard, I am also vulnerable to this sort of appeal. Then there's the prospect of cash . . .

"What would it be?" I ask. "What would you want me to do?"

"We have a patient—our other harpist used to play for her on Wednesday afternoons. She's a very frightened old woman. The music seems to help. Then there might be others."

"I think I can do it this once," I say. Then, panicking, I add, "But this Wednesday is too soon. Can it be next Wednesday?"

"Sure." she says. "You may do it once and realize it's not for you, but it *can* be rewarding. And I'll talk to the board about compensation."

"All right," I say. I look over at Eleanor, who smiles, looking down at the carpet.

Marcia gives me her card and we make arrangements.

"So nice to meet you, Matt!" Marcia says, shaking my hand with both of hers.

"See you," I say, already feeling a pang of remorse over the lost practice time.

7

~~~

TOWEL OVER MY shoulder, wearing only my unfashionably short navy swim trunks, I walk through tiny cool puddles on the tiles, making my way to the instructional pool. Among a long row of parents scattered on a wooden bench, Milena is looking down into a tote bag, showing me the new red highlights in her hair, putting off eye contact.

"Hey, Matt," she says, without looking up.

Audrey huddles with a friend, yammering the poor kid into submission. She doesn't seem to notice me.

"Hey," I say, sitting down next to Milena, though not too close. She finishes with her bag, from which she has extracted nothing, and looks ahead at the pool, which is so still and gleaming it looks like it's filled with Jell-O.

She smooths her hands over her thighs.

My armpits are sweating. A glimpse of her bare right leg has a strong effect on me—there's so much sexual pressure behind my wall of inhibitions that it threatens to burst out at the slight-

63

est opening from Milena—and I must take care not to embarrass myself.

"These kids look weak to me," I say, affecting disgust. "I hope these instructors test them the way they need to be tested."

"I hope so, too," she says soberly, playing along.

"Let's get 'er done!" I call toward the kids.

The instructor, Jean, a large tan woman in a brown one-piece, stands with her arms folded and gives me the eye, as do some of the other parents. But their looks don't bother me because I catch Milena controlling a smile. Then, all at once, Jean claps her hands: "All right, guys, time to line up!"

I'm nervous now and not just because I'm sitting next to Milena, but also from worrying about how Audrey will do, if she'll have a meltdown, if she'll have to be rescued, if the gangly older boy in the long yellow trunks will surreptitiously try to hold her head underwater.

Jean orders her charges to the edge of the pool and puts them through their paces: sit dives, back floats, treading water, and so forth. "That boy in the yellow suit wouldn't get in the water the first day," Milena says. The grand finale is swimming the twenty-five-yard length of the pool. Jean lines them up again and sends them in one by one. Some kids set out at odd angles like mindless wind-up toys; others bitch-slap at the water; few make steady progress. Audrey jumps in, bobs to the surface, and begins swimming, chugging slowly but steadily across the pool. Five yards from the wall, she seems to lose steam, but then she recommits, and she makes it.

"Look at that," I say. "She can swim!" And all without whining, a crying fit, or other demands for attention. We haven't destroyed her yet!

"All right," Milena says with a smile, and puts a power fist in the air. This is the old Milena, for sure.

After this final skill demonstration, Audrey runs instead of walks to get the pool toys out of the basket, but that type of disobedience seems downright reassuring.

"She did good," Milena says.

Jean invites the parents to come on in. We get up and walk toward the water. I let my hand touch Milena's as we walk.

Her hand slips away.

I lower myself into the pool with my arms at my sides, then crouch in three feet of water until my head goes under. When I surface, Milena also comes up for air on the far side of the pool. Audrey swims to Milena and clings to her neck, her pale green eyes lit with excitement.

I swim slowly toward them. Milena looks past me, it seems, as if someone is following me.

"Group hug!" Audrey proclaims, reaching one hand toward me.

I walk on the bottom of the pool, the water now up to my chest, taking heavy strides.

"Group hug!"

When I arrive, I put my hand on Audrey's small shoulder. At the same moment, Milena kisses the side of Audrey's head, then swims away, one stroke at a time. Audrey is left treading water, so I offer her my arm to hold on to if she wants. Instead, she grabs my shoulder and puts her arms around my neck from behind. "Swim!" she commands. Wearing her like a cape, I try to swim but find it hard to get my face above the water to breathe right. Soon I coast into shallower water and let her slip off.

I linger in the shower, convinced Milena and Audrey will take a while in the women's locker room. Terrific water pressure pounds up my spine, against my neck and down again—maybe enough to knock some sense into me. I know I shouldn't have touched Milena's hand the way I did. I know that, just to cop a jolt of sexual confidence, I am causing everyone pain, confusing myself, and betraying Cynthia, who needs support against this Whitaker prick. I finish showering, get dressed, and grab my duffel.

When I step out into the corridor, they have just emerged from the women's locker room. Milena walks by me without a glance, and I fall into step with them—we are not together but we are in the same place at the same time—out the doors of the Y and into the parking lot.

"Can Daddy come over and read to me before bed?" Audrey asks, holding Milena's hand.

"I don't think so," Milena says.

Audrey grabs my hand and Milena lets her. We walk all the way to Milena's car like this. Milena presses her remote and a vehicle beeps, lights flash. Turns out she's driving a new red SUV—a Ford Escape.

Near the end of our marriage, I said to Milena, "We're not getting an SUV just because everyone else has one." Despite their size, most are nowhere near as convenient for hauling a harp as a good old-fashioned station wagon. The argument escalated quickly, like a refinery fire, and two days later, Milena left the apartment with a suitcase. I'd called her "herd-minded" and a "TV slave" and other apology-proof phrases. I had no idea how much damage even one of those fights could cause, because my parents had stayed together despite thousands.

Milena opens the back door. I let go of Audrey's hand.

"Good night, guys," I say.

"Good night, Daddy!" Audrey calls.

"Good night," Milena says.

I walk away slowly. My own car is parked three blocks away so I wouldn't have to pay for the lot.

"Wait up!" Milena calls.

I turn. As she walks over, she puts her hands in the front

pockets of her jeans, which raises her shoulders in her fleece. Behind her, Audrey sits in her car seat, lit by the dome light, the door wide open.

Milena stops and looks past my shoulder.

"We might be getting engaged," she says. "Just so you know."

"I figured that," I say. "With the house and everything."

I have not actually figured this. Audrey's comments in the car on our way to the wake had made me discount the staying power of Steve, notwithstanding their current living arrangement.

We make eye contact, but her lazy eye makes everything feel wrong.

"Thanks for coming out," she adds. "Audrey was happy."

"No problem," I say.

Milena gives a low, awkward wave of her hand, and then she turns and walks back to her SUV.

8

~~~

THURSDAY MORNING, I sit down to the harp to work on audition pieces. I'm still catching up on the practice time I
lost last week for the funeral, yet despite a desperate sense of
urgency, I can't make myself tackle *Symphonie fantastique*.

With the harp off my shoulder, I hold the top of the soundboard with both hands. The weak sunlight through the window
seems to be detaching from objects and receding upward. I keep
hearing Milena say, *Just so you know.*

Is the joy of empty-headed lovemaking life's highest good?
Yes. And what are harps for? *No one knows.*

Though I've been touching the harp for minutes now, it
seems impossible to tip it back, raise my thumbs, and begin.

Once, as a nine-year-old, I hesitated in the frigid, ankle-
lapping waters of Lake Michigan, afraid to take the plunge,
prompting Bart and George to pick me up and hurl me in. Bart,
my oldest brother, is a butt-chinned marketing executive at
Harley-Davidson. He took my tentativeness as a personal in-

sult, and George has always had a weakness for mischief—together, they tossed me about fifteen feet. After that minor humiliation, I adopted a method of running full-tilt down the beach and into the water until the waves tripped me and I would dive under. As I ran across the sand toward the lake, I was essentially telling myself, *Here comes the pain; your way is through the pain.* And something like that mantra has saved me thousands of hours of angsty procrastination before practice sessions. It has, basically, enabled my entire harp career.

So while *Symphonie fantastique* is insurmountable right now, I turn to another piece I'm unsure about, *Ein Heldenleben*. I find the score and quickly flatten it on my music stand, telling myself that these actions represent enormous progress. The piece's many double-handed arpeggios promise pain. I finally tip the harp back and, almost blindly, send my fingers running toward that pain.

Within ten measures I notice a buzz in the sixth-octave C string. I have to pull on it hard to get the volume I need, but the harder I pull, the worse the buzz. I tune that string again, but that's not the problem. I give the instrument a once-over, and sure enough, there's a hairline crack in the short hump of wood that connects the neck to the top of the soundboard. It wasn't noticeable just after I dropped the harp, and earlier this week, when I sometimes heard the slight tremors that herald a buzz, I had put off a careful reexamination. But now I see the crack exists. For their whole lives the neck and the soundboard have wanted to kiss, two thousand pounds of pressure pulling them together, and now they are a speck closer, and the bass string knows it.

"Shit," I say.

Unlike your violins and violas, which ripen over the centuries, all harps eventually fall apart or need overhauls, and this one, more than twenty-five years old, is aging. In other words, this buzz could be the beginning of the end. It's also possible that this is just one of those buzzes they can fix at the factory, which happens to be right here in Chicago.

I try not to freak out, but dizziness gathers behind my eyes. The likelihood that my dropping the harp caused the crack is poisonous food for thought. This is Ms. Beckwith's second harp, the one she kept at the high school and eventually sold to my parents for a rock-bottom discount because our family was large and financially pathetic and she had hopes for me. It's really the only harp I've ever played on, through college, through grad school, through my best performances—in Israel, Seattle, San Diego—and through my worst. And it's also a harp played by none other than Claire Houghton, Ms. Beckwith's stunning niece, who I believed would meet me at the end of my harping rainbow right up until she crushed my adolescent dreams. I'll not soon forget the day that I biked over to the high school in eighth grade and ran into her in the music room. She was just finishing when I arrived.

"You sounded good," I said.

"Ah, thanks," she said, wrinkling her nose, "but it's going nowhere."

Claire seemed in a hurry, cramming a few scores into her backpack. And though I lit more inane conversation starters, she was hell-bent on getting out of there. That's when I noticed a guy standing by the door.

Wearing bitchin' Nike high-tops and a letter jacket decorated with a ridiculous number of honorary patches, designations, and even actual medals, he was just as athletic and handsome as she was beautiful. I had successfully ignored the possibility of her dating someone else, assuming that her first allegiance was to the harp, which would give me an inside track when she would finally choose a mate. She went to him and they kissed on the mouth, his hands resting on the hips of her jeans. By the time they finished that obscenely long smooch, which they were still completing as they headed out of the room, my delusions were in ruins.

I sat down to the instrument, which was still warm from Claire, still smelling like her perfume. I felt the outer wooden edge of the soundboard against my thigh, knowing it had been warmed by Claire's thigh. I put my arms around the instrument and placed a palm on each side of the flat soundboard, which the strings divided in half. I closed my eyes. The rounded back of the harp was smooth against my chest, just as it had been against Claire's. I was alone in the music room, though I didn't know for how long. My heart started pounding and my spit burned away. I looked at the open door and sent my hearing into the hallway. A locker closed in the distance. "Crazy," I said out loud, but I knew the chances of stopping myself were not good.

I stood and carried the harp into one of the practice rooms on the perimeter of the music room. I closed the door. With my back to the tall narrow window in the door, I stood behind the harp, hugged it, and slid my hands down the front of the sound-board, imagining myself standing behind Claire, smoothing my hands on her thighs. The third oval sound hole was just about the right height. Trembling a bit, I took myself out of my pants and laid myself in the smooth wooden slot, which was softer feeling than you would think. I didn't care if anyone discovered me. I didn't care if I ever saw another person again. I used my hand and the lip of the oval. When I was getting close, I heard two girls enter the outer room, talking loudly. But I was past the point of no return. I knew they were as self-absorbed as I was; in this way, it seemed we were all in it together, and with that final, romantic thought I refocused on my beloved and ejaculated through the sound hole and into the harp.

I was nineteen before I successfully had intercourse with a

woman, but once when asked on a late night in college, in mixed company, how old I was when I lost my virginity, I blurted, "Thirteen." In response to the hoots and disbelief of my friends, I blushed and refused to elaborate beyond, "It was the whole harp thing, some people can't resist it."

In the wake of this appalling memory, sweat starts on my forehead and full-on dizziness washes over me. I walk slowly, hands out in front of me, to my bedroom and ease down face-first on the bed and close my eyes. And I know if I don't move for five minutes, I'll be able to lie here indefinitely without throwing up.

My doctor thinks my dizzy spells are related to my congenitally low blood pressure, but I'm beginning to think they might be something more psychological.

I lie on my stomach for an hour, maybe two, flipping the pillow occasionally so I don't overheat it.

All in all, this is just one of my garden-variety personal collapses. Pretty trivial, I know, compared to, say, the catastrophes in Iraq or Darfur. Yet I imagine the people who perpetrate such large-scale misery probably get their start by mishandling their small personal meltdowns, so I try to be on my p's and q's whenever I implode to limit the damage on those around me.

My apartment is quiet—T.R. must be out lunching with friends, and Max, the wayward boy occupying the attic, hasn't been around much lately—and I drift into a thin sleep, before the ringing phone on the nightstand wakes me up.

"Matthew, this is your mother. Are you still fornicating with that girl with the screwy eyes? I really wish you'd consider the priesthood."

The imitation is so spot-on that it takes me a beat to figure out who's calling.

"Adam, you bastard!" I exclaim. "It's great to hear from you, man!" And the last wisps of dizziness blow away.

"How are you, my dear Midwestern friend?"

It is in fact my best friend from college, Adam Brackett, calling from New York City, where he is enjoying what the general public considers B-list fame and fortune, but which appears to me as amazing success. He's had major supporting roles in movies like *Fear and Loathing in Las Vegas* and the *Scary Movie* franchise, starred in dramedies like *Rocket Man* and *The Love Letter*, was the lead in a Broadway revival of *Oklahoma!* for which he was nominated for a Tony, and has guested on a bunch of TV shows.

"I'm good," I say. This is entirely for Adam's benefit—a knee-jerk effort to appear happy and successful—and now it's too late to mention my father's death. "Hey, I saw that *Sex and the City* episode again last month," I add. "You and Sarah Jessica Parker!"

"Sarah is a lovely professional, and I enjoyed working with her."

Adam and I roomed together at Northwestern, in the fine arts residential college, freshman and sophomore year. Adam was tall, handsome, quick with a joke, a great actor with a great singing voice. Right after college, he did the Second City Conservatory, was in a touring company within a year, and on the main stage in two. Meanwhile, I was playing harp in the Civic, still taking sections with Eddie, who was in his twilight years at the CSO. Adam and I stayed reasonably close while he was still living in Chicago, but when he moved to LA and then to New York, we became less so. Even though what he did always got him more attention than what I did, for a while I thought our lives were more or less parallel. Then it became obvious that he was nearing the top of the mountain and I was clutching the base of a greased pole.

"And you were pretty convincing as that moody jazz pianist!" I gush, going on about his *Sex and the City* role.

"Thank you, thank you very much. But enough about how my career has fallen into guest appearance hell: I'm going to be making some short films here in New York and, fuck me, but I need a harpist."

He goes on to describe a kind of high-concept comedy thing called "Eighteen Breakups (with Music)," which involves horrific breakup conversations set in various venues around the city, some of which would involve live harp music. He tells me he's going to shop them to *SNL* and Comedy Central, and if they don't pick them up, he's going to post them on YouTube and ride the Internet buzz to new opportunities and idiosyncratic artistic satisfaction.

"I want some creator shit to start happening for me," he explains.

"Sounds good," I say.

"Come out to New York for two days of work, I'm thinking the twenty-sixth and twenty-seventh," he says, "and I'll pay you a thousand plus expenses—and don't say you'll do it for free or I'll whip your ass with a car antenna."

"Man, I totally can't charge you," I protest, though my heart's not in it.

"Matt, that's incredibly feeble, even by your standards. I'm assuming you're desperate for cash and I've got money for this, and have some respect for yourself as a pro, goddammit."

"All right, all right," I say, though this is just two weeks away.

"Beautiful," he says.

Then he tells me he has to run but he'll be in touch about details—don't worry, I can stay at his place, etc.

It's only when I hang up that guilt, with more dizziness, comes crashing back. I find the bottle of Tylenol by the harp and down two with half a glass of water that's been sitting there for who knows how long. It seems to offset the dizziness. I have further sabotaged my audition prep, but I feel powerless against the aura of success Adam Brackett emanates, and my worst insecurities seek validation via a New York gig of any sort. And what if it leads to something cool? This all makes me feel excited and somewhat out of control. In an attempt to settle down, I call Aphrodite Harps to make an appointment to bring my harp in—turns out next Friday is first available. And then, despite the buzz, I practice.

9

~~~

"Don't get weird about it," Cynthia says, standing naked at my dresser, rifling through the drawers.

"All right," I say.

"You're starting to, right there," she says. She turns around with one of my T-shirts in her hands. "The way you said 'all right' was weird."

"It was?"

"Yes."

She slips into the shirt, flips her shoulder-length hair behind her with the backs of her fingers, and for good measure reasserts the left-side part of her hair with a swoop-back of one hand.

"Look," she adds in a softer voice. "Your father just passed. Cut yourself some slack." Then she heads out of the bedroom, maybe making for the john, flashing her charming behind.

I'm sitting up on my mattress, with my back against the wall. During his time here, Charles painted this room red and purple, and I'm the sort of person who can't make himself correct an obvious flaw in his environment. Part of one wall slants over-head to accommodate a staircase that used to go from roughly the front door to the second floor, but which T.R. walled off when he converted this to a two-flat.

In the wake of what has just happened, or not happened, the lameness of my bedroom in general and my lack of a bed frame in particular suddenly seem emblematic of my condition. It occurs to me that if I had asked—and of course I never would have asked—my father would have made a bed for me. He was always ready to substitute your need for his own will. This positive recognition brings another: he was usually very friendly out in the world. At the grocery store, he was like a mayor on the campaign trail, chatting up shoppers, cashiers, stockers. It must have driven my mother nuts to see him cracking jokes with bank tellers and waitresses. Why was it *so* hard to bring that ease home?

I'm glad Cynthia is out of the room, because suddenly I can't talk. I close my eyes and tap the back of my head against the wall until it passes.

When she returns a minute later (carrying a refreshed glass of wine, which seems odd), I've gathered myself and the topic shifts to litigation.

"I wish these engine failure cases would just *go away*, thank you very much," she says, pacing high on her toes.

"Excuse me?" I say, because "engine failure" sounds suspiciously like a euphemism for my dysfunction.

"Aviation litigation," she says, still pacing. "It's this fucking litigation."

"Oh, the fucking litigation," I say. "Well, at least something's fucking."

"That's good," she says with some excitement, pointing a finger at me. "I'm glad you've got your sense of humor. We're going to joke our way through this."

"We are?"

"Yes."

"It's not as funny as it looks," I suggest.

She seems to ignore this, while pacing.

"But we were talking about a litigation," I say.

"Yes," Cynthia says. She stops and makes strong eye contact, locking me in, her one-man jury. "Three Cessna Skycruisers have crashed. Three people are dead, two seriously injured. Each plane lost engine power during a normal descent, possibly from fuel starvation, and the pilots crashed into trees and power lines and whatever. The NTSB couldn't settle on a probable cause, but now plaintiffs have a theory about the fuel selector system that ties the three accidents together—it's complicated but kind of makes sense. It's a new plane for Cessna and everyone wants to blame their design."

"And get compensated," I throw in.

"Get a shitload of compensation," Cynthia acknowledges. "Plus punitive damages." She turns thoughtful, rubbing two fingers around her lips, as if applying lip balm.

I adjust the sheet over my still-naked waist. I say, "How does it all look?"

She sighs. "A reasonable settlement would free me to camp happily to the end of my days," she says. "I'd hate to go to trial, but I can't give away the store, either."

She stops pacing, finishes her new glass of wine, crawls onto the bed, and tackles a pillow.

"Let's hope you don't have to," I say.

She frowns and stares at something within the rumpled-sheet landscape. She's afraid of failing, it suddenly occurs to me. Why so beautiful *and* so worried? Why insurance defense? I suspect that a person's career can be both a solution for, as well as a shadow of, the problems that dog a life. My heart goes out to her.

"You're a good lawyer," I say.

"You have no idea what kind of lawyer I am."

78

"See? That's how good you are." I smile, but she doesn't.

Nearly a minute of silence passes while she studies a ridge in the sheet where it crosses my knee. I tap my opposite thigh, counting the silence in 4:4 time.

"You know," Cynthia says, "when I first met you, I thought you might be gay."

"I know," I respond, not knowing what else to say.

"There's still so much fucking homophobia."

"There really is," I say. "But I don't know, maybe there's less—these days?"

"Just last summer the Eighth Circuit issued a terrible opinion upholding the constitutionality of bans on same-sex marriage," she replies quickly. "The people stealing T.R.'s yard signs aren't collecting souvenirs."

"Yeah, I guess I wasn't really thinking."

"Oh, what does anybody know about anything?" she says, exasperated. She breaks her death clench with the pillow.

And though there's no softness to it—more as if she's climbing onto my body like a koala climbing a tree—she embraces me and we hug there on the bed. She squeezes me hard in her arms, almost too hard.

"You're a real young man, aren't you?" she says. "My protector."

"Sure, doll, whatever you say."

We're quiet for a bit, then I ask, "So when you came up to me at that party, you weren't hitting on me?"

"I thought you were cute," she says, pulling back from the embrace.

"And I thought you were my ideal. You kind of move like a gymnast, and I had a Mary Lou Retton thing when I was a kid."

"You did not," she says.

"I like compact, muscly girls with great posture who can do flips and shit."

"I'm afraid you had a thing for the leotard up the butt crack."

We laugh, for no good reason, and this almost breaks the ice—the big ice, the melting of which would make me so happy I imagine it wouldn't matter if I won or lost any audition ever.

"First loves can be strange sometimes," I say, with mock gravity.

Eyes down, she smooths the bedsheet with her palm, breaking a wry smile.

"I tried stuff with women," she says. Her words arrive as if at the end of some boomerang arc, hitting me in the back of the head.

"Really?"

"In law school," she says and laughs. "Not the most romantic time of life! We got an apartment as 2Ls with another girl. We studied together a lot, and sometimes we ended up in one bed, just like sisters."

As if to illustrate, Cynthia picks up the pillow and holds it against her chest like an umpire's pad.

"I know everyone's supposed to have their moment in college," she says, looking down. "But I was a late bloomer."

Finally, she looks up at me and smiles sheepishly. I've seen her smirk often enough and her big smile, but I've never quite seen this. This smile makes me fall for her all over again.

"My dad was such an asshole," she continues quietly, "so nasty to my mom. He couldn't keep his dick in his pants, for one thing. I went through this time when I thought marriage was totally evil, and I was suspicious of men."

I remember that the nightshirt she sometimes wears is a cast-off from her father.

"I thought you liked your dad," I say.

"He's himself all the time—and I like that. He doesn't worry about anything—but I hate that about him, too. And when he didn't worry about hurting my mom, I *really* hated that about him. But they're apart now, so it doesn't matter."

"Sure it matters," I say. "Everything matters—more and more all the time, that's what I'm starting to feel."

She smiles at this, though I don't know why, but I'll take her smile because it makes me feel as if we've almost broken through.

"Whitaker is keeping his distance," she says.

"Nothing to make amends?"

"No, the weird thing is, he's acting like he's mad at me, like *I've* done something to him. He doesn't get back to me like he used to. He's sort of icing me."

"Maybe he's embarrassed."

"That's not what it feels like."

"So are you, I don't know, going to the appliance committee or whatever it is?"

"I'm not sure. Doing something formal feels risky. I might go to this senior partner in our group, who's an asshole, but I think he hates Whitaker. Actually, I've been meaning to tell you, this partner wants me to go to Denver a week from Monday to oversee a document production because one of his senior associates is crashing and burning and can't do it."

"Sounds like a good time to wangle a favor out of him."

"This is one of those situations where the longer you wait, the more suspicious it looks when you say something." She seems to ponder this. "It's weird," she says. "I think I became a lawyer like some women take karate—so no one could mess with me. And now I'm getting messed with."

"But you know how to fight back."

"Well, I think he's icing me to let me know that he can make things hard for me. And his defense isn't bad: he's getting over his divorce. I don't talk much about my personal life at work, so he doesn't know if I'm seeing someone. We work closely. We've gotten along pretty well. He thought we had something. He takes a chance, kisses me, and when I get mad, he apologizes and leaves."

"But he kept going after you said no. You had to push him away."

"He trapped me with the chair, but that left no marks, and he had to stand somewhere. I'm the one who probably hurt his neck pushing him away. It's a fucking hopeless 'he said, she said' situation."

"But he's your *boss*. Some kind of abuse of power, right?"

"Not necessarily," she says, with an unbecoming curl of her mouth. It seems we're role-playing: she's doing to me what some defense attorney would do to her. "Yes, he has power over me," she continues, "but it's only an *abuse* of power if what he's done is abusive, and that goes back to his story, which, as I said, is a good one."

"Unless it's always abusive to come on to a subordinate."

Cynthia snorts. "You're about to turn millions of office relationships into rape cases."

"So he wins?"

Cynthia takes this moment to shift her position in the bed. She turns on her side facing away from me and uses the pillow as a pillow.

"Why'd you do that?" I ask.

"What?" She turns her head to face me.

"Make an argument against yourself. Persuade yourself you're in a bad situation."

"It's just the truth."

"Actually," I say, "I do that to myself sometimes. Maybe that means we're made for each other."

She barely smiles at that, and I remember a half hour ago, lying on my back with her half kneeling, half crouching over my hips, reaching to take me and put me inside of her, but it was clearly no use, and the position, with us both looking at what was happening, was mortifying to me beyond words.

I roll toward her now and let my nakedness touch where she

is bare under the hem of the T-shirt. I hug her from the side, which she allows.

She's my lawyer—a lawyer apparently taking the Fifth on the question of whether we're made for each other. And she's also a party to an ongoing humiliation that makes me want to run from this room, but I lie with her, because I live here, and because I think love is possible with her.

At the very least, I did fall in love with the person I thought she was when we started dating, and I can't bear the idea that I might not always feel that love because of how self-conscious I've become with her, which is not her fault. Of course, *I love you* is always shorthand for something complicated. I've heard that love is really just a commitment to stop second-guessing the other person, to stop asking yourself if you should be with this person, so you can just embrace the person and make them happy. But what if it's myself I'm second-guessing too much?

She reaches over and turns off the bedside lamp.

Surprisingly, I'm not ready to stop talking. She's never been quite as open with me as she has been tonight, and that gives me a sliver of happiness. After a dark minute, I hear myself ask, "What was her name?"

"Whose name?" she murmurs, letting me know that she's intent on sleep.

"Your roommate."

"Oh. It was Anna. We don't keep in touch. She took a leave second semester and never came back. She was a little mixed up about things." She sighs. "Good night, Matt."

10

∿

WEDNESDAY IS ANOTHER cool day threatening rain. Though it takes me a disturbing amount of time to get started, I finally practice in the late morning, still fighting the buzz that's been coming and going. Then I've got business to take care of in the afternoon.

First, scruples be damned, I'm going to see my GP, ostensibly for a routine physical, but really because I want to make a play for a Viagra prescription. Then I'll be heading out to Elmhurst for the hospice gig. I've thrown in the towel on being all-natural in bed, because I've started dreading physical intimacy with Cynthia, which is not likely to improve my performance or our relationship. And I suspect this fear has also infected my camaraderie with the harp. My unseemly dilly-dallying this morning—I actually cleaned my bathroom—suggests I'm afraid of practicing. My old associations between the harp and sex make it difficult for me to confine a sense of having lost my touch to the bedroom only. Not practicing enough will of course be fatal in many ways.

So I pack the harp into the Volvo for later and drive to the old Rogers Park neighborhood to see the talkative and baby-faced Dr. Hands. Unfortunately, the visit will be totally out of pocket. Since the divorce punted me from Milena's health plan, I've been resisting insurance through the American String Teachers Association, economizing until I really need it. Depending on how much the Viagra prescription is, it could be time.

Contrary to every cliché about brusque and indifferent doctors, Dr. Hands chats with backyard-barbecue length and familiarity, which means he's always running behind. Today I learn about his support for President Bush, what camps his children are headed to this summer, and his wife's favorite wine. As he does every visit, he tells me, "no offense," that classical music is not his thing. I embarrass myself by having tied the hospital gown his nurse gave me in the front rather than in the back, but otherwise the exam is routine and his palpations, peerings, and listenings turn up the expected: my blood pressure is still aberrantly low, and my prolapsed mitral valve—the cause of my heart murmur, which allows a bit of blood to slosh backwards with every contraction of my left ventricle—doesn't sound worse.

"You look a little worn out, but nothing that's showing up in your vitals," Dr. Hands concludes.

The room is windowless, the walls painted forest green. A poster of the mountains in Grand Teton National Park adorns the wall across from me. I'm perched on the examination table, feeling like a child, with my feet dangling and tissue paper rustling under my ass.

I stare at a mountain and let fly. "One more thing, Doc," I say. "I have certain psychological problems that I don't want to burden you with, but—"

"*Psychological problems?*" he asks, with vaudeville intonation.

I keep my gaze on the snowy peak. "Anyway," I continue, "long story short, would you be willing to write me a Viagra prescription?"

Cary Area Public Library
1606 Three Oaks Road
Cary, IL 60013

I blush horribly.

He rocks back and forth for about four beats, looking down at the top of his fancy tablet computer on which he takes all of his notes with a little stylus. He's about five years older than me, but he seems younger. His sweep of sandy brown hair swells as if pumped with air.

"You're kind of young for that," he finally says, looking up. "Usually . . ." He smiles fatuously. "Look," he says, changing his tack, "it's a pretty serious drug, and with your low blood pressure and dizzy spells, you'd risk fainting every time you took it."

"What do you mean?"

"Well, it'll lower your blood pressure even more. Plus your heart murmur. I just haven't seen enough data on this stuff and heart irregularities—"

"Doc, I'd much rather be unconscious but functional than the other way around. You know what I'm saying?"

He purses his lips, looks past me. Then he reengages, lowering his voice. "Ah, maybe it's the divorce, you know, getting used to dating again?" He holds his computer like a kickboard and squints at me.

"It's always been bad," I say, lowering my voice, too, though of course this wasn't true with Milena. It occurs to me to mention my father's death, as if to explain everything, but I'm afraid I'll start crying. I've been disturbingly dry-eyed about my father, but thinking about losing him and my impotence at the same time threatens to send me over the edge.

"I know you don't want to hear this," he says, "but right now I can only recommend some talk therapy." He reaches out and slaps my left biceps. "Sorry, guy."

I park illegally, nearly sticking out into an intersection, and stare up at the third-floor left unit, where Milena and Audrey and I used to live and where I had erections to burn. There's the front porch, with its brick pillars, where we grilled burgers and salmon steaks and kabobs and drank daiquiris, where I gave Audrey more than a few bottles and showed her a cicada up close on her first birthday. "Bug right there," she said astutely, not late-to-speech like I was. I can see through the walls where my harps used to stand, all the way to the kitchen where Milena and I tended to have our fights.

Near the back of the apartment was also our bedroom, where, for a few years, we tried to sustain our undergraduate ways, smoking pot and listening to Brian Eno and Pink Floyd (from before they hit it big: *More, Obscured by Clouds, Meddle*), making love almost whenever we were both awake and in bed, never mind the time. I remember falling asleep with her head on my chest, listening to *Another Green World*. I had never been able to fall asleep while touching someone, and even with Milena I only did it a few times.

A few blocks away is Touhy Beach, where we played checkers on the jetty and, on several occasions, indulged our short-lived but intense mutual interest in public sex. Milena somehow turned my self-consciousness completely inside out. But maybe there was no place to go from there, and overall the move from Evanston to Rogers Park was like transplanting a flower from Tahiti to Chicago. Things eventually withered when my ambition turned desperate and Milena's bourgeois needs grew ascendant, but for a time I was happy with her, sitting around, saying almost nothing, eating pizza turnovers and drinking RC Colas, and sometimes it seems I have never really been happy before or since.

What a fool I was for blowing it with Milena! That's all I can think until I finally tear myself away from the place.

Now in the proper mood to confront a building full of dying people, I take Lake Shore Drive to the Ike and cruise toward Elmhurst, my hands getting clammy.

The Golden Prairie Hospice is a sprawling one-story complex with gray-stained cedar siding, ornamented with about twenty peaked roofs. The overall impression is of houses that were once separate—like balls of cookie dough on a baking sheet—but which have melted together to form one large building. I park, remove the harp (my backup, a smaller Lyon & Healy 85P, because it'll have a less overwhelming sound in a patient's room than my concert grand), and get it rolling across the fresh black asphalt. The wind blows in cool gusts. A sign on a parking lot island says you can't smoke *outside* in this area. The long covered walkway from the lot to the front door also has a high peaked roof, with exposed beams supporting it. The point of the airy space, I guess, is to avoid the impression that you're entering a crypt.

To open the automatic door, I gently press a round aluminum button emblazoned with the crude outline of a blue wheelchair-bound figure, then pull my harp into a vestibule where an empty wheelchair sits pushed into a corner between a bucket of driveway salt and a green snow shovel with a bend in the handle. Another button admits me to the heart of the building, where I have my eye out for a receptionist, but there is none—not even a station where a receptionist might receive. Straight across the shallow lobby, two French doors open into an area a wall plaque labels "Great Room." At one end of this room, flanked by tall bookshelves, is a monumental, nearly *Citizen Kane*–scale fireplace. Arrangements of living room furniture anticipate semi-intimate gatherings, à la the Marriott's lobby. The people here—wherever they are—are dying in style: no linoleum hallways or buzzing fluorescent lights.

I stand still in the lobby with my harp and my gear and I listen. The building is so quiet I hear my own surprisingly quick, shallow breathing. My stomach twists. It was easy to keep my head down and just live when I was like a cyclist unaware of drafting behind my father. Now that I've looked up to find him gone, the frightening awareness of my own mortality blows silently but bitterly in my face, a headwind I'm not ready to brave without the shield of some major accomplishment or a close companion.

Just as I begin to hope that no one is here and I can leave, Marcia appears, coming down the corridor.

"Our angel has come—hooray!" she says. She bops her head to the side and throws her fists weakly into the air. "Come on back to my office," she says, "and I'll tell you some unpleasant things before you set up and play."

Her office is also set up like a living room, with two small couches, armchairs, lamps, and end tables. The large windows look like the old-fashioned, multipane variety, but they're really just single rectangles with a beige vinyl grid pushed against them to make the glass seem partitioned. There's a writing desk facing the wall in a corner, but no big desk behind which she might preside, benevolent and official, when family members park their dying for the last time.

We sit in two stiff armchairs, and she asks me if I want something to drink.

"No, I better not."

"I was just thinking water or a Coke." She laughs.

I smile my hapless tight smile, as if my face were stretched across a loom. She's bringing out my desire to say *the right thing*, which of course leaves me tongue-tied.

"Ah, I see," she says to herself. "Well, now, Matt, are you ready for this?"

"I don't know."

"Good. Not knowing is very good. Let me just go over some things and then we can get you set up." She runs a ringless left hand through her hair, tucking it back behind her ear. "Now, you're an excellent musician—wonderful—but when you're playing at our hospice, you might think of yourself more as a nurse giving medical care. I know that might sound strange, but

I hope you can see that it's about the clients and their families, not your performance."

"Of course," I say.

"Music, especially live music, has amazing therapeutic properties. It lowers blood pressure, it releases endorphins. You're like a morphine drip to these people, believe me. How does that sound, being a morphine drip?"

"It sounds great. I've always wanted to be—or have—a morphine drip."

"Being and having, not so different in this case, Matt. What you do for them you're doing for yourself—that's the secret here. That's how we get through our days with a smile on our collective face. All right, rule number one: *Listen*. Listen to the nurses and the family and the client to find out what would be best to play. Some people want hymns, some people *hate* hymns; some want their favorite songs, some need songs they can't recognize, and so on. Then, as you play, watch the client and use common sense. If the client is getting agitated, maybe the song is calling up a bad memory—or maybe the client needs something. It's okay to stop and ask if the client would like you to call a nurse or play something different. Rule number two: Keep your hands washed. Leave the room if you have to sneeze. Don't come if you have a cold—don't get any more colds, Matt. They're inconvenient." She smiles. "We don't want your germs to finish someone off, understand?"

"Killing someone with my germs is my worst nightmare," I say.

"As well it should be." She peers at me, recrosses her legs.

It takes all my effort to keep my eyes on her eyes during the recrossing. Maybe she's ringless because directing a hospice suggests a level of soulfulness and moral seriousness a guy might not feel he could live up to. I think, *Just my type!* My head wobbles slightly and I chuckle.

Her look turns quizzical. "Can I ask you something, Matt?"

"Sure."

"Are you psychologically stable?"

All the molecules in the room rearrange themselves, departing from, then reassuming the shapes they were in before, as if they all decided to make a break for it but then realized that would be pointless. I don't know if her comment was prompted by the extended eye contact, or my chuckle, or every move I've made since we've met. I don't know if she's wholly serious, either.

"I think I'm almost *too* stable," I venture.

"This is going to work." She smiles. "One way or another, this is going to work."

"You're a bit strange yourself," I say. "In a good way."

"Yes, well, there's another thing you really need to know: the client's metabolism will have a tendency to match the tempo of your playing. We call this *entrainment,* and you need to be careful with this. If you play rhythmic music, especially a song the client recognizes, the client's heart will try to keep up with you. If the person is actively dying, trying to let go, your music might actually keep that from happening."

"Not a good thing?"

"I'm afraid not. On the other hand, I've also seen a harpist calm a panic attack by meeting the client's anxiety with intense music and then bringing him to a quieter place."

"Nice."

"Very risky, very difficult. All right, let's talk about your first client, Mrs. Rosemary Fennelly."

She goes on to tell me that Rosemary is eighty-three, a widow, mother of two children, grandmother of six, and she's dying of pancreatic cancer.

"No hymns for Mrs. F.," Marcia says. "Not happy with God right now. She likes snappy thirties and forties stuff. Anything with a guy, a girl, and a dance floor. Do you think you can manage that?"

"I brought a little bit of everything," I say lightly, starting to relax. Her suspicions about my sanity notwithstanding, Marcia is positive and friendly, the place *does* feel homey—or at least is not depressing in a predictable way—and the residents are apparently still firmly tethered to life's delusions. Maybe I can deal with this for an hour or two, and at least for once I'm not behaving like a selfish schmuck. If only Milena could see me now.

Marcia escorts me down a broad hallway lined with "cottages." Each door is a few feet wider than normal and appointed with a welcome mat and a porch-light sconce. A sign under each sconce reads "Oxygen in Use." Several doors are open and I can hear TVs set to various channels, one featuring the caustic questioning of Judge Judy; another sounds like a *Pokémon* episode. As we approach Rosemary's cottage, number 17, I hear a disco beat coming from inside.

Marcia knocks and calls out, "Hello." I leave my harp beside Mrs. Fennelly's welcome mat and follow Marcia into the room. Mrs. Fennelly is lying on the bed and a man sits in a recliner facing an open armoire in which a TV plays *The Ellen DeGeneres Show*. The audience members dance in front of their seats, some stylin' in the aisles.

"Hi, Gerald," Marcia says to the man. "This is Matt, our new harpist."

Gerald kills the TV with a remote and slowly rises and extends his hand. He's graying and dressed like someone who works at Cynthia's law firm: penny loafers with tassels, winecolored shirt, tie and suspenders. I say, "Hi," and we shake, but he doesn't make eye contact or speak, easing back into his recliner without having stood up completely.

The room is almost as nice as Milena's new house, with hardwood floors, two alcoves at an angle to the rest of the room, the one closer to the door with a small kitchen table and chairs, the other featuring a loveseat under a bay window, with the armoire resting between. An inert overhead fan is suspended from the peaked ceiling.

"Good afternoon, Rose," Marcia says warmly to Mrs. Fennelly. "This is Matt, your one-man band."

Mrs. Fennelly is turned toward Marcia and me, but she is unresponsive. It's even hard to tell if her glassy eyes see us, and her slack mouth also suggests no one's home. Patches of her frizzy white hair are gone, and her puffy face has a greenish cast. The skin on her thin arms appears pleated. Unless there's a pillow under the bedcovers, her belly is distended, and her ankles and the tops of her feet, which stick out of the quilt, are swollen. A pillow has been placed under her calves to raise both heels from the mattress. A musty urine-like smell—something I've never quite smelled before—pricks the air.

"Hi," I say, trying to speak as if she were fully sentient. She blinks, possibly in greeting. I look to Gerald, who I assume is her son, but he has folded his hands over his stomach and peers down his chest like he's assessing a poker hand.

"Thank you, Matt," Marcia says quietly, touching my arm, and she slips out of the room.

"Okay, then," I say, still addressing Mrs. Fennelly. "I'll bring in my harp." Each word I say to her has become quieter, as if her stillness is entraining me.

As I carry in the harp, her eyes stay unfocused, her mouth slack. The smell is now something I can taste. I quickly tune and open my book of *Fifty Great Years of Movie Songs* to "I've Got a Gal in Kalamazoo" but wonder if Marcia was joking about Mrs. Fennelly's preference for swinging dance numbers. Throwing caution to the wind, I finger the opening bars to no reaction. I play the song.

I move on to "Forty-Second Street" and "Shuffle Off to Buffalo." During the shuffle, Rosemary finally moves, twisting her spine slightly and bringing her hands up to her chest, which actually causes me to miss a note. Her fingertips fidget there for a while—some knitting-like movement I can't figure out while I'm playing. Is this agitation? A cry for help? The son's eyelids are getting heavy. I try something slower—"It's Only a Paper Moon"—hoping it might be calming, and Mrs. Fennelly and her son close their eyes, as if they're trying to guess the answer to a question. In another minute, I have put them both to sleep.

I play "I Only Have Eyes for You" as a love song for Mrs. Fennelly. I play "Evergreen" because the line about the easy chair references the son's seating arrangement. I play "Born Free," though as I get into it, it starts to seem like ironic commentary on Mrs. F.'s condition. Lying in sprawled positions that remind me of the St. Valentine's Day massacre, the Fennellys remain stubbornly asleep—though the son stirs once during "Born Free" in a way that suggests maybe he's wondering what I'm thinking.

At last, I stop, lean my harp forward, and listen to their breathing. Gerald respires regularly and quietly, laying down a basic beat. Mrs. Fennelly solos in a wild and halting manner: her breathing seems to stop for ten or twenty seconds before she takes two or three more or less consistently spaced rattling breaths. I notice a small black sore on the edge of her left heel.

I pack up and tiptoe out of the room before she can die. The corridor now feels relatively cool. There are a few visitors moving about the hallways. I think of my father, not on his exercise mat of death, but in a psychiatric hospital, on his back, on suicide watch, pumped full of meds, maybe wondering if he would ever make it out, feeling the responsibility of seven children and a wife, knowing there was something seriously broken about him. A thought wobbles into view like a butterfly, alights between my eyes: *If I stay impotent with Cynthia and blow this audition, will I lose it like my dad did?*

I tell myself I'm all right, despite the fact that it feels as though someone is standing on my chest. My breath gets short, and dizziness descends like a cloud of nerve gas. My hands saddle the harp's neck, precisely where my Aphrodite is cracked back home, and I lean my cheek against the wood. My knee bones dissolve. I breathe deeply, trying to control the dizziness. I console myself with the fact that it's just dizziness and not a nervous breakdown, and then wonder if this *is* a nervous breakdown.

A nurse (I'm guessing from her shoes) passes me in the hall. The harp's neck hides my face, but I speak to the sound of her passing: "I need to lie down."

"Excuse me?"

"I'm sorry, is there a place I can lie down? Right away? Otherwise, I'll vomit."

"Oh dear," she says in a way that makes it impossible for me to tell how my problem rates on her scale of concerns. I can tell, though, that she's not used to having a strapping, squared-off guy like me turn out to be a dizzy pantywaist. She touches my arm, but I don't dare shift my head to look at her.

"It's not that I'm freaked out," I say, though it's uncomfortable to speak in this state. "I just get dizzy sometimes." When I stop speaking, I sense she is gone. An instant later, a curved plastic basin rises toward my face.

"Here you go," she says. "Come this way."

Having an ergonomically correct vomit receptacle on hand steadies me somewhat. I take the basin from her and carry it at the ready as she guides me down the hallway to an unoccupied cottage. The door's creak echoes in the room, which is furnished exactly like Mrs. Fennelly's. All the blinds on the half-dozen windows are open and the room glows with sunless light.

The nurse leads me to the bed, which is fitted only with a mattress cover. Despite a flash of concern about having my shoes on, I lie down, place the basin an arm length away on the mattress, lower my cheek to a caseless pillow with my head turned from the windows, and hold still. As the nurse leaves— I still haven't seen her face—I say thanks. She comes back and drapes a blanket over me. I say thanks again and, breathing minute by minute, sink into shallow sleep.

After some time, I open my eyes and focus on the door to the bathroom in this cottage. I can't sleep here. My gig is over. I need to be elsewhere.

I sit up and feel a negotiable amount of dizziness. I stand and lurch toward the bathroom. I splash lukewarm water on my face and pat my cheeks dry with a scratchy paper towel, then raise my eyes to the vanity mirror but see only a dark square. I flick on the light and find that the door to the medicine cabinet is not a mirror but varnished wood. I suppose by the time you've moved here, you don't want to see your face. Then again, it's disconcerting to expect your own eyes and instead see something that looks very much like a casket lid. I peer more closely, into the grain, and wonder if somehow this is a special mirror for examining one's second face.

Not right now, I say to myself.

11

~~~

A FTER I GET back from the hospice, I restore myself at Big
Tony's Pizza with two large pepperoni slices and a quart-
sized syrupy fountain Coke and spend Wednesday evening and
all of Thursday indoors, willing away dizziness, teaching two
students, and practicing with the focus of a very frightened
man. But suddenly, in one of those unexpected, life-saving
shifts, it's not the harp I'm afraid of but rather the scene in Mrs.
Fennelly's cottage, and I seem able to improve on almost every
piece I touch.

On Friday morning, the music for Moncayo's *Huapango* arrives in the mail. While listening to a recording I bought on
Amazon, my fingers and I look over the score, and we find that
it requires tenacious dexterity. I set aside four precious days to
learn it. I'll need to start playing through every piece at least
two or three times a day, to get all twenty-five into my hands
simultaneously. But first, I must go to the harp factory to fix this
buzz.

As I roll the harp past T.R.'s garden, I'm hit with a lot of changes I haven't been noticing. If you've ever been trapped in a refrigerator only to have the door flung open just before you black out, you have some sense of what a Chicago spring feels like. There's a dogwood in bloom and red and yellow tulips and blue-purple hyacinths. The mercury has vaulted into the seventies, and small puffy white clouds hang in the blue sky. As I drive west on Cermak with all the Volvo's windows open, maple seeds propeller down.

Chicago happens to be a global hub of harp manufacturing, including the big kahuna, Lyon & Healy, and a smaller, scrappier operation, Aphrodite Harps, run by Stanley Nowak, a third-generation harp builder. Stanley's factory is a long, low brown-brick building, with glass-block windows topped by transoms that are levered open. I park in the back and walk around. From the street, the only indication that musical instruments are made here are two folk harps drawn facing each other on the rusty gray steel door one step up from the sidewalk.

I head inside, and beyond a tiny vestibule is an open room with a hodgepodge of worker stations. A man in black shorts, T-shirt, and a leather apron, with his white gym socks pulled over his calves, is using a piece of equipment to shave a small metal part, sending sparks into the air. Another man etches something into a neck plate. Two others are clamping a neckless, stringless harp onto a rack padded with skanky purple carpet. They barely glance at me before returning to work. An old caged gray fan, as tall as a sunflower, blows air. Sunlight slanting in from the high windows illuminates enough dust to make the air seem as thick as water, but no one's wearing a mask. A tape player broadcasts *Capriccio Espagnol*, which happens to be on the St. Louis list. Maybe these men would rather listen to something else, but Stanley's shtick is to be totally focused on the artistic ends of harp making.

Through a wide doorway to the left is the much larger woodworking room, with all the saws and planing machines and gluing vises. But I go to the right, past a time clock labeled with a hand-lettered sign in Polish, and into another small dingy room, where the only woman in the shop—Stanley's sister Marge, heavy in a collarless shirt, with a nimbus of gray hair—sorts neck hardware in a long case.

I used to love everything about this place, where meticulous attention shrinks the world to the piece of wood one is carving, the hole one is drilling, the eyelet one is inserting. It resonated with a positive sense of my robothood—that I could play with something like perfect concentration and mechanical precision. I used to imagine that if I were ever injured, the ambulance should bring me here instead of a hospital, both for physical repair and psychic rehab. But since my divorce and my troubles with Cynthia, I'm more worried about the downsides of robotic behavior: moving herky-jerky through the world, holding myself too tensely, projecting a disconcertingly blank affect to conceal my inner hijinks.

I go through one more door, and in the quiet showroom, with its low dropped ceiling and rec-room paneling, I find Stanley and his second-in-command, Carl. Stanley is a short, sleepy-eyed man with lead-gray hair combed straight back and huge hairy forearms that he proudly displays year-round in untucked, short-sleeve dress shirts. Carl sports bushy sideburns and aviator glasses with a classic tape repair between the eyes; his long brown hair is pulled back in a ponytail. Shaped uncannily like a bowling pin, Carl towers over Stanley, bringing out the bowling ball in Stanley's physique.

"Matt, take a look at this," Stanley says in greeting. He leads me to a new harp. "Sit down, tell me what you think. It's just wood and metal until a musician plays it."

"And glue," Carl says, smiling and extending his hand, which I shake. "A *lot* of glue."

"Sit," Stanley commands. "It's tuned."

I sit and play some *Symphonie fantastique.* The bottom of the soundboard is unusually broad and curved and gives the instrument a deep, clear sound.

"Sounds great," I say.

"Consider it, Matt. We're going to do everything we can to make your harp right, but you deserve a new instrument, huh?"

I play a few more licks with an expression of consideration on my face, but I'm impatient to get my harp diagnosed. "Should I bring it in?" I ask.

"Of course," Stanley says, tight-lipped.

Carl and I lunge and march, respectively, down a back corridor to the parking lot where we fetch the cracked concert grand.

"Jesus!" Stanley exclaims, as Carl wheels it in. "At least get a new cover, for the love of Pete!" The fluorescent lights of the showroom are particularly revealing: along the pillar, where I grip to lift the harp, the golden mustard color has darkened into a sort of sweat-stain brown. No wonder Vikram went nuts over it. But a new cover is $450 and there's no way I can spend that much money on something I don't absolutely need.

I play a bit to demonstrate the buzz. Carl winces, then gets to work. He clips a small pickup to the soundboard. A wire runs to a boom box–sized electronic tuner with an oscilloscope, set up on a music stand. He begins tuning, lines rippling and coalescing across the screen, reminding me of an electrocardiogram. I think of Mrs. Fennelly's heart clenching and unclenching in time to what could very well be, at any moment, her final dance number. As sounds go, the heartbeat is almost too beautiful and terrifyingly fragile to be believed. It seems a sort of cosmic joke that something so essential makes a sound that isn't constant but leaves and comes back, over and over.

After Carl tunes, he replaces the two metal disks that pinch the sixth-octave C string into sharp or flat. He tightens a few screws in the neck plate with a tiny Allen wrench. The buzz persists. Finally, he says, "I think we need to open it up."

Stanley motions with his head, and I follow him into his office. The place is small and tidy, with a metal desk, a few file cabinets, and a table to the right that's covered with binders and wood samples. Rows of eight-by-ten glossies of Nowaks, harps, and harpists cover the walls. I take a seat in a low-slung vinyl chair, while Stanley climbs into a high-backed executive chair, the headrest of which rises well above his head.

"Matt," he says in a tired voice, "just let us finish the job, okay?"

"Finish what job?"

"I'm saying, you leave it here, we have a little accident. You call your insurance company. Damaged in transit. It's standard."

"I can't do that," I say. At the same time, I'm thinking, *Maybe I can do this.*

"Sure you can. It's standard business practice. That's what insurance is for. You *did* have an accident, didn't you?"

"Yeah, but it's not like it's destroyed."

"Maybe not to some numbnuts adjuster, but if it's no good to you, a musical artist, it's basically totaled, am I right?"

"I'm not sure it's totaled," I say. "I've got an audition, I can't be switching harps right now. Plus I'm dating a lawyer who defends insurance companies."

"Do I do things right?" Stanley asks, raising his prodigious forearms and his voice. "Look at me. I do things right. You want a good harp for the audition, you have to do what it takes. The harp you just played is available—that's not a floor model. We made it for a lady in the Houston Symphony and, long story, but now she's not taking it."

"How much is it?"

"I take a thousand right off the top. Eighteen nine. You heard how it sounds."

I lower my voice as if the office is bugged. "How much would I get . . ."

"It wouldn't cover everything. Insurance would pay out ten, maybe eleven thousand."

Which means seven, maybe eight thousand.

"The rest—payments," Stanley says. He leans forward and chops his hand across his metal desk, spacing out the payments. He smiles.

Winning the audition is the only way I'll have the salary to make such payments. On the other hand, the insurance money plus selling the 85P, which would be quite painful, would bring me close to that new harp. No one would give a hoot about the little lie, really. Except maybe Cynthia—if she found out. But then, the unpredictabilities of a new instrument disturb me, and why commit a crime to go through that if I don't have to?

"Do you think Carl can fix the buzz?"

Stanley growls. He rubs his mouth and chin with two downward strokes, as if erasing that part of his face. His voice goes quiet: "We'll try everything. But I'm telling you, it's on its last legs. A crack like that is just going to get worse. Could be a fast mover. I'm being honest with you, Matt: you can't rely on that instrument anymore."

This last statement hits me like a haymaker. This harp was practically brand-new when I started playing on it at the high school. I've squandered the gift, let a decades-wide window of opportunity close too soon. I stare down at my ratty tennis shoes. I crack my knuckles like an ingrate. I realize, once again, with crushing certainty, that it was incredibly stupid of me to have devoted my life to the harp.

"What about rebuilding the neck?" I say.

"I put a rush on it, you have it back in four, five weeks. Six thousand dollars."

I stare back at him.

"Let's think about this," Stanley says, trying to check his exasperation. "*All* the possibilities. Let's give Carl until Monday. Then we'll know where we stand, which is always good, Matty."

I get home, make lunch, then sit dully at the dining room table, chewing my peanut butter sandwich and staring at the empty space in the living room where my blonde Aphrodite used to stand. *Huapango* beckons. I don't like the idea of getting down on it with the 85P, but letting the difference between the two harps keep me from practicing would bode ill. Just as I'm dumping my apple core in the trash, the phone rings.

It's my hospice buddy Marcia Marquardt.

"How are you feeling?" she asks.

"Not bad," I say. "Sorry I flaked out the other day."

"You didn't *flake out*. Have you ever seen a doctor about that dizziness?"

"It's just a weird thing—it's not medical."

"Well, you ought to get it checked, just to be sure. By the way, did you really play 'Born Free' for the Fennellys?"

"I know," I say. "That was bad."

"Oh, no." She laughs. "Actually, her son told me you 'greased the skids' for her—that's how the man expresses himself."

"Really."

"He was so *appreciative*. He's just not that good at talking to people. So much going on in his life I can't even tell you. He's been at the end of his rope for months, and yet he spent so much time with her. Anyway, she passed on about an hour after you left."

"Oh," I say. "I'm sorry."

A strong feeling sweeps past me, like the brief wind off a speeding car when you're standing too close to the road. *You didn't even know her,* I tell myself. Still, I wonder if she was satisfied with her life, if she had any consoling thoughts or beliefs to protect her when the end arrived, or if it was just a slow, terrifying slide into oblivion—which is what it felt like when I was with her.

"Listen, I'd like you to come back on Monday and meet some people."

"Oh, gosh," I say. "I don't know."

"A very nice couple and a very nice dying father. And the board approved a hundred dollars each time you come out."

The redemptive power of serving others is a form of protection against death that I repudiated when I set out as an adult, but maybe I need to hedge my bets. "All right," I say, though it sounds like someone else's voice. "Anything for you, Marcia," I add dryly.

She laughs.

As I hang up, what I'm really doing to myself flashes in the corner of my mind, like the mouse that I discovered darting across my kitchen floor last night: either I'm going to lose my marbles once and for all or I'm going to prove that I'll never lose them, no matter what.

12

≈≈≈

L ATE SATURDAY MORNING—a warm day with an armada of
big white clouds overhead—Audrey and I head up to a wedding I'm playing in Glenview. I can't afford to turn down a gig
and I can't afford to give up one of my days with her, so I sometimes impress her into service as my roadie. Surprisingly, she
doesn't seem to mind, maybe because she gets to wear her frilly
white dress with the green sash and her shiny Mary Janes, or
maybe because she gets a roadie's prestige without having to
perform any of a roadie's tasks.

Today, for example, she's only carrying her stuffed unicorn
that had its electronic guts removed one grim day, just before I
was asked to leave the Rogers Park apartment, when Milena
apparently heard the unicorn's song one time too many. Now,
rolling my 85P harp up a broad concrete walkway to the church
entrance, with Audrey and her mute unicorn in tow, I can't help
but feel we're a pair of refugees from the land of nuclear families, making a bid for repatriation.

St. Patricia's Church, built in 1975 according to its cornerstone, looks like a sombrero: it's a circular mass of stucco and metal that gives way to a ring of stained-glass windows right under a Superdome-like roof with a rounded steeple rising in the center. As we approach the entryway, a young man in a white button-down shirt and blue jeans holds the door open for us and the dollied harp.

"Thanks, dude," I say.

"You're welcome," he says, with a touch of passive-aggressive stiffness.

I settle Audrey in a pew close to where I'll be playing, tune, warm up, and meet the large wedding party. Heading behind the chancel looking for a restroom, I run into the doorman again, now dressed in green and white vestments, straightening up at the drinking fountain. His hair is short on the sides but makes a pleasing dense wave across the top of his handsome head, JFK-style. I'm struck by how young he is—I'd heard they'd stopped making new priests. His white collar cuts a clean demarcation on his neck. His sacred garments drape and conceal his torso, giving the impression that his elite noggin is traveling like a jewel set on a green and white pillow.

"Oh, hello," I say.

"Hello again," he says. "Do we need to work anything out?"

"Sorry I didn't recognize you when I came in, Father."

He smiles and shakes his head, once, to dispel the notion. "I'm Fred," he says, extending a soft hand, and he proceeds to enlighten me on my major entrances: the tricky segue from prelude music to "Wagner's 'Bridal Chorus'" (he's not about to call it "Here Comes the Bride" like a civilian), the unity candle ceremony, the recessional. Stagecraft under control, he sighs.

"Weddings just don't pay, do they?" he says, one vendor to another.

"How so?" I ask.

"Well, you're here all Friday night for the rehearsal. Saturday everyone wants to come early to get dressed and take pictures and so on. Then they have more pictures and the reception afterwards. Someone has to stick around and lock up."

"And that would be you."

"I can't attend the reception, even if they invite me. I can't stagger into church Sunday morning for the eight-thirty mass." He laughs incredulously.

"Yeah," I say.

"I guess you have to look at it as a labor of love," he concludes, and lapses into a thoughtful silence.

"Well," I say, "I've got to make a pit stop before we start."

"See you in a few," he sighs.

When I exit the restroom, the bride bustles by, holding her skirts up in her fists, all stifled tears and white crinoline. She dives, arms outstretched, into the nearby women's room. The door threatens to close on her train, and she turns and grabs up cloth in one hand while holding the door with the other. I stare stupidly: her eyes are full of tears, yet they suggest an intensity capable of lifting a car to free a crushed child. I bow my head and turn away. Her sobs echo against the tiles. On my way down the corridor, the maid of honor bursts through a back door and scurries past me, carrying a small purse in two hands like a first aid kit. She's followed seconds later by the bride's mother in a yellow dress with a huge corsage roosting below her clavicle. The mother's measured nod to me says, *You are hired help and will not speak of what you have seen upon pain of death.*

I restraighten my tie and head back into the church, where the first guests are being seated by the ushers. The pews are arranged in a broad arc with several aisles to the front, creating a sort of altar-in-the-round feel. I take my seat at the foot of the steps of one approach to the altar, pull the harp into my arms, and jauntily plink out prelude tunes.

The bride appears on cue during the processional, arm hooked against her father's elbow. She's a pale blonde whose updo has been piled and knotted extravagantly. It's hard not to call out, "Let's hear it for the bride's hair!" Her makeup has been well restored, but her lips quiver slightly. The groom is an anvil-headed jock with an appealing grin. He wears a sharply tailored black tux with long tails and a white bow tie. As if to best display these beautiful humans, someone has decided to give them seats and kneelers in front of the congregation, on the dais to the right of the altar.

With a tiny black microphone clipped to the neckline of his chasuble, Father Fred barrels through the first half of the liturgy at an exhilarating pace, like a downhill skier on the very edge of control. There's something old school about the way he reduces the service to a mere verbal sequence, shorn of emotion and sense. You've got to admire his enunciatory chops, at a minimum. Then he takes the podium for his homily. Done playing for the moment, I am sitting in one of the front-row pews off to the side, with Audrey next to me. I've promised her an ice cream cone if she can keep still during the ceremony.

"What a beautiful day!" Father Fred begins, in a much slower, more cornball tone. "And it's so exciting to see Jennifer and Todd looking their best on their big day." He pauses ever so slightly, as if to assure himself that he's used their correct names. "And Jennifer and Todd, I know you couldn't have prayed for better weather—I know . . . I know I couldn't have."

He looks down at the lectern, absorbing the stillness. Maybe he botched a weather joke? He lifts his head and troops on: "You're young, you're with family and friends, on this, your most exciting day. You can look forward to a delicious meal, dancing the night away. And this celebration of God's love for us will seal your love for each other. Magnificent!"

He wags his head in happy disbelief at their good fortune, yet as he prolongs this gesture, it acquires rueful overtones.

"But I hate to break it to you," he continues. "Just you wait, because it's not always going to be so magnificent. Not always so perfect."

Father Fred pauses to let his bold gambit sink in. A new sort of silence settles on the congregation, as before a verdict is read in a courtroom.

"Jennifer and Todd, there are going to be trials down the road, rain when you want sunshine. Disappointments. Bummers. Sometimes the dog makes a mess and we step in it. That's a part of life, too."

Titters pass over the pews, and he nods. Audrey pulls on my sleeve and whispers, "Dog poop," in my ear. I nod thoughtfully and pat her leg to keep her quiet.

"And those are the times I want to talk about with you today," Father Fred continues. He looks over to where the bride and groom sit rigidly with their hands on their knees, staring at him like a pair of pharaohs. He smiles warmly as he proceeds:

"I know it's hard to believe right now, but little habits of your spouse will get to you: Jennifer doesn't squeeze the toothpaste from the bottom; Todd always tracks mud into the house. You won't have as much to say to each other as you used to. You're going to have terrible fights, where you'll say things just to be hurtful. You may not even be true to each other. Oh, I know you're not thinking of that now, but you, Jennifer, you may be tempted by a handsome fellow at work who gives you a lot of attention. And Todd, you're going to have some wild oats. You may go out to the bar right after dinner instead of helping with the dishes."

An odd look appears in the couple's eyes.

"But these are just the everyday challenges, and in any strong marriage we need to meet those challenges. But let me tell you a little story about a couple I married before I came to St. Pat's.

"Aaron and Beth started their married life on a magnificent day very much like today. Right off the bat, God gave them two beautiful children. Aaron had an excellent job, and Beth stayed home to raise the kids, something she had always wanted to do."

The bride looks down in her lap.

"Then one day Aaron was playing softball and got hit in the head with a line drive. The impact damaged a formerly benign brain cyst that began to swell, causing terrible nausea and occasional seizures. Aaron started to struggle at work. There was an economic downturn, and Aaron was 'downsized.'

"With no salary coming in, Beth was forced to take a telemarketing job, using her home phone so she could keep raising her children. Meanwhile, after the cyst proved to be inoperable, Aaron had a reaction to an experimental medication and lost sight in one eye. Then one of their children, two-year-old Sarah, suddenly came down with a very high fever that just wouldn't go away. It was caused by a mysterious virus. The doctors said it was one in a million—Sarah died in the hospital a month later."

The bride stares saucer-eyed at Father Fred. Her mother sits straight-backed in her pew with her eyes closed. The bride's father has the crotch of his meaty hand wedged under his nose, his eyes apparently fixed on a hymnal holder. A stream of tears suddenly rushes down the bride's cheek, and she brushes her face with a gloved hand.

"Beth hung on," Father Fred affirms. "But it was hard. She was honest with me: She told me she wanted to run. Pick up and go. Get out of her marriage. Abandon her family to Social Services. She had even lined up a job as a cook on a cruise ship. And do you know what I said? I said, 'This is a time when *your love for your husband* can be truly magnificent, when *your love for your husband* can be truly perfect.' "

The bride covers her nose and mouth with both hands, as if to muffle a scream. Audrey sits forward in her seat, watching intently, her unicorn in her lap.

"The stress was getting to Beth. She suffered migraine headaches and hallucinations—but she stayed. After years of living off social security insurance and the generosity of friends and relatives, Beth and Aaron moved into subsidized apartment housing with their remaining child, Jared, who hopes to start kindergarten next year. Though often bedridden, Aaron takes calls on a helpline for a computer company and spends every waking moment of his free time with his wife and son, hoping for a miracle treatment that will halt the growth of the cyst. Meanwhile, Beth cooks and cleans and loves them all—and with a smile on her face. Now, that's what I call a marriage."

With a strangled cry, the bride rises from her seat, says something half under her breath, negotiates the carpeted stairs, and runs down a side aisle.

Father Fred clutches the lectern and gazes after her, his mouth drawn in a slanting line. Murmuring rises from the congregation. The maid of honor goes in pursuit, but the bride's mother sits stonily for a time, until a nudge from her husband rouses her and she drifts out of the pew. The groom looks around, ashen-faced. Then he leaps to his feet and jogs down the steps to seek his betrothed.

Meanwhile, Father Fred gathers himself and speaks:

"Let us all spend a few moments in quiet reflection."

He looks at me, nods meaningfully, and withdraws to his chair behind the altar. I slip over to the harp and fire up "Clair de lune," which I know by heart. A feeling of intermission descends on the church, but no one gets up to leave. After I finish the song, I notice Audrey looking very upset.

I want to go to her, but find myself looking at Father Fred, waiting to be excused. Meanwhile, I'm playing nothing, and centrifugal force threatens to hurl everyone out to the parking lot.

Father Fred takes the podium again: "As we reflect, let us pray for the hearts of Todd and Jennifer, that they may see God's truth." Then he gives me another nod.

Just as I pull the harp back, the bride's mother pokes her head in the doorway through which everyone has been disappearing. Father Fred, reseating himself, pauses and lifts his chin expectantly. Before the congregation can turn to see what's going on, she shakes her head emphatically. Father Fred calmly returns to the lectern.

"Ladies and gentlemen," he says, "the vows of holy matrimony will not be celebrated here today. This mass is ended. Go in peace to love and serve the Lord."

When I get over to Audrey in the pew, she is fighting off tears. "Is he going to be okay?" she asks.

"Who? The groom?"

"Aaron."

"I hope so. The doctors are helping him."

"Are they going to get a divorce?"

"Aaron and Beth?"

She nods. She is working very hard not to cry. Every time her chest begins to swell into a sob, she stops it, like holding back a sneeze.

"They're staying together, looks like."

"What about Jennifer and Todd?"

"Well, they didn't quite get married," I say. "I don't know what's going to happen with them."

I'm waiting for her to mention Sarah, the two-year-old. Her chin flexes in a trembling pout that suddenly breaks and she starts to cry and then it seems her inability to stop herself from crying makes her cry even more. I hug her.

"Sweetie," I say. "Sweetie, it's okay."

"It's not okay," she says, which is something Milena started saying around the house after she was in therapy for a month, just before we separated. This replaced Milena saying "That sucks wind" to describe a bad thing.

I hold Audrey. She cares and feels, and this shouldn't be a bad thing. She fights with her sobs, until she lets out a tremendous hiccup.

"Oh, now, hey, that was some hiccup!" I say.

She hiccups again.

. . .

At Maggie Moo's, an ice cream "shoppe" in an upscale Wilmette strip mall, Audrey is crying because the hiccupping won't stop.

"Peppermint ice cream is just the cure for hiccups," I say.

Ten minutes later, most of the cone and a tree's worth of napkins go through the slimed swinging door of the trash receptacle. Audrey's lack of appetite may be the most disturbing symptom yet. And the hiccups persist. "It hurts!" she complains, putting her hand on her chest. Her eyes have a wild, haunted look. Now that it's crunch time, her unicorn proves useless. In fact, when I suggest that she imagine her unicorn has the hiccups, she shrieks, "That's not funny, Daddy!"

The unicorn is a poor substitute for what she really wants—a dog. But Daddy is nervous around dogs, and fragile harps and pets don't mix, so Audrey has her unicorn.

It's only two-thirty, and I'm not supposed to bring her back to Milena's house until four, but Audrey has been crying and hiccupping for almost an hour now, fifty minutes longer than any bout of hiccups I've ever witnessed. I've suggested holding her breath, the only cure I know, but this hasn't worked. The dangerously thin girl behind the counter suggests drinking a glass of water from the wrong side of the rim, and Audrey tries this to no avail.

"I can't make it—stop!" Audrey cries miserably, hiccupping, flaying my last nerve and breaking my heart all at once.

I take her outside Maggie Moo's, into the open world, the only space commensurate with her pain. "Look at those clouds," I say. She leans back, looks straight up into the sky—and sneezes! Surely this has reset her upper respiratory tract.

She blinks a few times, smiles, and hiccups.

"Let's go see Mama," I say.

On the way, the hiccups occur roughly every five seconds. We pull up in front of Milena's house an hour early. Milena answers the door in yoga pants, bare feet, and a T-shirt with super-short sleeves and an inch-of-midriff-revealing hem.

"What's going on?" she says, tucking some hair behind her ear.

"Mama!" Audrey shouts, and she runs into Milena's arms, dropping her unicorn in the doorway. Milena crouches to give her a hug and looks at me over Audrey's shoulder.

"We just did a wedding. She's got the hiccups," I say, picking up the unicorn. "Really bad."

"The hiccups?"

"Like for the past hour and a half," I say.

"I can't stop them," Audrey whines.

"We've tried everything," I say. "Or, actually, we've tried *a few* things."

"Come on in," Milena says, her eyes wary. She sits on the couch with Audrey on her lap. The couch is fine caramel leather, no doubt Scandinavian, and probably cost close to what I'll pay T.R. this year in rent. "My tummy really hurts," Audrey says, putting her hand near her diaphragm. She hiccups yet again. Now, fully aware that her mother is no magic cure, she lapses into nerve-shredding wails of pain and despair. Milena gets a paper lunch bag, stands over Audrey, and says, "Breathe into this bag." She brings it toward Audrey's mouth, then abruptly crumples it. "I can't do this," Milena says, turning to me. "What if she passes out?"

"I don't want to pass out," Audrey says, total terror in her eyes.

"Oh, sweetie," I say.

"Maybe I should take her to the ER?" Milena says more quietly.

The singular pronoun stings. I wonder where Steve is.

"Maybe," I say, though I don't want her to do this. I want us all to stay in this living room together for as long as possible. "But what do you think they'd do?"

"Give her a shot of something?" Milena says.

"I don't want a shot!" Audrey yells.

Milena closes her eyes and puts her slim fingers to her temples.

"You know, I could play harp for her," I say, because it occurs to me that maybe I could entrain Audrey's hiccups to a safe stop or at least use the attempt to show I'm a helpful egg whose presence might be suffered a bit longer. I give Milena a smooth explanation of why entrainment might work, which makes her stand up and pace. "And if that doesn't work, we'll take her," I say.

"I don't know, Matt," Milena says. She looks away with her arms down straight and her palms parallel to the floor. It's her trying-to-keep-catastrophe-at-bay pose. Maybe she's thinking about Steve.

Audrey hiccups as violently as ever. "Ow!" she whimpers.

The distant echoing roar of a plane coming in for a landing at O'Hare grows in the room. It sounds like someone rolling a laundry cart on the roof.

"It'll relax her," I say. "It can change her breathing. It's magic."

"Yeah, okay," Milena says in a low voice, one hand to her brow.

I go out to the Volvo and get my axe. Despite Audrey's agony, I catch myself wishing she'll still be hiccupping when I get back, so I can be a hero. I'm too impatient to put the harp on the dolly, so, glad my 85P is slightly lighter, I just pick the sucker up, one hand gripping the column, one hand hooked in a sound hole, and walk up two sets of stairs and through the door Milena is holding open.

I put the harp down and have a terrific headrush that nearly makes me pass out. My heart is racing. Taking stairs too fast exacerbates my mitral valve leak. I smile, a little dazed, and pause to catch my breath.

Then the old family unit assembles in Milena's new living room: Audrey lies supine on the fancy-ass couch, Milena sits next to her, and I'm across the room, standing at the harp, facing them.

I choose the first ten notes from the third movement of Saint-Saëns's *Fantaisie,* a duo in which a supporting harp eventually draws even with a pensive and lyrical violin. These notes at the beginning of the third are low and stealthy in the bass, and I play them over and over, trying to land the tenth on Audrey's hiccup, which is still coming about every five seconds. After a few tries, I am timing it perfectly, and when Audrey notices, she smiles briefly and looks up at her mama, who smiles, too. Audrey and I are in sync for about two minutes, and then very gradually I begin to slow down.

By the end of the next minute, I'm playing ten notes in six beats, and Audrey's hiccup still lands on the fifth note. I bust a sweat, because keeping in sync with her feels as precarious as balancing a bottle of beer on my nose. But my training kicks in, and I make myself into a metronome running down: ten notes in seven beats, ten notes in ten beats, ten notes in fifteen beats. Ten notes in thirty beats. One hiccup every five notes—and Audrey's eyes close.

And then comes a tenth note with no accompanying hiccup, but instead an all-but-silent snore. Milena puts her hand on Audrey's forehead, smooths her hair to the side. Personally, I wouldn't touch Audrey when she is this shallow in the ocean of sleep, and if we were still married, I probably would have said something sharp about that. No wonder Milena kicked me out.

Milena looks at me with no small amount of gratitude in her eyes. She rises carefully from the couch and motions for me to follow her around the wall and into the kitchen. Near the sink, she turns and faces me.

"What a head case, that kid," I say, louder than I want to.

Milena puts a finger to her lips, then she puts her hand on my neck to pull my ear toward her and whispers, "Thank you."

I pull away and look into her smiling face. Her misaligned eyes peer into mine.

"Do you want some water?" she asks, keeping her voice down. She grabs two pint-sized blue glasses from the cupboard.

"Dang, Mil," I say involuntarily. Between the touch on my neck and her vulnerable eyes and the view of her stretching to retrieve the glasses, she's acting on me in a powerful way.

"Dang what?" she says, working the faucet. I wish I could see her face.

I don't answer because I sense she knows.

She turns, with her eyes down, and hands me a glass.

I lift it. "Here's to getting along well enough to do right by the kid."

She raises her eyes to me. "Yeah," she says, smiling shyly.

We clink and have a sip.

"How are things?" I say.

"Things are all right," she says evenly.

We get very interested in drinking our water.

"Better go," I say. I put my glass on the counter and she does, too. I raise my hand toward her in an ambiguous wave, half pointing at her, half suggesting I want to bring her close for a pat on the back or a hug.

"Good seeing you," she says. "You're not as bad as they say."

She makes frank eye contact and steps in my general direction, though maybe just to lead me to the door.

I move toward her, and our bodies decide on a quick hug good-bye, because after the Audrey trauma we can't part as distantly as we usually do. As we separate, my hand touches her hand and she holds on to my fingers. She looks up at me. I smile at her but fear I'm staring like a robot. The side of her mouth opens, possibly just from nerves, possibly on the way to an encouraging smile.

I lean down and she rises up, lifting her lips, and we kiss.

Soon we're making out standing up in her kitchen like a pair of teenagers. Then she turns and, holding my hand, leads me downstairs into the family room, where there's a knockabout couch, a TV, an elliptical machine pointed at the TV, and an expanse of carpet populated with Audrey's toys. A dark beer bottle stands on an empty plate on the floor near the couch.

Over the years, she taught me what she likes, and I kiss her and undress her and touch her in those ways now. This is how she breathes and puts her head to the side and shows her lower teeth. She stills wears the same sly floral perfume that mixes with her Caress soap. She undoes my belt and corkscrews her hand into my underwear. Her first touch on me is almost scalding, creating a crazed ticklishness I have to get past, but in no time I do. When I touch her, she's as turned on as I've ever felt her. She slips back onto the couch and pulls me on top of her.

My pants are still around my ankles, but I'm inside her, and it's as if I never met Cynthia and my father never died and we're twenty again and Audrey isn't born and everything is possible. The familiarity of her body is so profound that I seem to get my own body back. Pleasure rushes up with surprising force, like being pushed from behind off a high cliff.

I pull out at the last second and finish myself. And maybe it's this gesture that turns everything from loving passion to something else, because when I'm done it's like waking up from a dream.

Through sliding glass doors that lead to the patio, I see a vehicle, a red Ford Escape, slow in the alley, and then I see the garage door rising.

"Shit!" Milena says. She bounds off the couch and pulls her

underwear and yoga pants over one ankle. She hops three times before she can get them over the other ankle and pull them up.

My pants never got past my shoes, so I quickly follow suit. The faster I try to button my shirt, the clumsier my fingers behave.

"Shit, Matt, shit!" she says, making for the stairs blind with her top over her head.

I follow, doing my belt.

"Hey, girl!" Milena says in a totally new and loud voice, suddenly stopping at the top of the stairs. "Feeling better?"

My whole body seizes on the stairs at the glimpse of Audrey I get from around Milena's hip. It's like seeing a ghost. I hunker on the steps and tuck in my shirt, though I'm not finished buttoning.

Milena steps into the kitchen and crouches down to give Audrey a hug. I continue up the stairs and onto the landing, crowding them a bit, trying to get as much out of Steve's view as I can. Audrey stares at me over Milena's shoulder, as if she's not sure who I am. I try to imagine Audrey's angle of vision from the top of the stairs, or what it would have been had she come down a few steps.

"How about a glass of water, sweetie?" I ask.

"Yeah," Milena says, breaking the embrace, moving toward the cupboard. Audrey keeps staring at me, but her eyes move from my face to my chest.

The door on the lower level opens.

Milena runs the faucet with a glass in her hand. "Go sit," she says.

I button my last two buttons on the way to the living room, glad Audrey is following me.

"Hey, Steve, Matt's here," Milena calls out. Her voice is not natural.

I sit in a chair in the living room and Audrey sits on the couch and flicks on the Cartoon Network to an episode of *The Power-puff Girls*.

I can't hear what's going on on the lower level. There's probably a smell down there. Steve could be brooding over discoveries, making inferences, because he doesn't come upstairs right away.

"How does it feel?" I ask Audrey. "No more hiccups, hey?"

"Good," she says, staring at the TV.

Milena hurries into the living room carrying two glasses of water. Her face is still flushed from sex. She gives me a glass and puts one on a coaster on the coffee table near Audrey's knee. Then she sits on the edge of an armchair. Steve finally comes upstairs, carrying a box, and Milena rises to greet him near the passageway to the kitchen.

Steve is tall and handsome in jeans and a nice dress shirt. He actually looks a lot like Brian Williams, the news anchor, with a forehead the size of a billboard, keen blue-gray eyes, and large feet. It's very hard not to like him, just looking at him—his big loafers and the way his legs angle give him a big-lug/gentle-doofus stance—though in his eyes you can see the streak of canny coldness that I imagine it takes to make big bucks as a securities analyst. The box in his arms has a picture of a bread machine on it.

"Hey, it's the breadwinner," Milena says, slyly getting in a dig on me that Steve might appreciate, and she kisses him on the cheek.

"Hi, babe," he says, with half an eye on me over her shoulder. Then he disappears into the kitchen with the bread machine.

"We had a medical emergency with Audrey," Milena says. She's twisting her hands together at her waist. "It's all right now, though." She reaches for Steve's hand as he comes out of the kitchen and leads him into the living room, until he pulls his hand away. I stand and put down my water glass.

"Sorry I brought Audrey back early," I say to Steve. "She had a bad case of the hiccups and wanted her mommy." This sounds unbelievably idiotic, and I'm so keyed up I almost burst into laughter.

Steve looks to Audrey, who is in full slouch, apparently lost in her TV show. I can sense the wheels turning in her head; every instant she is quiet is a good instant. Steve seems about to say something to her.

"What's with the harp?" he asks instead, hands on his hips.

"Believe it or not," I say, "we used it to get rid of the hiccups."

Steve makes a face. He doesn't trade in hiccups bullshit.

"Audrey had hiccups for *two hours*," Milena says. "She was freaking out. We were ready to go to the emergency room."

"The hiccups, Audrey cat?" Steve asks her in his fun, aspiring-stepdad voice.

Audrey nods, eyes on her show. The Powerpuff Girls are kicking ass again.

"Matt played music to calm her down and the hiccups stopped," Milena explains.

"Never heard of that," Steve says to Milena.

"It was scary," Milena says, looking warmly into Steve's eyes, as if it's Steve who saved everything.

"I should take off," I say.

Steve looks at Audrey, who is not reacting with glee or gestures or talking to the TV as she often does when watching her shows.

I turn to Steve. "I guess I'll just take this with me, eh?" I say, referring to the harp.

"What?" he asks, his eyes sharpening just enough to let me know he's capable of punching me, if it ever comes to that.

I put on the cover and pick up the harp. At first no one rises to get the door for me. Then Steve moves to do it.

"Watch your step," he says as I carry the instrument over the threshold.

13

~~~

HOUR BY HOUR, I swing between elated, guilty, hopeful, and unsure. Then there's poor Audrey. I don't know what she saw.

Meanwhile, Cynthia's Denver trip has drawn nigh, and after apparently working crazy hours to get things in order before she flies out tomorrow morning, she suggests a Sunday afternoon Rollerblading excursion.

Though I haven't used them in years, I happen to have a pair of stiff blue Rollerblades from some desperate phase in my marriage, when Milena and I were going to "get out more," a euphemism for escaping the b.o. and anxiety that clouded our apartment after I practiced every day. This is definitely a nineties dating activity, and maybe marks Cynthia and me as aging, work-obsessed dorks, which only makes me more sympathetic to her for having the idea.

We're lucky to snag a free parking spot by the Diversey Marina. Sitting in our seats with the car doors flared open, we put on our skates. The giddy intimacy that often overtakes bowling parties, I think, has a lot to do with that brief interlude of stockinged feet as shoes are changed before hitting the lanes, and I get a fizzy version of that.

Almost forgetting Milena, I take Cynthia's hand as we set out on a wide path of fine-packed white gravel. I try to stride forward, clack against Cynthia's skate, she cries out, I fall on my ass.

"I forgot to tell you that I fall constantly," I say as a jogger swerves to avoid me. "I rarely get more than fifty yards from the car before it's time to turn back." When Cynthia laughs, I add, "Sorry about banging your skate."

"Make sure you fall forward," she says, possibly misunderstanding the essence of being uncoordinated. "It's safer." She manages to stay stable as she reaches a hand and helps me up. "There you go," she says.

We follow the path past beds of yellow daffodils, take the Fullerton Parkway underpass beneath Lake Shore Drive, and soon we're cruising down the busy lakefront trail. As we roll, I wonder why Cynthia is apparently interested in making this relationship work. Why does she like me? Is my general lameness appealing in a nonthreatening sort of way? Does she hope, as I do, that we can get back to our happier early days? Or is she still afraid to see herself as the type of woman who would dump an impotent guy with a freshly dead dad?

We skate south with the brisk wind mostly at our backs toward a huge postcard of downtown stretching from the Ferris wheel of Navy Pier to the Sears Tower with the Hancock anchoring a massive cluster of buildings in the center. Sand blows across the path, making tiny dunes on the other side, and occasionally the lake splashes against a cement wall and sends water under our skates. Bicyclists pass us at freeway speeds. At North Avenue Beach, there's a snack depot shaped like an ocean liner, complete with twin red funnels on the roof, blue railings, and portals. We buy burgers and ice cream, then smile at each other and don't talk much. We skate back north, squinting against the relentless sand-flinging wind. At long last we come to a small grove of trees on a jutting point by the Theater on the Lake, where we commandeer a south-facing bench and rest.

All sorts of Chicagoans pass by, walking, jogging, bicycling, even Rollerblading: the garb of a hundred nations, a hundred neighborhoods, from shorts to saris, dashikis to nylon bicycle pants. We all seem suspended in innocent civic harmony. It's the first really nice weekend since winter grayed the city last November.

"This is great, isn't it?" Cynthia says, smiling.

"It is," I say. "This was a great idea."

She takes my left hand. "You're all right," she says. "You know that?"

"I am?"

"Don't worry anymore," she says. "We're both too hard on ourselves. We've got to stop that."

"I'm trying not to worry," I say, and smile. I remember her sheepish smile when she was talking about Anna, and it seems that now we're showing totally different faces to each other. Things feel warmer between us than they have in weeks.

And what if *now* we go to her apartment and try to have sex and I can't do it?

"Give yourself some time to get over your father," she says, her voice a melodic humming under the wind that is parting the hair on the backs of our heads. The fact that she's said things like this before makes me wonder if she's using my father's death as a rationalization for our difficulties as a couple. And maybe this is a half-truth we need until we can stumble our way to something more solid.

"I know," I say.

I remember my father once stood at the edge of the sand at McKinley Beach in Milwaukee, took off his brown shoes and his socks, and exposed his long feet with the badly yellowed toenails, as pale and strange as creatures from the lightless reaches of the ocean floor. I never saw him in running shoes or sandals, ever, and that day he had cuffed his khaki pants and put his shoes and socks into a plastic drawstring bag that he pulled up onto his wrist. He and Bart grabbed an end of our enormous red Coleman cooler, into which Mom had packed half our kitchen, and led the rest of us, toting umbrellas, chairs, baskets, canvas bags, toward Lake Michigan. Soon after we set up camp, Dad passed out in a beach chair for the duration. He always slept at the lakefront. I remember that particular day I ran out of the waves and yelled to Dad to come in the water with us. Mom ran across the sand to shush me. "*Please* let him sleep," she said, so emphatically it scared me.

"I didn't mean that—getting over it," Cynthia says. "I'm sorry."

"That's all right," I say. "I'm not a stickler about grieving, believe me."

I'm tempted to tell her about my father's breakdown and my own fear of unraveling, but my problems with my father and my problems with Cynthia feel too entwined to risk bringing it up.

She sighs and looks out over the emerald-green and white-capped water, which—bounded at the shore by a retaining wall, not a sandy beach—sloshes up and down more than it rolls in waves. There are a few psychotic jet-skiers in wet suits, braving the still-frigid water, and some distant yachts.

What can I offer Cynthia in return for her kindness? Even as I feel a surge of warmth and affection for her, my renewed connection with Milena makes it even harder to see things clearly with Cynthia. I feel dizziness gather and I take some deep breaths to fend it off.

"Are you going to make it, with Whitaker and all that?" I finally say.

"I don't know," she says, trying to keep her hair from blowing across her face. "He's a manipulative bastard. I was supposed to work on a section of a brief he's filing, and when I emailed to ask him when he needed my chunk, he didn't respond. I ran into him and he said he didn't get the email—said the email server was freaking out on him—and then he said he needed it the next day, which really put me under the gun."

"Is it possible he didn't get the email?"

"Seems unlikely, but I can't call him on it. Which makes it the perfect way to mess with me. I *have* to do well on these plane cases."

"He seemed like a good boss for a while, didn't he?" This is a stupid tack to take with Cynthia, and I don't know why I'm bringing it up, except that it strikes me as interesting, even mysterious, how people can look so different from different angles.

"He didn't seem like a typical guy," she says. "He seemed to really care about the associates. But I think it was all about getting us to love him, to show everyone he was *the cool partner,* the one we could trust, or something. I don't know."

"Think that bastard will be brought to justice?"

"I'm just glad to be getting out of town for a few weeks."

It occurs to me that I could take this personally, but I don't.

Just then, a man who looks exactly like Osama bin Laden—complete with long, unkempt salt-and-pepper beard, sunken eyes, robe, and headcloth—Rollerblades by. Everyone turns to watch him, and he leans over and really begins to work his arms, skating faster and faster.

We go to the grocery store to pick up supplies for a chicken and veggie stir-fry dinner. When we get to Cynthia's loft apartment on Lake Street, I start to worry about how the night will end and begin drinking a little aggressively.

Her apartment has a lot of exposed piping and ductwork and dangling track lighting. No interior wall reaches the twenty-foot ceiling. The bathroom is a cubicle with a lid on it. On one wall there's a framed print of Warhol's *Double Elvis,* with guns drawn, and the furniture is all fifties thrift-store kitsch and pop debauchery—candy-colored, saucer-shaped, tubular. Near the windows, there's a high-rise scratching post with several platforms for her reclusive black-and-white cat.

"How are things going for the audition?" she asks, when we're at the candlelit table.

"Pretty good," I say, though I'm not sure this is true.

"Really? That's good. And are you still going out to the hospice?"

"Tomorrow," I say. There must be more to be said here, but I'm stumping myself.

"Is that good for you—right now?"

"I think it's more like I can't say no."

There's a long beat of silence, and then, simultaneously, I reach for my beer and Cynthia reaches for her wine, a coincidence we notice and laugh about.

"I want you to sleep over," she suddenly says. "But no pressure." She raises her palms in a hands-off, no-pressure gesture, but I can't tell if this refers to accepting her invitation or to whether we'll try to have sex.

"No pressure," I say, mimicking her hand gesture. I smile beatifically, though I don't mean to.

Cynthia's got a 7:50 a.m. flight, and we agree to hit the sack early. I hand off the bathroom to her, and find her cat curled up on the down comforter, right in the middle of Cynthia's bed. The apartment is drafty and I shiver in my boxer shorts and T-shirt. I could use a shower, but I'm afraid that will put me on the spot as wanting sex. I pick up one end of the comforter and give it a shake, trying to dislodge the cat, which holds down its spot like a brick. "Don't make me thwap you with a pillow," I say, picking one up. The cat regards me impassively. "We can be friends, you know. Plenty of mice in my apartment for you to bat around." Finally I slide into bed, then work my foot under her, and she stands, leaps to the floor, magically sheds her momentum, and struts away, meowing once over her shoulder.

Cynthia takes forever in the bathroom. *No pressure,* I think as my beer buzz evolves into a headache. The bottoms of my feet seem to break a cold sweat. Her apartment is still but for the sound of water coming through the pipes in discrete bursts.

At long last, Cynthia comes out of the bathroom and walks through the apartment, turning off lights. I hear each click, notice the subtle change of illumination in this space. There's nowhere here not to be with the person you're with. She enters the bedroom, wearing a baggy T-shirt and panties and her glasses. She takes off the latter while seated on her side of the bed and puts them on her nightstand. She half rolls to face me, and I half roll to face her. Our noses come closer and we kiss, dryly. She props her head up on her hand, and then I know for sure we're not going to try to have sex, which brings a relief that's marbled with sadness.

"When I come back, let's just start from scratch," Cynthia says.

"We can go back to the beginning," I say.

"We can start fresh."

This is the dream: to not be the person we are and always have been.

"It could be great," I say.

"It *will* be great," she says.

I look at her with an expectant expression on my face. I think of Milena with a confused ache. I have no idea whether I'll be true to Cynthia while she's on her business trip. I feel another rush of dizziness, even though I'm lying down.

"Yeah," I say.

The word feels like a sort of bathtub ring: ever since we returned to her apartment and I started fretting in earnest about a possible attempt at sex, my personality has been leaking down a drain, growing less full, becoming less and less available to me, and this word-residue is all that's left.

As I drop Cynthia at the airport the next morning, she enthusiastically charges me with getting a bagel at H & H Bagels when I visit Adam in New York, and I promise I will. We hug tight. Back at my apartment, I shower, practice on the 85P for two hours, then head out to Golden Prairie to meet the new couple Marcia told me about. The day is still overcast, refusing to warm up, but I'm trying to feel good about things—or if not good, at least open to better possibilities, which I hope will minimize my chances of another dizzy collapse.

I set the harp and my gear against the wall and enter the Great Room, where Marcia is in animated conversation with a couple sitting on a large sofa with massively padded armrests.

"Matt," Marcia says, getting up, "good to see you. I'd like you to meet Erin Kael and Malcolm Glazier."

They rise to shake hands. Malcolm has a fashionable, stubbly beard, round, wire-rimmed glasses, and a Caesar-style haircut. Erin has sparkling direct eyes and a pointy chin. Both look fit and trim in their Eddie Bauer–type clothes. I feel scuzzy in my striped dress shirt that has tiny wear holes at the collar edges and cuffs.

We small-talk for a bit: they met at Yale while earning PhDs, and now they teach at Northwestern. Malcolm does complex systems theory in the Physics Department, while Erin is an analytical chemist.

As we chat, it all comes to me like a cold breeze off a glacier: their large American Foursquare on a tree-lined street near campus; the kitchen stocked with organic vegetables and various soy products; *All Things Considered* on a stereo with an iPod port; the two kids, in first and fourth grade, literate since age three, alternate between reading Harry Potter novels, playing the piano, and building Bauhaus-influenced structures from raw Legos that are special-ordered from Denmark; a Subaru Outback in the driveway, but Malcolm and Erin walk to "class" and "the department" and "the lab," where they deal with fascinating scientific problems and mentor obsequious grad students and write papers they publish quickly. Then they run four miles, shower together, and fuck vigorously to simultaneous orgasm.

It's the life you should be willing to forgo when you dream your musical dream, but I've always thought I would be one of the lucky few who would somehow find my way to it.

"My degrees are from Northwestern," I say, feeling foolish.

Marcia brings her hands together on her knees, glances at her polish-free fingernails.

"My mother died from cancer when we were living in New Haven," Erin says.

"I'm sorry," I say reflexively.

"And the hospital," she continues, "had a wonderful music program."

"We were skeptical at first," Malcolm says, "but I did some research and found all sorts of cool stuff about music and the body. A lot of excellent studies have shown how music releases endorphins and increases blood flow and lowers blood pressure. Very persuasive, peer-reviewed stuff."

"But it's not just physical," Erin adds. "It's spiritual, too."

"The harp especially," Malcolm interjects, stepping through Erin's last word, making the sort of eye contact hypnotists favor. "The harp was hugely important to pre–Christian Gaelic cultures—that's no secret." He glances at me and discovers in my thick gaze that much knowledge of the world *is* a secret to me. "They thought it united the masculine and the feminine—

the phallic pillar and the feminine sound box. It's an incredible symbol of harmony."

"Gosh," I say, "I'm glad I don't play the bagpipes."

"I was actually thinking more in contrast to the violin family," Malcolm presses on. "The violin, viola, and cello all have the classic feminine, hourglass shape."

Marcia breaks in: "What would you like Matt to play for your father?"

"My mother loved to hear all the great Irish and Scottish folk tunes," Erin says, "and Dad likes those, too."

"Coming right up," I say.

I stop in a restroom to wash my hands and gather myself, then proceed to cottage number 8, the room in which Richard, Erin's father, will almost certainly die. I tell myself I won't freak out or get dizzy, that, in fact, I am carefully staging myself through an immersion therapy that will leave me inured to death and free from the risk of nervous breakdowns. Leaving my harp and gear outside per protocol, I step in, hunching my shoulders, moving my hands to my stomach as if I'm entering hat in hand.

To my surprise, Richard is not in the bed but sitting upright in the recliner. Malcolm sits on the edge of the loveseat in the alcove, ready, it seems, to spring forward. Erin stands over her father, with a hand resting on the back of his chair, and I feel like a photographer who has come to shoot a portrait of a patriarch with his daughter.

He rises slowly, careful of the oxygen lines that travel up his chest, hook over his ears and meet, as natural-looking as a pair of glasses, under his nose. Making firm eye contact, he extends a hand and smiles. "Hello," he says in a voice that is not strong but is not altogether weak. We shake, his grip firm, his hand cool, and I introduce myself. His face is not too lined; his gray hair is combed back from his forehead in a dashing sweep. He's got the prototypical old-guy mouth: lipless, prone to gaping, Muppet-like. It reminds me of the last time I saw my father's mouth, though his lips were sewn shut by then. Richard takes a while to sit down again, and I stand, frozen, wordless.

"Papa, why don't you put up your feet?" Erin says fretfully. "We don't want your ankles to get big." Above his slippers, Richard's bare ankles do look somewhat swollen, the skin dry and rough.

"I'm fine," Richard says.

"Okay!" I say. "I'll just go out and tune and bring 'er in."

As I arrange the instrument at the foot of the bed, Erin pulls a chair next to her father. She takes his hand and nods at me to begin. I play "Trip to Sligo" and "Flow Gently, Sweet Afton" before I glance at him. His face has gone slack. At some point he and his daughter have stopped holding hands. When I turn to Erin, she nods at me, like a drama teacher prodding a student from the wings: *Keep going.*

I power up "Gilliekrankie" to shift the mood. When I finish this tune, I ask him if he'd like to hear something in particular.

"How about 'Danny Boy,'" he says with as much sardonic emphasis as his short breath will allow.

"Oh, Papa," Erin says.

Malcolm is a coiled spring on the edge of the loveseat, his elbows on his knees, chin raised as if he's about to speak, but he's been that way for about the last ten minutes without a word.

I consider changing musical genres altogether, but I'm just the harpist, not the conductor. I try "South Wind," which is slow and beautiful and hard for anyone to resist.

After I finish, Richard thanks me without looking up and says he wants to rest.

"Okay, Papa, okay, Papa," Erin says, soothing him as if he's just had an outburst.

"All right!" I say too loudly. "I really enjoyed meeting you and playing music for you."

"Thank you, Matt," Erin says meaningfully as she helps her father out of the recliner. I carry everything out into the hall.

Just when I'm despairing over not having created Malcolm's expected harp-induced harmony, a nurse approaches and says a man next door has heard me playing and would like me to come by his room. "His name is Michael," she says. "He has AIDS," she adds, like I was maybe planning to have unprotected intercourse with him.

"Sure," I say. "I'd be glad to."

In cottage 9, a very thin, long-necked man lies stiffly, propped up in the bed. The part in his hair has eroded far down the side of his head, and his long bangs lay sparsely like dry grass over one side of his brow. There's a raised, purplish lesion at one corner of his small mouth, which seems contracted though his lips are parted. But the most striking thing about him is that his face is much thinner below the prominent cheekbones than above, so that the top half of his face with his large forehead and broad-set eyes seems mismatched with the sucked-in cheeks and narrow jaw. I can't escape the fact that the air smells faintly of diarrhea. His eyes are a quarter closed and watch me with an uncanny stillness.

"Hello," I say. "My name's Matt."

"Happy to meet you," he says softly, and he points his broomstick arm at something across the room. "Michael." It takes me a moment to realize he wants me to shake his hand. I smile, we shake. His hand is so cool my arm involuntarily shivers when I release it, but he doesn't seem to notice.

"Did she tell you I've got AIDS?" he asks.

"Uh, yeah."

"Not supposed to do that. Thinks I'm deaf."

"That's not good," I say, and laugh nervously. Sweat prickles on my forehead.

"I don't really mind," he says in a slow but steady voice. "Except dying from HIV is so nineties." He sighs. "Late to the party again."

He gives me a crooked grin.

I smile, but not too much.

"Would you play me something?" he asks.

"Sure," I say. "Whatever you want."

"Surprise me," he says.

I bring the harp in and take a look around the room for clues as to what he might like. His windowsills are filled with plants, and there's an antique lamp on his nightstand. Next to the lamp, there's an autographed black-and-white head shot of, if I'm not mistaken, Paul Lynde, the snarky, barely closeted center square on the old *Hollywood Squares* show. There are other homey touches—an afghan thrown over the recliner, a chalky portrait on the wall of someone who very well might be Michael, an old movie poster for *The Poseidon Adventure* that has a prominent image of Shelley Winters swimming in her bra and panties.

I take him at his word and play the unexpected "Don't Fence Me In," which makes him smile with half his mouth.

"I am surprised," he says, and he nods.

The picture of Paul Lynde sends me deep into my collection of cheesy pop. I play him some Partridge Family—"I Think I Love You," which gets Michael moving his shoulders slightly, as if dancing in bed.

I try a classical piece, Handel's Harp Concerto in B Flat, and he seems to like it.

"How about some opera?" I ask.

"Don't I have to love opera?"

"No."

"Well, I do. I love everything. That's my problem."

After I finish the Overture to Verdi's *La forza del destino*, which is on the St. Louis list, he brings his fingertips across his lap and pats them together.

"I saw *Tosca* at the Met in New York five years ago," he says. "That's the night I saw Gabe Kaplan."

"Gabe Kaplan?" I ask. His enunciation is somewhat impaired by his tight mouth.

"Kotter, from *Welcome Back, Kotter*. Leaving a restaurant in the East Village. He had a beard, but I recognized him." Michael smiles weakly, but there's pleasure in his eyes. He recounts other sightings of celebrities from his childhood: Julia Child at Savenor's in Cambridge, Massachusetts; Angie Dickinson buying contact lens solution at a Walgreens on Michigan Avenue; Wilt Chamberlain at a party on South Beach.

"Those were the coke years," he adds with a sigh.

"Sounds like you were living the life," I say inanely. "What did you do, if I can ask?"

"Sold business software."

"Ah."

"Traveled. Had fun." He grunts. His eyes turn toward the windows. "Is it cold outside? It looks cold."

"It is," I say.

He stares out the window. Once his head assumes a new position, it seems to lock into it like a mannequin's. It's hard to tell his exact age, but he's a lot closer to me than to Richard or Mrs. F. It's far too easy to visualize his bare skull, to see his cranium and his mandible as distinct parts, like a chattering skeleton.

I should get out of this building soon. "Well," I say. I stand up and bow to him, to ease my abrupt departure: "I should probably take my song-and-dance down the road."

"Okay," he says.

"See you, Michael. You take care!" I add, overcompensating with fake enthusiasm.

"Okay, thanks," he says quietly.

I'm schlepping my harp to the entrance when I run into Erin and Malcolm talking intently by the doors of the Great Room. Erin reaches out to shake my hand again.

"Thank you so much," she says.

"Glad to do it," I say.

"Listen," she adds. "We've been talking, and I don't know your schedule, but we'd like you to come by one or two times a week if possible." Something in my expression seems to prompt her to add, "I know that's asking a lot, but it would mean so much to him and to us, and, well, all we can do is ask."

Malcolm steps up and says, "We can pay you fifty dollars every time you come out." And to illustrate this, he holds out a check, apparently for today.

I stare at the check. Maybe playing for Richard can somehow honor my father, though I can't say whether Richard enjoyed my playing. My sense is he didn't. I am not feeling super about being here, but now that I'm out of Michael's presence I don't like the image of me bailing on him so quickly.

"That's okay," Erin says, because I haven't actually moved a muscle, am just staring at the check. "You must be busy."

"They already pay me," I stammer. I finally look up and see the disappointed look on her face. Guilt squeezes my head and chest. "Let me get back to you," I manage to say. She looks at me intently, a bit frozen.

"Thank you," Malcolm suddenly jumps in, the check vanishing. I shake his hand again, and, finally, we part.

Outside, the wind buffets me, and I stop at the harp factory to check on Carl's progress. Stanley is in the front workroom, talking to a guy who's stringing up a new harp. He smiles when he sees me: "Come on back. You're going to be pleased."

We go to the showroom, where Carl gives a detailed explanation of what he's done to my harp, starting with a lecture on how the pedal action gets transmitted to the disks on the neck plate via metal rods that pass through the column, and moving on to how he placed felt at certain places in the column and sheathed some of the rods in plastic, dampening vibrations while preserving the fluidity of the action. The man's aviators are practically fogging up with excitement.

"That's amazing, Carl," I say, though I've barely followed him, anxious to hear for myself. Finally, I sit down and play licks designed to aggravate the buzz, and yet there is no buzz, unless I totally whale on it—and then only the ghost of a buzz.

"Hey," Stanley says. "Don't break the thing!"

"I can't believe this," I say, standing up from the instrument. "How much do I owe you?"

"It's on the house," Stanley says.

"Are you sure?" I ask halfheartedly.

"I'm always sure," Stanley says, mindful, no doubt, that I'll be in the market for a new harp soon enough.

"Thanks, Stanley," I say. "Thanks a ton, Carl." And I give them both firm handshakes, which is all the payment any man has ever wanted from any other man.

Carl and I roll the harp into the back hallway. Through a window in the door, I see snow falling. So what if it's April.

"Damn," I say. "It's snowing."

"Fucking Chicago," Carl says.

That's when I realize I've already got the 85P in the Volvo, so I'll have to run that one home first. And by the time I do that, return for my Aphrodite, and get back to my neighborhood, the snow has whitened the grass like chalk dust. The snow throws me back to December, when I first met Cynthia, when my father was still alive, and I had lived for years with a reasonable sense of sexual potency. Let it snow!

As I drive down the alley toward the garage, I see T.R. and Charles unloading grocery bags from T.R.'s old BMW. I pull in and bound out of the car with a barely restrained desire to give them both a hug. "Hello, men!" I say. "How are you?"

"I'm sane," Charles says, pausing in the alley with a laden plastic bag in each hand. "And yourself?"

"Good, really good," I say.

"That's nice to hear," Charles says. "Oh, guess who I ran into up on Belmont last week." Before I can answer, he says, "Cynthia. Interesting girl. We went for coffee and had a nice chat about you."

"Oh, really," I say.

He makes a pouting face. "She's so worried about you!"

Not sure how to respond to Charles, I ask T.R., "Hey, what about your garden?" and I lift a hand at the snow.

"Worse things have happened," T.R. drawls, taking the last bag out of his trunk and slamming the hatch shut.

"Oh, don't believe the stoic," Charles says. "He's crying inside."

"Every few years it snows this late and most things make it," T.R. says. "Charles has his hands full with the present, so his memory is not good."

"Come along, Father," Charles says to T.R. "Time for your meds."

T.R. laughs briefly, like a cough—or maybe he coughs like a laugh. They go inside, and I begin to unload the repaired harp at the scene of its near-fatal injury. The Volvo is looking especially hearse-like. The alley, with its askew dumpsters and light poles and strung wires and dry weeds and trash and enormous rats in hiding, grows beautiful with snow.

When I was about eleven there was a midday blizzard, and nearly a foot of heavy snow had accumulated by the time I made it home from school. I started shoveling the driveway while it was still coming down. The snow was so wet and heavy I was wary of overexerting my heart, so I was basically lifting and heaving one shovelful at a time, especially near the street, where a plow had thrown up a wall of chunks as unwieldy as broken concrete. By five-thirty the sky was darkening, though all the snow still glowed, and my dad's white Pontiac station wagon rolled slowly up the street. I paused in my shoveling, head sweating beneath my snow-encrusted hat, and stepped up near the side of the garage, to give him maximum berth. I leaned on the shovel handle, breathing heavily but complacently, waiting for a "Good job" that would offset dozens of moments of his disgust with all my typical boyish incompetencies. The wagon turned in, fishtailing slightly, accelerated up to my line of progress, and stopped a body length from the garage door. He got out, hoisted his thick briefcase, put a cardboard tube of blueprints under his arm, and finally noticed me, snow gusting between us. Then, with a mere glance, no nod or any other gesture, he continued on into the house.

What I wouldn't give to be back at the top of that driveway, beside the pine tree, in that same heavy snow. "Helluva storm, Dad!" I'd say. "Damn straight!" he'd respond, though he never used that phrase in his life. What I actually did was pound my wet glove against my chest, trying to further fuck with the congenital backbeat of my heart's rhythm and bring on a paroxysm that would leave me dead in the snow and my father rethinking his ways.

But knowing what I now know about his state of mind, the moment appears different. Maybe he was looking out at me from the bottom of a well. Maybe to him, I was a mere silhouette against a distant circle of sky, someone who couldn't really help him, someone whom he couldn't hope to reach.

In this alley, it occurs to me to cry. But the intensity feels good, and as the feeling blooms, it actually seems that I'm happy. I'm not as bad off as my old man. I can see Malcolm and Erin for who they are and what they need, and I can see her dying father, and I can do something for them, and maybe for Michael, too. And though playing at the hospice will make me sad, it might also be a way to escape my anxieties and corrosive self-loathing. I don't believe it will absolve me for what I did with Milena, but at least it will be a step in the right moral direction. With Cynthia out of town, I can make up the practice time. I'll call Erin and Malcolm and play an extra day at the hospice until the audition. At that point, if I fail again, this may be a way to avoid my own well on an ongoing basis. For now, with my harp miraculously fixed and an April snow falling and Cynthia landing in Denver and Milena in her office downtown and Audrey learning at school, I'm just about as happy as I can be.

14

～～～

ICALL MILENA AT work. Since the early days of the divorce, after we reestablished regular contact centered on Audrey, I often call her on Mondays at the end of the day. I have Audrey at my place on Tuesday after school, which likely means we have things to discuss. Now, it's also an easy way to call her without goosing Steve's suspicions.

I'm not sure what I want to say to her, but I'm resigned to the fact that whatever path I take will cover the shady valleys and fetid swamps of human motivation rather than the moral high ground. I'm going to betray Cynthia by exploring how Milena thinks about the future, and I'm going to betray Milena by having feelings for Cynthia at the same time. In short, I'm going to be a two-timing bastard until things get figured out.

"Hi," I say when Milena picks up. "It's your ex, Jimmy Malone." Why the persona? Not sure.

"Jimmy the deadbeat? Please hold." She puts the receiver down, has a brief muffled exchange with a co-worker.

When she gets back on the line, she says, "What's on your

mind, Jimmy?" in a voice that is guarded enough that my heart starts taking on water.

"Look, if I made things bad, I apologize, but it wasn't just that moment. I've been thinking about you."

This is more than I wanted to say right off the bat. There's silence on the line.

"I've been thinking about you, too," she says finally. Her quiet voice reminds me of Audrey apologizing in the car.

And with that, all of my equivocation is gone. It's all I can do to keep from proposing to her again, right on the phone.

"I think it would be good to talk," I say.

"Yeah," she says.

"How about we get together for lunch, downtown?"

She considers this for a beat that could contain the consideration of a million unresolvable pros and cons, or her gathering the resolve to put on the brakes, or just a look at her planner. "Not tomorrow—I've got a meeting," she says, steady. "How about Wednesday?"

"I'm driving to New York on Wednesday, like I think I said?"

"Oh, yeah. Why are you going out there again?"

When I brought the trip up a week ago, I actually didn't say why, just that I would have to leave town by 10:00 a.m., and would she let me switch my Friday night with Audrey for Saturday night.

"It's to make a good chunk of money," I say. And then, because I've entered this conversation having already exceeded my deception quota, I add, "Adam Brackett called. He wants me to play harp in some videos he's making."

"I thought you were getting ready for an audition." There's an edge of challenge and hurt in her voice.

And with this it appears we're passing from getting remarried to getting redivorced.

Milena knows too well the family things I blew off, the chores I didn't do, the times I rolled out of bed after lovemaking way too soon just to put on my headphones and work on a score. I did take her for granted to some degree. Many uncleared mines are buried in these marital fields.

"I do have an audition," I say. "I've got a lot I'm dealing with."

"You worship that guy," she says flatly.

Adam Brackett may not be Milena's favorite person. There was an off-campus party in college at which Milena ventured a joke that involved seafood, exercise, and "pulling a mussel." Adam took that moment to assert his superior comedic genius by projecting through cupped hands, "Boo! No! Please develop a sense of humor before attempting further jokes!" The drinking had been going on for a while, and though Adam's comment fit within the bounds of the raillery permissible among friends, it was also typical of the dismissiveness Adam often directed toward Milena. She startled at Adam's words, as if her hair had been pulled from behind, then turned red and gave him the finger.

On top of this, by the end of our marriage, nothing made Milena madder than me protesting about not having time for things around the house and then jumping to go out with a friend—sometimes Adam, who occasionally dropped into town to play as a guest in the third set of Second City shows. Now it must look to her that Adam is even more important to me than one of the auditions that she always took a backseat to.

"He's paying me a thousand bucks," I say. "I just can't say no to that much money. I wish I could, but I can't."

Near the end of our marriage she admitted that my lack of earning power was "disappointing."

I can almost see her at her desk, the phone clamped to her ear with both hands, as she does during traumatic calls. "I do want to see you," she finally says. "But it has to be different, Matt. You know?"

"I am different, Mil. If you could know how much I miss

you, how much I need you, you wouldn't be thinking like you might be thinking. I've been through stuff. I know myself better now."

She sighs heavily enough to blow a sail taut.

"Okay, meet me in my lobby at noon next Monday."

"You got it."

Then I add, by way of good-bye:

"Take care, sweetie."

"Take care, Matt," she says diplomatically, though perhaps sincerely, too.

15

~~~

THERE'S ONLY PARKING on one side of Adam's underlit West Village street, and the vehicles are jammed tight. After fruitlessly circling the neighboring blocks, I pull up over the low curb onto the sidewalk in front of his townhouse to honor my agreed-upon arrival time and to avoid blocking the single-lane street. I put on my flashers and get out, road-buzzed, limbs numb and creaky, smelling like something that's been deep-fried and left out in a waxed paper bag. From dirt squares surrounded by tiny fences, spindly trees rise and intertwine in the darkness above the quaint streetlamps. The narrowness of the street, the lighting through the trees, and the walls of town-houses make the space feel almost more indoors than out.

I press the buzzer, footsteps skip down the stairs, and Adam opens the tall wooden door. When he notices my car on the sidewalk, he steps all the way outside.

"Brother man!" he shouts, with an indeterminate amount of irony in his voice, but he greets me with a fairly convincing embrace.

"Dude!" I thump his back a few resonant times.

He's grown a bit bearish and his dark eyes are tired, but he's still got long sideburns and all of his thick hair combed back off his high forehead in a borderline pompadour.

"How was the drive?"

"I loved the Soviet-era vibe of the Penn Turnpike, with all those state-sponsored service plazas." I feel an enormous duty to be funny and clever and punctuate this sentence with an ingratiating laugh.

"That's very nice," he says. "Is that your car?"

"Yeah, and I couldn't find a place to park."

"Well, you can't park there."

"I know, I know."

And thus follows a discussion of how to handle parking: larcenous garage versus absurd space-finding odds and street-cleaning protocols. He also mentions that he has several locations in mind for his breakup scenes, and the first we'll shoot tomorrow is a few blocks away. It's clear that the unwieldiness of the harp has not figured prominently in his plans, or in mine, but we decide to worry about other locations later. I can't leave my concert grand in a car parked on a street, so we unload the instrument and carry it up to his duplex.

"God, this thing is heavy," he exclaims.

The apartment looks completely rehabbed, with sleek and boxy leather-and-chrome furniture, track lighting, blond hardwood floors, and art on the walls between built-in bookcases. I smell coffee. We put the harp in the living room, where there's a fireplace with a polished oak mantel and a brick skirt—the only sign of how old the building is. Through a half-opened door into an office, I spy a slice of wall crammed with glossy photos, and a distressed brown leather sofa chair. The space gives off a certain heat; it's the boiler room of his ego. The rest of this level seems strangely un-lived-in.

"Nice view," I say, looking out the living room window, unable to shake ass-kissing mode. The lit-up top quarter of the Empire State is visible.

"Better be nice—it probably cost me an extra quarter of a million dollars."

"Are you serious?"

"No, yes, I don't know." He waves his hands. "Let's move your car somewhere before it gets towed."

I hustle downstairs and take another fifteen-minute tour of the neighborhood, finding a just-opening spot only four blocks over with no street cleaning until Friday. We toast this small victory—beer for me and bourbon for the Lord of the Manor.

In the living room, ensconced in black leather that gives off new-car smell, I finally tell him that my father has died.

He freezes in his armchair, holding his half-raised glass in the air. This is his code for extreme shock.

"Matt, I'm very sorry," he finally says. "Sudden?"

"Yes."

I tell him about the heart attack, the meditation CD. My small wry smile brings no smile from him.

He asks for a more in-depth Milwaukee report, which I give, including details about my brother George the felonious inside trader, whom Adam has met and taken an interest in.

"Totally bald and beardless," I say.

Adam whistles. "I love that," he says.

"So what are you up to? I rarely watch TV or go to movies—I have no idea."

"That's very supportive, Matt. Well, *Scary Movie Quatro* did fine, so there's going to be a *Cinco,* but not right away."

Trying to be loose and breezy, I've insulted him. "Of course," I say.

"Then, you know," Adam goes on, "there are *things* that I know I'm being considered for, and *things* I'm auditioning for. We'll see. The good news is, tomorrow you're going to meet some fabulous actresses."

"And you're going to break up with all of them?"

"That's the idea."

"People do love a good relationship meltdown," I muse. It occurs to me that these scenes might have some personal practical value.

Adam explains that we'll be working with a director named Hugh Gallagher.

"He's great," Adam says. "He's a Groundlings guy. I did my massage talk show with him. Listen," he adds, "are you okay improvising? Everything is going to be improv tomorrow, including the music."

"Sure," I say.

In fact, I am not okay improvising; the idea of responding musically, in the moment, terrifies me.

"Tomorrow's going to be intense, brother man, and I'm fading fast," Adam says, a bit abruptly, clapping his palms to his knees. He does look exhausted. "Let me get you some fabulous towels spun from the butt cotton of baby lambs."

Fifteen minutes later, lying on my back in the downy guest bed with its bazillion-thread-count sheets and surprisingly homey fabric softener scent, I press a remote control button and the skylight shade unfurls and locks into place, blocking out a leering moon. I kick myself for not asking Adam exactly how this was going to work ahead of time, and mentally run through riffs that might work for when a couple is talking, moves composers make when they're heightening tension or accentuating dissonance, pop tunes that could be commentary. In short, I lie awake for several hours, trying to wring as much improv out of tomorrow as possible.

Midmorning, Hugh Gallagher shows up. He is a surprisingly serious man, clearly over sixty but trying to pass for forty, with a tan, taut, varnished face and a pie wedge of short thinning hair pointing down his forehead to his Roman nose.

After Hugh and Adam huddle in the kitchen, talking in low voices over coffee and a huge breakfast pineapple, Hugh wants to hear me play my theme music ideas: "Julia" by the Beatles ("John wrote that about *his mom,*" Hugh says scathingly); "Sometimes When We Touch" (he bites a fingernail); and a very plinky New Agey song I made up with some badly deformed notes. It's my on-the-verge-of-a-seizure masterpiece.

"That one," Hugh says.

At a tiny park a few blocks away, we meet the sound-and-lights guys and Adam's scene partner, Celeste, an acting grad student at NYU. She has long, center-parted brown hair, the smallest and most narrow nose I have ever seen, and a little red pyramid of a mouth. Enormous circular sunglasses dominate her face like eyes on a fly. It's absurdly difficult not to look at her.

She and Adam start the scene with some babble about nurturing their relationship "no matter what it costs," but soon it emerges that Adam's character has been flamboyantly unfaithful, something he can't quite admit though she punctures absurd lie after absurd lie.

Musically, I'm a bit off at all times, like the English dub of a kung fu movie.

Celeste storms off; Adam is duly crestfallen; Hugh calls, "Scene!"

And then Hugh wants to know how everyone feels.

Adam's mouth prunes for an instant before he puts his game face back on.

"Celeste?" Hugh asks.

"Meh," she says.

"If he's been cheating," Hugh says, "you need to be more upset from the beginning."

"I know, I know," she says peevishly.

"No, it's good," Hugh says. "We found something good."

Something in the tone of this exchange suddenly makes me wonder if I'm the only one getting paid here.

I get up and intercept Adam's pacing. "Sorry, I was fucking clueless," I say.

He closes his eyes and waves a hand rapidly back and forth. I can't tell if he's pissed at me because of my playing or because I'm breaking his focus. I go back and sit down at the harp. Adam and Hugh talk for a minute, and then we try again.

In the afternoon, we shoot in Washington Square Park with a different actress, which goes a bit better for all of us. And after some rerecording of me alone for use in editing, Adam says we're going to have dinner with a "special friend." Adam has dated people like Helen Hunt and Amy Adams, so I'm curious.

Walking to the restaurant, Adam says, "You remember Mindy Sheperd, don't you?"

Mindy was also a theater major at Northwestern, a year behind us. She was part of the theater gang that I sometimes hung around with because of Adam, but she and I were not close. Adam says she's been living in New York since graduation, doing mostly stage stuff as well as the occasional TV commercial, and it turns out we're having dinner with her.

When we walk into the restaurant, Mindy is already at a table by the window.

"Hey, Matt," she says, getting up for a quick hug. "It's been a while."

"Yeah," I say. "Wow, you're looking great."

And in fact she *is* looking great in a black cardigan over a black-and-white flower-print dress. Her dark hair drapes in tousled waves around her pale face and sad brown eyes. Her upper lip swells over prominent choppers, which I find sexy, though when she smiles fully, she reveals a career-limiting amount of gums and tragically short teeth. I wonder if her old designs on Adam are in play again—or if they're dating. I remember Adam making an odd reference to licking someone's gums in today's first scene and wonder.

I was expecting Adam to choose some place trendy and swank, but the restaurant is old-school Italian, with worn wooden tables covered with sheets of brown butcher paper jammed into an open room. The tessellated white tile floor looks chewed through in spots.

I ask Adam and Mindy a lot of questions about their lives as actors and they name-drop and trade war stories. I grill Adam about his *Conan* appearance, and, with the air of a cruel father disabusing his son about Santa Claus, he tells me that everything that gets said on those shows is prepared ahead of time.

I listen intently, nod, enlightened though not surprised. The ache to be successful gathers enormous pressure into my head, but it's not clear how the harp could ever take me from where I am to there, even if I win the audition. In fact, just moving to a place like St. Louis, for whatever reason, would look like failure to these people.

We're on our third bottle of wine and finished with our entrees when Mindy starts asking about me. I don't mention my father but talk about the upcoming audition and about how I've been playing harp for dying people.

"It's pretty weird," I say.

"What's weird?" she asks.

"Playing for dying people."

"You should come live out here," Adam insists. "Chicago is a pussy city."

"It is not!" I say.

"All right, it isn't, but it is—you know what I mean?"

"Listen to you, '*pussy city*,'" Mindy mock-scolds Adam. Then she turns back to me, leaning in. "How's Milena doing?"

"We got divorced about a year and a half ago," I say evenly.

Her face becomes a perfect mask of tragedy. "Oh, Matt, I'm sorry to hear that."

"Well . . ." I look out the window. "I don't know," I say aimlessly.

"She never had a lot to say, that Milena Ceban," Mindy adds, looking at Adam as if for backup.

"She was sweet," I say. "She *is* sweet." I should add that she is shy with most people, that she doesn't crave attention.

"If by 'sweet' you mean a great piece of ass," Mindy says with a smile.

"No, Mindy, you're a great piece of ass," I say, smiling back. "Milena is sweet."

" '*Officer and a Gentleman* is the *best* movie I've ever seen!' " Mindy says, imitating Milena disturbingly well.

"What she's trying to say," Adam jumps in, "is that, as your friends, we were concerned when you set out in your little dinghy for the tropical island of Idios, and we've been dying to tell you for almost twenty years."

I of course knew that some of my friends thought that Milena wasn't the brightest person, and, I'm ashamed to say, I've had my own versions of these thoughts.

"What is that?" I say to Adam. "Why do you think you can say stuff like that to me? You're basically calling her an idiot. Seriously. What the hell is wrong with you?" My voice ends much louder than it began, much louder than I wanted.

"All right, brother man," Adam says. "Easy now. The truth is painful, and yet we must embrace it and French-kiss it."

"What about Lucy Varnum and what's-her-name, the alcoholic soprano?" I practically shout. "And that girl with the harem pants!"

"I didn't *marry* those women."

"Of course not," I say, trying to get Mindy on my side.

"Ah," says Mindy. "I'm thinking your ex is not as ex as we thought."

"That's nowhere near the point," I say. "It's just rude to insult her like that."

"All right, bronco," Adam says, hands raised. "Mea culpa, if you insist."

I stare at the candle flickering in the white paper bag in the center of the table. Suddenly, I can't bear the idea that I've ruined things here, even though I don't particularly like Mindy.

"Look, it's all right," I say miserably, trying to nice up the situation. "Let's talk about something else."

When we're back in Adam's living room, drinks in hand, I still feel twisted up about the incident at dinner. On the drive out, I actually considered talking to Adam about getting back with Milena and had vaguely hoped for some support.

I try to act as if everything's cool. "How do you think the scenes went today?"

"You mean when you blew up at the restaurant or earlier?" He puts his stockinged feet up on the coffee table and holds his drink in two hands on his stomach. I remember this pose from our room freshman year. I can't help but think that we stood together at the same starting line twenty years ago. I get the sick sense that my failure is being fixed right now, even though the audition is still over a month away.

"Dude, sorry I got *that* defensive, but give me a break."

"No, I get it," Adam says quietly.

This catches me off guard and I don't say anything.

Adam sighs. "It's so awkward when I'm sincere." He takes a swig and returns his glass to his lap. "We made some usable stuff," he ventures. "I guess I'll really know when we edit it."

"I'm amazed you guys did improv all day today."

"Well, you did, too."

"And I totally dicked it. How do you deal with just winging it?"

"I like that anything can happen," he says, and shrugs.

"Like you could just run off a cliff. I mean, there were times today when I was just twisting in the wind."

He pulls his feet off the coffee table and leans forward. His eyes bear in on me; he looks pissed. "Don't let fear become a problem. Don't run away from it. Just walk along next to it and you'll be fine. You've got to be confident."

"Yeah, but how can you be confident if you're afraid?"

"Listen, motherfucker," he says, "confidence is a *choice.* That's what they beat into our heads at Second City. It's got nothing to do with talent. It's a fucking choice. And it's totally on you."

The phrase "confidence is a choice" falls into my arms like a child jumping out the window of a burning house. I catch the child, because I must, but the impact hurts. There is suddenly one less excuse in the world. It makes me think of my father, on whose impatience and sharp critical eye I have occasionally let myself blame my obsession with failure, when I should have known and accepted it was on me.

"Makes sense," I say, which is the easiest, truest, and possibly only thing I can manage to say right now.

Adam retreats to his slouching position, like a genie sucked back into its bottle.

"I thought that maybe you and Mindy were dating," I say, to change the subject. I drink from my beer.

"Now, why would we do that?"

"Ask Mindy."

He takes a swig of his drink. "I'm single—for the moment."

He sounds more morose about this than I would expect. "A man of your fame and means . . ." I say, marveling, encouraging.

"A man who loves women, a man with a horse cock, a great sense of humor, a willingness to commit, to love, to love passionately, and yet I tend to fuck things up."

"I'm surprised," I say.

"Come on, haven't you ever seen a biopic?"

"Not having success or money doesn't exactly help, either," I say.

"There's really no escape. It's not just me. I see it all the time. People I know, people who are huge, as famous and as successful as you can get, and . . . If you're a drug addict or clinically depressed or a soulless manipulative fuck, you're still that shit even after your movie grosses a billion. If you've got a problem with your girlfriend, that problem is still there after you've been onstage. You may be able to forget about it for a while, but it's still there. Actually, what really fucks with you is how the good shit convinces you that the problem is really with the other person, because you're getting unbelievably intense validation. Trust me on this, motherfucker."

"I know you're saying it in the nicest possible way, but please, ease up on the 'motherfuckers' with me. I'm a fragile individual."

"You're not fragile," he says in his simplest voice. "Stupid and self-defeating, yes, but not fragile. I know you, you neurotic *motherfucker*."

16

~~~

WHILE AUDREY DEVOTES herself to a slice of cheese pizza and an orange soda, I ply her with questions about first grade that she quickly answers. I stay silent to let her say something—nothing doing. I point to people walking past the window of Big Tony's and ask what she imagines they're thinking, and she shrugs.

Is she sad? Is she troubled? Her eyes don't seem to focus on anything. She swings her feet forward and back under her chair. She chews lazily, with her mouth half-open, but I don't correct her. I want to ask what she saw, if anything, between Milena and me on the lower level of Steve's house. Instead, I ball up our greasy napkins, sweep our crumbs onto our paper plates, and announce in my friendly-Russian-giant voice: "We go home now!"

Back at my apartment, we have ice cream and watch *Happy Feet,* which is about a penguin who can't sing his love song. The movie is surprisingly good, though Audrey doesn't laugh when I expect. Then she asks me to read to her more from *Where the*

Red Fern Grows, so we sit side by side on the futon couch and I oblige, though I know what Billy's adventures with his coonhounds are likely to prompt.

"When you get your own house, then you can have a room for your harps and we can have a dog, right?" she asks.

"Maybe, sweetie, but it's going to be a long time before that happens."

"I could teach the dog not to run into your harp."

"You'd be great at teaching a dog stuff, but dogs can't always help themselves."

"We could put her in a cage when I'm not here."

"Well, dogs don't like to be in cages."

"We could get her toys for her cage."

Only the Jaws of Life can extract me from this conversation.

"I'm just really, really sorry, sweetie," I say.

"It's not fair," she says in a tremulous voice.

"I know," I say. I hug her with one arm, but she begins to cry.

When she finally gets sleepy, I turn off all the lights in the living room and retreat to my room with audition scores and recordings to listen to with my headphones.

Around midnight, as I'm emailing congratulations to one of my students who has just decided to attend the undergrad harp program at the University of Michigan, I hear a soft knock on my bedroom door and I jump at the sound. I open the door and Audrey stands there in her nightgown, holding her unicorn and a bath towel. She's looking down, her eyes squinted against the light on my desk.

"What's up, sweetie?" I say.

Rubbing an eye with the fist holding the towel, she silently enters the room. She climbs up onto my lap, sits sidesaddle, and begins making high-pitched, whiny noises and babbling sounds, as if she means to complain about something, but the only possible word I can pick out is "him." She rests the unicorn on her knees, and her free hand plucks at my arm several times. The gesture is uncanny and makes me suspect she's sleepwalking, though as far as I know she's never done so before. Then she pulls my wrist up and holds it there. I don't say anything and finally she lets go of my wrist and stops making noises and leans her head against my chest. She is warm and smells like she needs a bath. I consider asking her if something's wrong. I consider asking her if she saw Milena and me. If she's sleepwalking, she might answer but not remember answering, which would be ideal. But instead I just rock her, holding my hands around her hip to keep her slumped against me.

I'm very glad she's come to me, but I read on the Internet that sleepwalking correlates with subconscious turmoil.

After several minutes of rocking her in silence, I decide that she is either fully asleep again or at least soothed. I start to pick her up, to carry her back to her bed, but she gets down and walks back into the living room without a word. I follow her in the light from my room. She climbs into bed with the towel and the unicorn, and I bend to give her a good-night kiss. She is aware enough to expect this, leaning on one elbow in the bed, not letting her head sink down to the pillow. I offer her my cheek, because it's hard to avoid her lips if I try to kiss her— Milena kissed her on the lips a lot when she was younger, so she still tries to kiss on the lips—and she kisses me on the cheek, as if she is putting me to bed, and I say good night and she says good night.

T.R., bless his heart, babysits Audrey while I play brunch. It's not ideal to abandon her for five hours on one of my custody days, but because of the New York trip, my weekend day fell on Sunday and things are too precarious with Vikram to bring her to the Marriott. After I drop her at Milena's Sunday afternoon, I return home and notice something on Audrey's unmade bed. She has written in black marker on her white fitted bedsheet: "I am Stoopid." And below the "I" she's drawn a stick figure of, apparently, herself, her eyes vertical slits, her mouth an upside-down "U," her hair on the side of her head in two short straight lines, her arms extra thick and extended from her shoulders like bird wings.

Half a bottle of Spray 'n Wash and a trip through the washing machine later, the essence remains:

"I am Stoopid."

Cynthia emails me pictures of the office in Denver where the documents are stored, and of their worktable spread with documents, and of herself holding her gun-shaped hand to her head, with her tongue sticking out to the side. I write back telling her that practicing excerpts can also involve sifting minutiae. I assert that she and I are "soul mates," united in our efforts to wring meaning from tedious detail. She writes back: "You don't know from tedious. These documents! There is no meaning! I miss you, sailor boy. I've been remembering our night at the Art Institute and the first time you came back to my pad☺. (And nursing you after all of your bar fights!) We are two crazy obsessive people, working way too hard at EVERY-THING. Thank you for being cool when I've been stressing. I will be a happier camper soon, I hope, and better to be around."

It's strange how we seem closer in writing than we do in person. On our third date we went to Second City, laughed at mostly the same jokes, got mildly drunk, and went back to her place, where we had, on our first try no less, something very close to normal sex. It was over almost before I knew it had happened—though not in a bad way. Not at all. Remembering happier times makes me hopeful, but I worry that her reference to what happened back at her pad is her way of saying that something very close to normal sex is a key ingredient in our happiness, which of course is exactly what I'm afraid of. I write back that I know she's been stressed and no worries on that front and I miss her, too.

Sunday night I call her, and she tells me she took a break from producing documents to fly to Wichita for negotiations on the Cessna settlement. Apparently, it's just about 100 percent nailed down and she's forwarded a draft final agreement to Whitaker for approval because the size of the settlement is beyond what she is authorized to approve. She sounds happy but nervous.

I try to commiserate with her about those awful moments when something huge and on the brink of finality is not yet over and done with. I don't say how many of those excruciating moments I've endured: Philadelphia, Charlotte, San Diego, Seattle, Orlando, Milwaukee, Salt Lake City, the Lily Laskine International Competition, the Israeli International. Finalist, semifinalist, eliminated. The suspense—it always seems perfectly designed to pry open my vulnerabilities. I tell Cynthia, "It's out of your hands now," but the fact is, seven years ago, waiting for results in Seattle, I bit and drew blood from the meaty part of my left hand, between my thumb and forefinger. I had made the finals and played my ass off. It may have been the high-water mark of my thus-far fruitless strivings.

"Ah, I'm getting sleepy," she says. "You know, I wouldn't kick you out of bed if you came through the door right now."

"I know what you're saying. If you tried to leave the bed, I would grab your ankle, so, you know, you couldn't go."

She laughs. "Oh, how were the bagels?" she asks.

I forgot to go to the bagel shop she recommended.

"Fantastic," I say.

On Monday, I wake up at 4:19 a.m. beset with figuring out what to do about Milena and Cynthia. I pit the choices against each other in a manic rock-paper-scissors-style smackdown: At first,

I resolve to (1) "choose confidence" and make things work with Cynthia, which will spill over into my harp playing and catapult me toward New York–style success; which is defeated by the fact that (2) any mental action like "choosing confidence" will, in the twitchy hands of my monkey mind, turn out to be another source of self-consciousness and therefore impotence, which will spill over into my harp playing; which leads to a desire to (3) beg Milena to take me back, solve my impotence, reassure the increasingly troubled Audrey, and make everything okay, which is undermined by the notion that (1) having to play it safe to keep my shit together is why I always lose as a harpist and will never be happy; in other words, I should "choose confidence."

And so on.

This thinking wears me out yet creates wide-eyed wakefulness. It adds up to a feeling of being trapped in an airless, one-man submarine at the bottom of the ocean, and I can't escape from these thoughts and get back to the surface. So, as I take the El downtown to have lunch with Milena after a morning of intense, fear-driven practicing, I'm still not sure what to do.

Feeling disingenuously clean-cut in a blue button-down shirt and tan khakis, I step through a slow revolving door into the Harris Bank building on LaSalle, where I find my dear ex-wife standing near a racing electronic stock ticker like a nervous job interviewee. We're both early.

She starts toward me in a business suit and nylons, absolutely regulation, and, with a shy, crooked smile on her face, looking cute as hell with her sheepdog bangs.

"All dressed up," she says, and she laughs at me.

But this is in fact what I want her to notice: I am different, things will be different, due to lessons learned.

"And you're looking lovely," I say with a smile.

"Hey, it's what the well-dressed businesswoman is wearing this spring." She smiles, pleased with her joke.

"Where do you want to go?" I ask.

"Let's just pick up something," she says lightly, leading the way back out the revolving door onto the street. "There's a decent food court pretty close."

For a second, the informality is disappointing, but then this isn't a date, it's just us again, familiar.

"How's work today?" I ask.

"Pretty good, pretty good," she says, with something guarded yet giddy in her voice.

She takes us across Clark and down rough marble steps to a sunny plaza at the base of a skyscraper. A huge square fountain with a grid of jets shoots foamy white water into the air while people with 401(k)s and health insurance sit eating at metal tables on one side of the plaza. We pass them and go through a heavy glass door into a thronged food court. Milena makes a beeline for Asia Express, and I follow her. She gets sushi and I get chicken stir-fry.

Outside, all the tables are full, so we sit with our trays on the edge of a long marble planter filled with violet tulips in full bloom, a few just beginning to lose their petals. Pigeons with iridescent blue-green necks scavenge around the tables and between chair legs.

"How was New York?" Milena asks.

"It was good in some ways. Kind of wished I had stayed home and practiced, I guess."

"How's Adam?"

"Ahm, good and not good. I think he's kind of in between things—not dating, not making a movie. You know, you came up, and he apologized for being a dick about you."

"Thanks a lot, Adam, really appreciate it." She dips a piece of her sushi into her sauce and lifts it to her mouth with her slender fingers.

This is as sharp as Milena's sarcasm gets, yet underneath

that, I can tell she is glad to hear this, and it has taken the edge off me going on the trip. I smile at her, and we eat more of our food. We are co-conspirators, just like any couple acting as a team, placing their friends around them just so. Milena should know about Audrey writing "I am Stoopid" on the bedsheet, but I'm not sure this is the moment.

"How have *you* been?" I say. My intonation is the shameless equivalent of putting a hand on her thigh.

"Things have been a wee bit *unusual,*" she says, with something like flirtation in her voice, alluding, I think, to Unusual Exhibit A: us humping in her family room.

Suddenly her phone goes off in her purse—her ring tone is from Barry White's "You're the One I Need."

"Stop!" she says as she paws through her purse.

As she checks the number, both of us, I bet, are thinking, *It's Steve.*

"It's Montessori," she says, which means she must answer it. "Hello? Yeah, hi, Rachel, what's up? . . . Oh my God . . . But how did she get them?" Milena's face crumples into disgust, disbelief, and her lower lip trembles. The voice on the phone is saying a lot. "Oh my God . . . Oh my God . . . What hospital? . . . Rachel? . . . Rachel? . . . What hospital? . . . Okay, I'm going there right now."

She closes her phone, looks at me. Her eyes quickly brim over and spill.

"What's happening?" I ask. "Is she okay?" I know Audrey is not okay.

"Audrey took a bunch of Tylenol this morning—like maybe fifteen pills," Milena gets out before bursting into tears. "She wouldn't eat lunch." She gasps, gathers herself. "She told the teacher she had a tummy ache. It's toxic, really bad. They're taking her to Children's Memorial."

I make sounds that are not words, something between a

cough and a moan. If she dies, I will die, too—this comes to me as an absolute certainty. I will know as soon as it happens, no matter where I am. I will lie down and shut off.

Flagging a taxi is not as instantaneous as one would hope, but eventually we are heading up Dearborn. The cabbie goes right on Washington, and we hit every light working our way east to Lake Shore Drive. Milena sits on the edge of the backseat, hunched slightly, her knees tight together, fists on her thighs. She hasn't bothered to get any tissues out of her purse. Her face is running with tears and makeup. The cab smells of Febreze and spoiled steak, which makes me feel more sick and short-breathed.

I can't believe Audrey attempted suicide, yet that is what it looks like. I remember her crying fit outside the Montessori school on the way to my father's wake and how helpless I felt at seeing her suffering and not understanding why. I know the doctors can save her—they must—but the idea that she is this troubled is simply unprocessible; it will be the main thing to worry about for the rest of my life. I flash on the image of my always-handy bottle of Tylenol sitting next to a glass of water on the windowsill by the harp, six feet from Audrey's bed, and a telephone pole passes through my chest. I don't remember seeing it this morning when I practiced.

I reach across the seat and grasp one of Milena's hands. She puts my hand in a death grip and knocks her other fist repeatedly against her chin.

"She was awake, right?" I say.

"They didn't say."

"They've got her at the hospital," I say, as if I'm having a vision of activity in the ER. "They're helping her." I cover Milena's hand in both of mine and squeeze.

"Rachel doesn't know where she got the pills."

"I think—" I blurt out. "I think she got them from me."

Milena pulls away, gives me the feral, openmouthed look

that I remember from the time Audrey was twelve weeks old and supposedly immobile so I left her to take a quick piss and she rolled off our bed and clonked her head on the floor.

"I mean, I didn't *give* them to her!" I say. "She might have taken the bottle from my apartment. I'm not sure."

"She went in your medicine cabinet? How could she reach?"

"The bottle was out. I took some and, and . . . I didn't put it away. I am so sorry, Milena. God, am I sorry." I can't bring myself to tell her that I always keep the bottle near the harp so I can pop a few for my shoulder without interrupting a practice session.

"You don't pay attention!" Milena yells. She slams her fist sideways against my arm. "How could you let her leave your apartment with a bottle of pills! You don't pay attention to other people! You are so fucking selfish!" Her face is red and crazed with streaking makeup.

I remember Audrey coming into my room two nights ago and wish I could tell Milena about it, as if it would be a type of defense, but now it seems I've only dreamed that strange visit.

The cabbie doesn't check us out in the mirror.

I feel so rotten I'm surprised I haven't blacked out. My heart pauses, then picks up as if I'm sprinting again, a sign of my heart murmur under stress. My skin flushes. Am I having a heart attack? I'm extremely alert, nowhere close to crying. Maybe I can't cry because I'm focused. Maybe because I don't deserve to cry. But if Audrey picked up the bottle yesterday at my apartment, why did she wait until she was at school to take those pills? And how did she get the bottle open?

Exiting Lake Shore Drive, the cab speeds down the off-ramp before braking hard to avoid hitting a backup of cars at the light. To make the left onto Fullerton, the cab tailgates the last car through the intersection well after the light has turned red, setting off numerous angry car horns.

But we're getting close.

"Oh my God, oh my God," Milena whispers. She spreads her hands over her face.

Children's Memorial banners appear on light poles. Just past a red "Pediatric Emergency Entrance" sign, we turn and accelerate up a driveway and into a tunnel that passes all the way under the second floor of the hospital and out the other side. Halfway toward that daylight, the cab brakes—beside an entrance to the building.

Milena has her door open before we come to a complete stop. I page through my wallet; I don't have enough cash. Milena is already out the door and running.

"What's your name, your code, your badge?" I babble to the cabbie, though I can see his ID on the seatback out of the corner of my eye. "I'm five dollars short."

The cabbie turns around, looking down toward the money I'm holding out. "Just go," he says in a resigned voice. He's got a close-cropped beard, an island tuft of hair at the top of his forehead, hooded eyes that make him look sleepy. He takes all my bills. "Seriously," he adds. "God."

"I'll get it to you," I say.

When I catch up to Milena at the desk, she's drawing tissue after tissue out of a box the receptionist has proffered, wiping her face, shaking. People try not to stare.

"Take a breath, Mil," I say softly, stepping near. I resist putting my arm around her for fear she'll scream. "They've got her. This is a good place."

The receptionist nods at me and says, "Doctor will be right out."

And after a few minutes, a short woman with small wire-rimmed glasses does come out. A plastic koala bear clutches the stethoscope around her neck. She regards us soberly.

"Mr. and Mrs. Grzbc?" She pronounces the "z" because she can't know.

"We're Audrey's parents," Milena says, and sniffs.

"Okay, I'm Dr. Donahue. Let's step in here."

She leads us down a hallway into a small room with a sofa and a lamp and a table with a too-conspicuous box of tissues standing on it.

"Let me tell you what we know, and then we'll see her," Dr. Donahue says, very businesslike and calm. "She did vomit in the ambulance, which is good. She also went into mild shock, which is not good. But she responded well to fluids, and her blood pressure has been improving. We're waiting for the blood test, but just given how long the Tylenol's been in her system, it's likely she'll need to be on an IV with an antidote that's very reliable for this type of poisoning. It'll take about twenty hours for those treatments. Okay?" We nod. "Children do much better with this than adults," she continues, "and I think we got her in time. She's not out of the woods yet, obviously, but the most likely outcome—not guaranteed, but most likely—is a full recovery. Any questions?"

Hearing "full recovery," I look at Milena, ready to embrace relief, but she doesn't look back at me.

"Is she awake?" I ask.

"She's groggy. The IV will help, but this is very exhausting. Don't worry if she's asleep when you see her."

"I want to see her," Milena says, as if that's the only point. She swipes a tissue under each eye.

"Okay, last thing?" Dr. Donahue says. "When a child takes this many pills, the Department of Children and Family Services is automatically notified and their protocol is to talk to the parents. I expect someone will meet with you later today or tomorrow."

Then we're out and down another hallway to a large room partitioned with curtains.

"Hi, Audrey, look who's here!" Dr. Donahue says, sliding aside a curtain.

Audrey lies in a big hospital bed, looking small, her pale

green eyes blurred with fear, all tomboy haircut and skinny shoulders, surrounded by plastic and metal equipment. There's a cuff on her left arm with a lead to a machine. A wire is taped to her forefinger and more wires come out of different parts of her gown and connect to a screen up on the wall that is beeping in a reasonable rhythm and showing wobbling lines. An IV sends a clear fluid into her arm. Her mouth opens, but no sound comes out. A warm fizzing gathers behind my eyes, and a few tears leak out. Her eyes track Milena, who rushes over and kisses her face and head. I stand behind Milena, by a metal folding chair, waiting my turn.

As if to punish me for breaking vigil for fifteen minutes to get some food in the cafeteria, Steve now sits in the chair on the other side of the bed in intensive care, holding the hand of a sleeping Audrey. He wears a white shirt and tie, radiating cologne, his face covered in a perfect five o'clock shadow, looking like a father, while I, in my button-down and khakis, look like a high school kid dressed for Grandma's birthday party. He lets go of Audrey's hand when I enter, nods my way.

I give Milena the pink smoothie and say, "In case you change your mind."

She takes the sweating drink from me and places it on the floor.

To avoid standing there awkwardly, I lean against the windowsill. It seems as if Steve has just arrived, because he goes back to asking questions about what happened and what's going on. I let Milena answer most of them.

"She's doing good," I say.

"She's going to make it," Milena says, correcting me.

"I can't believe the school let this happen," Steve says.

"They didn't know what was going on. She probably got the pills from my apartment," I say.

He glances at Milena, then focuses on Audrey, rubbing his thumb over the back of her hand.

During the second IV infusion of the antidote, the intensive care doctor comes in. He is young and at least six and a half feet tall. Audrey's liver function test results are approaching normal values. Her blood pressure is up and her heart rate is down, which means the symptoms of shock are fading as well.

"She's a trouper, this one," he says, smiling at Audrey. "She's making my all-star team, which is impressive since she's only been in the building for five hours."

Audrey smiles at him with gleaming eyes—the first real smile I've seen from her since Saturday night.

The next morning Audrey is almost back to her old self, awake most of the time, so around lunch time I go home for an hour to eat, clean up and make some phone calls: to my mother, to the hospice, to my students—informing, rearranging, canceling. I note that the bottle of Tylenol is gone from the windowsill. When I come back to the hospital, Audrey has been transferred out of intensive care and into a regular room. Milena finally heads home for a bit in the late afternoon, and while I'm there at the hospital, I get my visit from the DCFS investigator, who takes me to one of the small consultation rooms on the floor.

Karen Grier is a middle-aged woman squeezed into a large black and red suit. The brown skin of her cheeks is dotted with small dark moles or freckles. She comes bearing the Tylenol bottle in a Ziploc bag. Though it is one of millions of look-alike bottles, I recognize it instantly as the very bottle from my windowsill; I would know this damn bottle anywhere.

She tells me she is here primarily to protect the best interests of Audrey and to ensure that she is in a safe home environment. It turns out Ms. Grier has already been to the Montessori school—and has spoken as well with Milena and Audrey herself. She appears to be as serious as hell and my heart beats fast.

She starts with a series of questions that establish what I've already admitted: I left the Tylenol on the windowsill in the living room and Audrey took it.

"Does Audrey routinely go in that room?"

"Yeah, her bed's in the living room, actually."

Her expression is not questioning but it seems to invite me to say more.

"I can't afford a two-bedroom apartment right now."

"Can you say why the medicine was on the windowsill this particular day?"

"I'm a musician and I sometimes get soreness in my shoulder if I play a lot. My instrument is in the living room, too, and I don't like to get up when I'm practicing, so I keep the bottle there."

"You don't like to go to a medicine cabinet if you've got some soreness?"

"I'm afraid that I'll let myself get distracted and won't sit back down."

"I see," she says in a way that suggests she does not see.

"It's super important that I focus during the time I've set aside for practicing," I add. I hear how this sounds in this context and wish I hadn't said it, but I did.

She goes on to ask me if I had known that Tylenol can be toxic ("No"), was the safety cap on ("Always").

"A friend of hers at school helped her get the bottle open," Ms. Grier says. She folds her hands on her legal pad, takes a deep breath and resumes: "Now, Mr. Grzbc, what is your sense of Audrey's emotional state before this all happened?"

She says my name right, which reminds me she's been talking to other people about this, and I resolve to be as truthful as possible, no matter how it sounds. I say general things about the effect of the divorce and Audrey's ambient anxiety level. I cop to the sleepwalking episode and Audrey's writing on the bedsheet. On a roll, I also describe the hiccup crisis and note the possibility that Audrey saw us having sex. Ms. Grier frowns at me for an instant, and I realize, too late, that I've gone too far. In our brief time together I've given her some good reasons to question my aptitude as a parent. She writes in a big, flowing, constant hand, like a river meandering across her legal pad, and she seems to have completely detached her penmanship from her eye contact, which generally stays fixed on me, making her seem equal parts polygraph machine and human being.

When I stop talking, she continues writing for another half a minute, then folds her hands, glances up at the ceiling, then back down to look into my face.

"Audrey told me she was trying to make herself feel better by taking the pills," she says. "Do you know where she got that idea?"

"She was trying to feel *better*?"

"That's not what I'm asking."

"Okay, but where she got what idea? What are you asking?"

"I'm asking if you know where she might have gotten the idea that taking some Tylenol capsules was a thing to do if she wasn't feeling right."

"Well, I guess she saw me taking a few one day," I say, "and she asked me why and I must have said something like they help me to feel better."

"Was this recently?"

"Maybe a month ago, six weeks ago, I don't know."

"Any idea why she would think so many were necessary?"

I almost say she was just being thorough, like her old man. "I don't know," I say instead. "Honestly, that worries me a lot."

"How many would you take?"

"Two. Just two."

"She said she didn't feel anything different after she took the first one," Ms. Grier says. "So she kept taking them."

Well, why didn't you say so! I want to yell. Apparently, her questioning strategy is designed to sniff out lies and withholdings.

"I mean, we give her liquid medicine when she's sick," I say, "so maybe she was trying to take a little cupful of pills to match the amount of liquid in the cup?"

"Everybody's thinking all the time, isn't that right?" she says, suppressing a smirk.

"Sure," I say.

"Did you have liquid cold medicine or liquid pain relievers in your apartment?"

"Probably. They'd be in the medicine cabinet. Pretty high. She'd have to climb up there."

She asks me how often I see Audrey. Am I in a new relationship? Does my new companion spend the night when Audrey is present? And so on. Five minutes later, with the interview winding down, she tells me she'd like to visit my apartment on Friday to make sure it's a safe environment for Audrey. Then there will be a report that will say whether neglect is "indicated" or "unfounded." Pending her report, which she expects to complete by the middle of next week, she is suspending Audrey's custody days with me, leaving Audrey in the care of her mother on those days. Apparently, she is an officer of the State of Illinois with significant discretionary powers.

"If our investigation concludes that neglect is indicated, this will go to juvenile court. If neglect is unfounded, you'll go back on your normal custody schedule. Do you understand?"

"Yes," I say. Before I know I'm doing it, I put both hands on my head, like a criminal being arrested.

"Thank you for your time, Mr. Grzbc."

What I would like to do is grab Ms. Grier by her red and black lapels and scream, *Can't you see it was a fucking over-*

sight that anyone might make! How dare you take my child from me!

Instead I say, "Thank you," with actual sincerity. "Thank you for what you do."

"Medicines in the medicine cabinet," she says, closing her legal pad holder with a sigh. "That's what I do."

"Of course."

"Glad to hear Audrey's doing well." She gets up with effort. "Good afternoon."

Once my surface embarrassment burns off and I can bracket the whole "being suspected of child neglect" thing, which, it turns out, is not easy, I'm left cautiously embracing a new and relatively joyous possibility: Audrey was not trying to hurt herself; she was trying to help herself.

If this is true, I can deal with everything else.

A moment alone with Audrey to confirm her motivations for taking the pills does not come until the third and final day of her hospital stay, after many thousands of hours of Cartoon Network and stupefying awkwardness as Milena, Steve, Audrey, and I share the same space. Steve is polite, alternately ignoring me and questioning me as if I am a long-lost uncle of Audrey's with an intriguing musical hobby. Milena mostly acts as if both of us are not there, focusing on Audrey or going down to the family lounge to make phone calls. At last, Steve and Milena go for lunch in the cafeteria.

While we're watching a *SpongeBob* episode, I turn to Audrey and say, "You've been a great kid during all of this. Very brave."

"I'm sorry I took your medicine," she says. Her voice quavers slightly.

"No, that's my fault, babe. I'm sorry I left it out. I didn't explain about it like I should have."

She nods.

"But now we know, right?"

"Now we know!" she says with some happy excitement. She leans forward into a sitting position.

And I'm tempted to stop here, because maybe just having her squared away for the future can be enough. But I hear myself press on: "Why so many, sweetie?"

She falls back on the bed and looks at me. It's a painful look to confront, filled with sadness and confusion and a need for simple approval and love.

"I don't know," she says. She starts to cry, though she's trying not to.

I move toward her and she moves toward me and we hug. She seems to put what strength she has into hugging me.

"Good kid," I say. "Good kid. You can cry as much as you want. It's okay."

I wait until she breaks the hug and I sit back. But I can't live with "I don't know."

"Ms. Grier—the lady from Family Services—she said it's because you didn't feel better at first."

"Yeah," she says, looking at the TV, wiping her eye with the back of her hand. It would have been good to turn off the TV before starting this conversation.

"So is that why?"

"Pretty sure." She nods as if to confirm this to herself.

"Okay, I know this is hard to talk about, but please look at me: did you want to hurt yourself? It's okay, if you did. I mean, it's okay if you tell me. Then we know, right?"

She looks toward me but not exactly at me. "Yeah."

"Yeah to what?"

"Alyssa was just being my doctor."

Alyssa must be the friend Ms. Grier mentioned, but it occurs to me that if I interrogate Audrey further she *will* want to hurt herself.

"Okay, please, sweetie," I say. "Never hurt yourself, okay?

You can always tell me or Mom if you're feeling sad, okay? You're a good, smart kid. Always know that, okay?"

She considers this for beat after beat after beat.

"I want to go home," she says. "I want to go back to school."

"Okay, sweetie," I say. "I'm super glad to hear that. But let us know. It's very important."

"Okay," she says, and her eyes fall back, irretrievably for now, into the world of SpongeBob, which is probably not a bad thing.

I watch the TV as well, but I can't help but worry. Of all the art forms, music is the one most open to and defined by prodigies, from Mozart composing his first works at age five to Yo-Yo Ma performing for President Kennedy at seven. This fact stabs my thirty-eight-year-old soul daily. And now here's a twist of the knife: my daughter is an anxiety prodigy, on her way to her first therapist at the age of six.

17

~~~

LATE WEDNESDAY AFTERNOON, Audrey is discharged into Milena's care. I make it home in time for a big evening practice session, and as soon as I stop playing, T.R. comes down for an Audrey update.

"I'll tell Charles," he says after I explain the good news. "He was concerned."

I mention the impending visit from the DCFS.

"All right, no bondage equipment on the front porch," he says wryly.

On Thursday, I practice intensely all morning. Then, after paying make-up hospice visits to Richard and Michael, I'm asked to play for a sweet Alzheimer's patient who communicates entirely in honks and lip smacks. I squeeze in a late-afternoon lesson with a student, and in the evening return a ton of phone messages from people who are concerned about Audrey. I had given my mother the all-clear as soon as I knew it, expecting she would then get the word out with the family. But detailed updates are required, it becomes clear.

My oldest sister, Mary Ellen, has two daughters, eighteen and twenty-one, both basketball players, and she's dealt with everything from torn knee ligaments and a broken jaw to an alcohol-related car accident that battered her younger daughter, Irene. The chief of staff for my mother during the mad years of intensive child-rearing, she cultivates a hard-bitten, changed-one-diaper-too-many persona, but under that she's a support warrior.

She doesn't like the sound of what Audrey has done. I pace from my living room to the kitchen and back, spilling my guts about everything that could be weighing on Audrey, except having sex in front of her. I tell her a social worker is involved and that I've temporarily lost my custody rights.

"Oh, that's terrible," she says, "but that's not going to hold up. You'll get custody back. You're not using heroin, are you?"

"Uh, no."

"I've heard all the great musicians do," she adds. "Something to think about."

I laugh and look out my front window at the empty night-time street. There's actually a dealer on our block who offers "rocks and blows," cocaine and heroin—"blows" for heroin because people around here snort it.

"We'll probably have to take her to a therapist," I say. "We *should* take her to a therapist."

"Well, yes, there's that."

"Listen," I say, shifting gears, "do you mind if I ask you something about Dad?"

"Depends what it is."

"Well, I know we tend not to talk about this kind of thing, but George told me about some of the mental health stuff Dad went through, you know, back in the day, and I'm kind of wondering what you remember about that."

"Uh, boy," she says.

"George said he was actually hospitalized. I don't remember that."

"Well, you were too busy savanting with the piano. Yes, he got really sick." She takes a breath and seems to do something away from the phone. I wait out the pause. "But what I remember are the paintings. For a while, Daddy was an amazing painter."

"A painter?" I take a seat on the futon couch.

"I know, right? But he was. He'd paint when he couldn't sleep, which was basically all the time, or when he was freaking out. He told Mom he was dying in his head—something like that."

"Is this the whole 'crisis of faith' thing?"

"It was, kind of. I mean, there was that also. I remember for maybe six or eight months he wouldn't go to church—oh, that blew Mom's mind."

"I can imagine."

"It's a total mess, Matt. Back then Mom was always confiding in me—all kinds of crap—and when I was fifteen, I didn't want to be Mom's best friend. We got into big arguments about it, and then she stopped telling me things, cold turkey."

"Was he actually hospitalized?"

"Yes. He told Mom he was afraid he was going to hurt himself. Hard to believe he'd admit that to her, but that's how bad off he must have been. They had fights about the paintings. Mom really didn't like them."

Feeling a little dizzy, I ask why and lie down on the couch.

"Well, they were very odd. He claimed that the large-scale integrated circuit was the most beautiful object ever made. He painted computer chips obsessively."

"I don't remember him painting at all."

"He stopped. I'm not sure when. When he came back from the hospital after a couple of weeks, he was on medication and went back to church. Then he started screwing around with the appliances, but I think Mom actually liked that—because, you know, he fixed things for people. Neighbors, people from church were always bringing him things. And his medication kept him more or less in balance—though, as you know, not completely."

He was nicer to me, easier to talk to, as I grew up, especially after I moved out, and I need to keep that in mind.

"Mom told us he was on 'a trip,'" Mary Ellen adds. "You know Dad traveled a lot for the bridges. But I knew where he really went. And I think Bart had some idea, too. And maybe Bart told George something at some point. Honestly, it was scary, and when he came back and he was better, we all just didn't want to rock the boat."

"This is where she sleeps," I say, going for matter-of-fact but not quite making it.

Ms. Grier sizes up the living room, notes the proximity of Audrey's freshly made bed to the Aphrodite harp, to the TV. It's no place for a bed.

"She *will* need her privacy," she affirms. "Where are your cleaning products?"

These are high in a cabinet in the enclosed part of the back stairwell where the washer and dryer sit. I didn't just move them there for her visit, but I fear if I make a point of telling her this, she will hear it as a confession that they've been in an accessible spot until today. She asks me to bring them down so she can check all their safety caps.

"Any mousetraps, rat poison?"

This could be a trick question.

"No," I say.

"That's a beautiful harp," she says, looking back across the apartment. The Aphrodite is uncovered, while the 85P is shrouded.

"Thank you."

"*You* play that?" She laughs a bit under her breath, giving me a sideways look.

"I do."

"Good for you," she decides.

She inspects my medicine cabinet, wanders through my kitchen, opening drawers, looking for knives, firecrackers, plutonium. She enters my bedroom, notes the paint colors, the bed on the floor. Her expression doesn't change.

No firearms, drug paraphernalia, or signs of meth production.

She swabs for lead paint on the living room wall closest to Audrey's bed.

"No lead," she says. Her lips frown, as if she's disappointed.

"Do you want to see the bedsheet?" I ask.

"No, I got that," she says.

She takes some notes. Then she asks:

"And that's the windowsill right there?"

"Yeah."

"All right," she says. "I've got what I need."

She goes upstairs and talks to T.R. for about ten minutes and then she is gone.

18

~~~

THE AUDITION IS now less than a month away. While being true to my pledge to practice extra in Cynthia's absence, I listen for the buzz, hoping it will stay silent. Sometimes it seems to be there, sometimes not. On humid days, it seems maybe more there. Mostly, it slips below my awareness, like the ringing in your ears that's only present when you consider it.

Cynthia and I talk regularly on the phone. She was moved by the Audrey saga, and it was good to have her to talk to about it as Milena turned to Steve. Things seem almost normal between us, as though a thousand miles apart is the right distance for us.

I don't reach out to Milena. I figure that will be pointless until she's ready to accept my apology, which won't happen until she is through hunkering down with Audrey. It kills me to remember the flirtation in her voice before the call came from Rachel. Some stubborn hope survives there.

Adam sends me a disc of his first batch of breakup videos. He's still editing them and hasn't sent them around yet. They could be funnier, I think, but what makes them basically work, no matter how wild Adam's associations or how unfunny the dialogue might be on paper, is that Adam and the actresses are absolutely committed to their lines. They seem not at all worried about whether they're funny or not. I'm surprised by how steady my playing sounds.

At the hospice, Richard and I settle into something manly and almost affectionate. I usually see him without Erin or Malcolm around. One afternoon after I finish playing for him, Richard and I watch the Cubs on TV, and, in between bouts of coughing, he makes loaded observations about "the timelessness" of baseball. It's "a game without a clock," after all, and therefore, he seems to think, offers a wormhole into immortality, if we would only give ourselves over to its mysterious rhythms.

"It's not our national pastime for nothing," I say, trying to sound earnest.

I suspect he's dabbling in some sort of delusion—the kind, I think with a kick of pride, my father would have never fallen for—but I play along because the first unwritten rule of hospice volunteering is a complete evacuation of your self—all your opinions, interests, and needs—until you're as soft and air-filled as a pillow, offering pure comfort to the dying person.

When Richard gets tired or Erin shows up, I have more time to play for an impromptu client or two and to see Michael, who has become prone to window-gazing, or curling in the fetal position, or lying still with his eyes closed, sometimes with the back of his wrist to his forehead. I've never seen a family member in his room—only a chubby, bearded man, who left with a staring expression on his face when I came to the door.

One afternoon, between songs, Michael opens his eyes and asks me, "Do you live in the city?"

"Yeah," I say. "Humboldt Park."

"Ah, Puerto Rican boys," he says smiling. He mumbles something playful that I can't make out.

I smile back weakly. He appraises me with his heavy-lidded eyes.

"Where did you live?" I ask.

"All over. Before I moved in here—" He lifts his hand to take in the room. "Wicker Park. On Augusta."

"Right by the Lava Lounge!"

But my sudden excitement seems to add another degree of fatigue to his expression. Of course, there's no reason for me to be excited about the Lava Lounge, scene of many a failed pickup attempt.

"Guess so," he says, in a way that suggests he's never been there and would never think of going there. He looks out the window. Then he turns back to me.

"You don't know what it's like, do you?" he says, in a quieter voice.

I look back at him, stymied for a second, in part because he could be referring to any number of things. But then my answer comes easily: "No," I say, "I don't."

He closes his eyes. His face, in any paused state, appears alarmingly deanimated. I sit with him and watch his frozen face and what little I know of the person dying behind it. Then, with his eyes still closed, he says, "So you're . . . straight as a whip . . . as my father used to say."

"Yup," I say.

"Is that a real expression?" He opens his eyes and smacks his lips awkwardly, moving his tongue slowly. " 'Straight as a whip'? Bizarre."

"I don't know," I say, though I think I've heard "straight as a pin." There's a glass of water on his bedside table. "Do you want some water?"

He nods.

"Do you want to drink from the glass?"

He shakes his head.

So I go to the top drawer of his bedside table and pull out a small plastic package, with what looks like a little pink lollipop in it, but the head of the lollipop is a cube of sponge. I've seen the nurses use these sponges with him when his mouth is dry but he doesn't want to swallow something. The bodies of these dying people are shutting down, closing off rooms, turning off lights. They need and want less and less, which makes dying seem like a sensible process. There's a white residue on the inside of his drawn lips, like the stain salt leaves on pavement in the winter. I have no idea what it's from.

I open the package, sit as weightlessly as I can on the edge of his bed, and dip the pink sponge in the glass and move it to his mouth. His eyes open halfway and watch me. He has bad eyebrow dandruff, like I sometimes get, and I want to brush it away for him. Black and gray whiskers stand up all over his gray face, with a longer cluster right under his nose, where whoever shaved him was probably wary of venturing. I touch the sponge to his lips, paint them with it, dissolving the chalky film, and then his lips take the sponge into his mouth and hold it there loosely. He rolls it in his mouth a little and closes his lips around the stick. Finally, he nods, and I take the sponge out of his mouth.

"More?" I ask.

He nods. And we do the same thing.

"Thanks," he says.

I tip my head down.

"I drank too much, when I shouldn't have drank at all," he says softly, looking out the window. "That's why I'm here. I couldn't handle the side effects."

"Of the drinking?" I say uncertainly.

He turns his head and looks at me. "Of the drugs that saved everyone else."

"Oh," I hear myself say.

I don't feel equal to what he needs right now, and the sadness of that, and of the situation in general, pushes my chest backwards. Saliva jets from under my tongue and dizziness walks into my head, tilting my equilibrium wherever its weight presses.

"So what're you doing here?" he asks. "This is women's work, fag duty." He doesn't seem to have the energy to put scare quotes into his voice or inflect the right teasing tone—if that's what he wants.

"I'm not sure," I tell him, though this is not the nicest thing for a caregiver to say to a patient. It seems easier than mentioning my father or trying to care about someone besides myself or running at my fears. "I guess because they asked me."

"Ah, just messing with you," he says. He grins hideously, but I can see what his personality was like when he was healthy.

"Want to hear another song?" I say, though I really need to go.

"No," he says. "Gotta sleep."

19

~~~

O<small>N</small> T<small>HURSDAY</small> I get a call from Ms. Grier telling me that the case against me for neglect has been declared "unfounded" and my custody rights have been restored. A report, including her recommendations, has been sent to me via email attachment.

"Thank you," I say.

"Not a 'thank you' situation," Ms. Grier says. "I know you mean well, Mr. Grzbc, but we're all about doing over meaning to do."

I'm barely able to read the report, since my heart is banging on my ribs like a man hitting his head against a wall. Still, a few sentences get through and lodge in my memory for all time:

> Despite knowing that Audrey was an unusually anxious and precocious child, Mr. Grzbc did not take typical precautions to ensure the safety of her environment, resulting in extremely serious demonstrable harm. . . . Mr. Grzbc's willingness to have sexual intercourse with his ex-

wife in his daughter's playroom in the middle of the day suggests he puts his own desires ahead of his daughter's emotional well-being.

Still, according to Ms. Grier, my actions did not rise to the level of a "blatant disregard" of my responsibilities as a parent, which is apparently the standard for neglect.

No matter how I mentally twist and turn, I cannot seem to escape these facts and judgments. They are true as far as they go, and what they're missing may exist only in my own mind. These were accidents. I didn't mean to hurt her. But I did.

Not surprisingly, Ms. Grier recommends therapy for Audrey, and as sad as this is, it'll be a relief to have a professional on the case. She is not convinced by Audrey's answer to the question of "Why so many?" and neither am I.

When I pick Audrey up from school on Friday afternoon, I lift her up in a big hug and, still clutching her to my chest, carry her to her locker, which makes her giggle. I make her a proper meal of baked chicken, corn, and rice, with a glass of ice-cold milk. Then we clear the dining room table for arts and crafts. She makes a plastic heart with Hama beads and incorporates it into a Mother's Day card cut from construction paper. As she works intently, I remember when she was small enough for me to carry her around like a violin, my hand cupped under her neck, her little body tucked against me.

While she is playing a game on her Nintendo DS, I get an email from Milena. She says she is glad I have custody again. She tells me she is "thinking about everything." And then she writes: "All right. Gotta go now," as if pressing business calls. She signs off with just her name.

I wait until Audrey is asleep before giving Cynthia a call in Denver. It's good to report that I'm in the clear from the State of Illinois's point of view.

"I'm used to being suspect but not actually a suspect," I add.

"Oh, it's a short trip, believe me," she says.

"Really?"

"Yeah, I've been walking around feeling like a criminal lately."

"Why is that?" I ask.

"Oh, I don't know, when I'm feeling down in the dumps, I think of myself as a criminal. It's just something I've always done."

"Dang, Cynthia, what's going on with you?"

"Documents are going on with me. My mind is going on with me. I need all kinds of sleep and I need you when I get back."

"Why down in the dumps?"

"Whitaker is weighing. In case you haven't heard, being an associate at a corporate law firm is sometimes a very, very bad job for a human being to have."

"It's a lot of work."

"A lot of soul-crushing work. And there you have it, Matt."

"Which is making you feel like a criminal?"

"Oh, it's more than lawyering. Lawyering is just a whipping boy for my free-floating feelings of worthlessness."

"What about 'no worrying'?"

"That's my role in this relationship—truth-teller."

"Are you kind of drinking?"

"Not this instant. But before and likely immediately after, yes."

"Oh, Cynthia."

"I agree. I'll be sure to tell her. Until I see you again, which I'm glad will be very soon, you have yourself a good night."

On Sunday, I perform at the Mother of All Brunches: Mother's Day at the Marriott. There are a lot more song requests than usual to pay tribute to the moms, including some oddball choices: "You're So Vain," which I have, and "House of the Rising Sun," which I don't.

After brunch, I tool up to my parents' house. Normally, Mary Ellen hosts Mother's Day at her place in Greendale, but they're remodeling and people have decided it would be fun to "bring the party to Mom" this year. Everyone who lives in town is at the ancestral suburban split-level, drinking beer and soda and eating burgers and brats on the deck.

Mom seems both more animated and more sad. Widowhood has given her a wistful, showy air, almost like that of a retired movie star. My father is not around to contend with, and she's surrounded by her children, whose attention she deserves and gets. Everything has its compensations, I guess, though she hasn't given up on the belief that she murdered him. "There are some things I wish I'd never done—at the end," she says when Mary Ellen asks if she wants another glass of wine.

I'm my usual quiet self around my family and their spouses and kids. People ask about Audrey, but I can tell they've moved on. George has brought a plastic wheel of shrimp and eaten about half of it. Mary Ellen drinks a little bit too much and grows bemused when Christine, Luke's wife, tells an elaborate story about a clash among parents at one of her daughter's out-of-town volleyball tournaments. Bart and his wife use the communal conversation to snipe at each other, but no one says anything. The food is great and I don't have to be anyone in particular right now—it feels like a holiday before Cynthia comes back tomorrow.

I have half a mind to call Milena and wish her happy Mother's Day, something I didn't do last year with the divorce papers freshly filed. I haven't spoken to her directly since the hospital, but maybe the Family Services decision has put her on the road to forgiveness, and maybe calling on Mother's Day is a way of reminding her that though I screwed up, we're together in whatever happens to Audrey.

I take a cordless handset to my old upstairs bedroom, which is still furnished with a bunk bed my father made. I lie down on the bottom bunk, looking up at the U-curves of the metal spring overhead as I did hour by aimless hour as a youngster.

"Happy Mother's Day," I say without identifying myself.

There's a pause. Maybe she's deciding whether to hang up.

"Thanks," she says.

"Is Steve there?"

"He's grilling outside."

"Are you having a good day?"

"I'm sorry about losing it on the way to the hospital," she says in a quiet, defeated voice.

"You didn't lose it," I say. "Actually, you were very in touch with it. I'm still sorry. It just never occurred to me."

"I know," she says. "You didn't think of it. It's okay."

"How's Audrey? She seemed good at my place."

"Maybe sometime when I haven't cried in the last ten minutes, I'll tell you about the Mother's Day card she made me."

"She's a good kid," I say. I'm tempted to say I helped her with the card, but even I can see it would be a sly manipulation.

"Look, I need to tell you something," Milena says. "Steve proposed last night. And I said yes."

I imagine the top bunk coming down to crush me. I roll off the bed and stand up, but what Milena has just said is still present wherever I am.

"Oh," I say, politeness twitching my extremities. "Congratulations."

There's silence on the phone, then the sound of the air between us getting covered up by her hand. I expect to hear her hang up, but this doesn't happen.

"Are you still there?" she says, and I can tell she's been crying.

"Yeah," I say.

"Well, I have to go now," she says, and she hangs up.

I click off the phone and catch a glimpse of myself in the mirror. My expression is the blank but forbidding look of a zombie—not a crazed, brains-hungry, rank-and-file zombie, but one in administration.

I put the phone back on its charger and wander to the kitchen, where Luke and Christine are putting food in the fridge. I help them clean up, until my mother comes in from the deck.

"I hardly got to see you," my mother says. "Just come and talk with me for a minute."

She leads me into the living room, where dusk is more apparent than in other parts of the house, and we sit on the beige furniture.

"How's your music?" she asks, with deadly earnestness. This question, which seems so supportive and empathic, is actually quite painful, because she manages to put everything into it: she's a mother searching for her child's happiness, for whether or not my life has been good as a whole, and that's not a question I want to face right now.

"Coming along," I say. "How are you doing?"

She nods and purses her lips. "I'm okay, can't complain." Then she adds, "God must have thought it was time. I shouldn't argue with Him."

I grunt awkwardly. I just want to walk away, then drive far away.

"Matthew, I don't mean to upset you, but after what happened to your father, I know how things can happen so fast. So please make yourself right with God before it's too late. Can you do that for me?"

A gusher of anger spouts from my chest, filling my head. I almost shout *Leave me alone!* like a teenager. But I don't. Maybe it's the dismal memory of yelling at Audrey in the car on the way to my father's wake that warns me against indulging this not entirely explicable upsurge of feeling. And resisting yelling gives me just enough time to realize that yelling is an unusually sad activity.

"I'd like to," I say.

"All you have to do is ask Him," she says. "He'll take care of the rest."

She looks at me with damp eyes, head canted just so. This is a moment of extreme widowhood—nothing to hold against her.

"You know, I'm curious," I say. "When Dad wasn't doing so well, he did some paintings, didn't he?"

"Who said that?"

"Mom, please."

"I don't know what to do with them," she says miserably. "He wouldn't let me throw them out."

"Can I see them?"

"They're down in the basement," she says.

"Well?" I ask. "Could I look at them?"

She goes to her bedroom and fetches her key ring from her purse, and we head downstairs. The basement is more damp and musty than I remember. The dehumidifier is silent, with its red light on. I imagine Mom has trouble emptying it, so I go over and pull out its collection bucket, pour it down the floor drain, snap it back into place—and the fan and the compressor automatically come on.

"Oh, thank you," she says, paging through her keys, standing in front of a squat gray metal cabinet jammed in among boxes and cannibalized small appliances against one cinder-block wall. The cabinet is about four feet wide, with about twelve three-inch high drawers. She turns the key in the lock on the top corner of the cabinet, which pops out, releasing all the drawers. She pulls the top drawer open. It is full of canvases.

On top is a three-foot-by-three-foot painting composed of a series of rectangles, different sizes and colors, nested together and bordered by black bars. Within the rectangles there are very thin horizontal striations of orange and yellow or aquamarine and yellow or pink and blue. At first it doesn't seem as if it's something painted with brushstrokes. The lines have mechanical precision. All of the colors glow, as if lit from within, as on the surface of a TV screen. Some colors are so strong they seem to flame out of the painting and some seem to recede into it, creating a surprising depth of field.

"I like that," I say, and I imagine Cynthia would, too.

I lift it out of the drawer and place it on top of the cabinet. I look through more. A few are on the same scale. A few seem to be closer and closer views of individual sections.

"He was losing his mind," Mom says, looking over my shoulder.

"Did he ever paint anything else?" I ask.

"Never! I begged him to paint something outside—or Lake Michigan. He loved to go to the lake."

"I'm sorry, Mom, but I don't know if this was so bad."

"He thought this was the *meaning of life*! He didn't believe in God—he believed in *computer chips*. And apparently that was so wonderful he wanted to kill himself!"

She's crying now.

I want to cry, too, but instead I hug her—I hug my mother.

"I'm sorry, Ma."

"Uhhgh!" she suddenly cries out. "He made *me* crazy!" And now she laughs a bit as the tears subside.

"Would it be okay if I took a few of these home with me?" I ask.

"I knew you'd like them," she says morosely. "You both get lost in strange things. I guess that can be good, but it's so sad to me, Matthew. It *hurts* me. No beliefs, nothing to say. What about people?"

"People like to make things," I say.

"Well, people go crazy, too," she says.

. . .

I pull into the garage a little after nine-thirty, and I'm wondering if I can lose myself in the harp for an hour before listening to recordings until I sleep.

As I walk down the brick garden path, carrying several of my father's canvases rolled in one of his old cardboard blueprint tubes, someone calls out: "Hey there, sailor."

I make a high-pitched *yeep* sound and turn toward the voice. A safety light strapped to a telephone pole in the alley illuminates Cynthia, sitting on a wood and wrought-iron bench in a back nook of T.R.'s garden.

"Sorry," she says, getting up. "Didn't mean to scare you."

"Just testing my smoke alarm?" I say.

She laughs, walking down one of T.R.'s carefully raked gravel paths. "We finished last night," she says, "and I couldn't resist coming back to surprise you."

"I'm glad," I say, and I mean it.

She's wearing a light black sweater over a simple top and tight Capri pants, plus sandals. A bottle of wine in her right hand and my blueprint tube don't stop us from embracing. I press her up against me, breathe in her perfume, and we kiss. We kiss quite a bit.

"Is that a flashlight in your pocket or are you just glad to see me?"

"Just glad to see you," I say. In fact, I am crazy-grateful that she is here, feeling every bit of love and possibility surging back.

"And what's in the *little* tube?" she asks, tapping the cardboard.

My reply sticks in my throat. I smile unconvincingly. Eventually I'll show her my dad's paintings—she really might like them—but I don't want any wrenching thoughts coming between us right now.

Then we enter my dark apartment, where anyone with a nose would know that the garbage needs to be taken out.

I turn on the light in the kitchen. Suddenly revealed, a mouse on the counter is flat-footed for a millisecond before he disappears down the wall behind the stove.

"Should we open the wine now?" I say.

"Sure," she says, "if you want."

My garden erection is gone, but I'm hoping the renewal of physical contact will bring it back, and maybe she didn't see the mouse, and maybe she'll understand about the trash. I'm choosing confidence.

"Wish I could've cleaned up for you," I say.

While I pour some wine, she drapes her sweater over the back of a dining room chair. We wander into the living room, where she slips out of her sandals, leaving them on the floor by a plastic Polly Pocket beach house world. She's braless.

I consider quizzing her about the outcome of her document production, but instead I say, "Race you," and drain my glass of wine in one huge slurp. She follows suit, laughs, and we step toward each other, go into an exploratory clench. I take her to the bedroom, trying not to notice that I'm aroused again. We make out and undress, and her body is thinner and tauter, which weirdly feels like a type of accusation, like I've been failing to make a woman out of her, but the fact that I'm more or less completely with her as a person is amazing, and we could come through all of this, right now, and everything could be good.

We grope and rub and lick and kiss. Like a team of civil engineers, we get our genitals lined up. I've got just enough to penetrate, which I miraculously do, though the going is not totally slick and I wonder if I've blown the foreplay thing. There's enough surprising pleasure for me that I just about come right away—and stop moving entirely and realize that I have either ejaculated or had a muscle spasm *like* ejaculation that has drained away some pent-upedness. I'm still hard enough to keep the old in and out going but wonder if I've already actually come, which is a recipe for fruitless humping, and after Cynthia's sounds of enjoyment plateau and subside, I offer one final thrust, without coming, then relax as if sexual intercourse has been completed.

It's a moment when I wish mysterious human sexuality didn't exist, that the handshake was the beginning and end of physical intimacy, that pregnancy occurred after drinking a special protein shake mixed in a blender.

We lie together on the bed, neither of us willing to talk.

Finally, I say, "Welcome back."

20

I GET UP BEFORE Cynthia, take out the garbage, clean the mouse poop off the counter, and get breakfast rolling. I put out a grapefruit half and a box of Cheerios, then start cooking bacon and scrambled eggs, enough for both of us, but I'll eat her half depending on what she's in the mood for today. I'm focusing very hard on stirring the eggs to hold off any memories from last night, when she enters the kitchen and embraces me from behind.

"Sleep all right?" I say, and I turn to hug her with a greasy spatula in hand.

Fully dressed in yesterday's clothes, she puts her head against my shoulder. "I've got a bad feeling about today."

"That's an empty tummy talking," I say, and I kiss the top of her head.

But she's hiding her face against my shoulder, an otherwise powerful person most likely scared shitless about returning to her office, where she'll have to breathe the same air and walk the same carpets and use the same elevator bank as Whitaker.

"You haven't ever done anything wrong that I've ever heard of or seen," I say.

She grunts ambiguously.

"Let's chow," I say. I lead her into the dining room and move aside scores, CDs, and notes to clear two places at the table.

After I follow with the food, she says, "I'm going to talk to Whitaker in person about the Cessna settlement."

"Only makes sense," I say.

She politely eats a bit of everything except the Cheerios, but it's not much altogether. "I gotta get going," she says. "I have to stop home and get dressed."

And then she's putting her sweater on and heading out.

"Call me," I say at the front door. "Let me know how it goes."

"Okay," she says. She's got bags under her dark eyes, and it occurs to me that maybe it's not just Whitaker but also the less-than-thrilling homecoming, thanks to me.

After doing the dishes, I drift into the living room. I take a seat on the futon couch and stare into space. Each minute that changes on Audrey's Hello Kitty alarm clock reminds me of the audition's inexorable approach. The disturbing notion that working toward this audition also means working on separating myself from Audrey—a thought I'd successfully tied to a sunken lead weight—comes loose and bobs to the surface. When I finally sit down to practice, dizziness curls at the edges of my consciousness.

I didn't exactly *sleep* last night, which is no doubt part of the problem, but there are fewer than three weeks until St. Louis, and the more stressed I get, the more dizzy I get, which keeps me from practicing, which makes me more stressed, which makes me more dizzy.

I'm at the stage where I make recordings of myself, listen,

and give myself notes. I actually print these memos and put them in an in-box on my desk.

I look at one intra-office memo from two days ago:

Date: May 12, 2007
To: Matt
From: Matt
Re: Nutcracker
    Would it kill you to crescendo properly on the high A,
just once in your whole fucking life? I mean, crescendo
like a musician and not a monkey on a hurdy-gurdy.

This appeals to my sense of humor, in some way, though I guess I can see why Cynthia finds this sort of thing disconcerting. Regardless, I can't give in to the dizziness. I have to practice, even if it makes me puke, so I spend a few less-than-totally-focused hours playing through trouble spots in a few pieces.

During *Ein Heldenleben*, I start to hear the buzz in the sixth-octave C in a way that I can't deny. Maybe I'm freaking out, but it seems to get worse as I play. This threatens flat-out vertigo, and I only make it as far as the couch, where I lie still.

After a sleepless hour filled with bursts of panic and denial about the state of my instrument and my life, I hear T.R. and Charles outside and decide that fresh air and a chat might help—anything to get away.

I find them on the brick path, with a woody plant that sits in a burlap bag, inside a wheelbarrow. Charles has on tight black jeans and a shiny green polyester shirt—not exactly gardening wear. T.R. looks slightly more appropriate in his usual chinos and an old green Chicago Mercantile Exchange windbreaker, his big hands hidden in tan work gloves.

"Well, well, well," says Charles. "What do we have here?" He picks up a long-handled shovel and positions himself protectively in front of the wheelbarrow. "Leave our shrub alone—it's not your kind!"

I smile like I'm squinting into sunshine. The cool wind on my face feels good.

"Hello, Matt," T.R. says.

"What's up, fellas?"

Charles bites his tongue while T.R. goes on to describe what they're doing in the garden: removing a monster forsythia and replacing it with another, of a more restrained variety.

"Your playing was very nice today," T.R. adds, with unusual sincerity.

"He's trying to seduce you," Charles says. "Your cheap apartment, this garden, his attic—one big spiderweb for catching boys. You'll see."

"Charles is doing his best to act appropriately," T.R. says. "He really is trying."

"And don't pretend you don't want to be caught, *Mr. Harpist*," Charles adds.

"Thanks, T.R.," I say. "But I think there's something wrong with my harp."

"So I've heard," Charles says, smirking.

I remember that he's talked to Cynthia, but it's such a typical Charles joke that it probably doesn't mean anything. Still, I turn red.

T.R. gives me a quick look and then says, "Matt, would you mind giving us a hand here?"

I help them chop and saw apart the old shrub. T.R. has us leave about two feet of stump sticking out of the ground, and, using this stump as a lever, Charles and I rock the roots loose. It's hard work—the roots are unbelievably strong. Our hands overlap, our heads come close together, and I can smell Charles's cigarette breath and his sweat. T.R. jabs the sharp edge of a spade around the perimeter, breaking up the soil and cutting off root tips. Just as the whole thing is coming loose, Charles hisses, "Let go of my root, you pervert," and he pulls the stump toward him, breaking the back-and-forth rhythm we had going. But the joke misfires, because at some point during our work a different atmosphere formed. Charles realizes it and smiles what looks like a sincere, I'm-through-messing-with-you smile.

We drop the new shrub in a new hole and replace as much dirt as we can. I'm moved to shake hands with T.R. and then Charles, making manly eye contact. Though they seem slightly taken aback, they go along, possibly used to rolling with the curious impositions of straight men. I feel on new terms with them.

A phone rings that sounds like it's coming from my apartment.

"I think I'm going to get that," I say, and I jog toward the back door.

"Hurry, it might be an important call!" Charles cries after me. "Your mother has an extra ticket for *Cats*!"

I pick up just before the machine takes over. It's Cynthia.

"Matt," she says, keyed up as hell. "It went so fucking badly."

It turns out that at almost the exact moment we were having poorly lubricated sex in my mouse-infested apartment last night, an apparently fuel-starved Cessna 174 made a forced landing in Monterey, California. The pilot suffered only minor injuries, but Cynthia's plaintiffs got wind, of course, and all bets are off with the settlement.

"Whitaker's blaming me," Cynthia says.

"For what?"

"He's saying I had settlement authority, and everything should have been wrapped up before this happened."

"I thought it was over the limit."

"I think it was—plus I definitely had to cover myself because of how he's been acting—but he never actually set hard-and-fast limits. He always says, 'A good lawyer has good judgment.' He resent me an email from before I went to Wichita that said, 'I trust you to wrap this up,' but we still had a pretty big range of settlement possibilities, some beyond what I could have authorized. He said his email was 'explicitly empowering me' to settle it on my own." Cynthia is speaking extremely quickly. "I was just in his office. It was abso-fucking-lutely horrible. He was like, 'If you want to be a partner, you can't come running to someone every time you need to make a judgment as an attorney.'"

She stops abruptly, and it takes me a while to figure out that the noises now coming through the phone are the sound of her crying. I've never heard her cry before.

"Cynthia," I say, "you didn't do anything wrong. You emailed him the final terms two week ago. He was stonewalling you. He was messing with you!"

"But it looks like I screwed up," she struggles to say. "He's such a manipulative bastard." And she loses it again.

"Let's get you out of there," I say. "Let me take you to lunch."

"I don't have time for lunch!" she says in an uncharacteristically whiny voice. "I mean, I already ate . . . or maybe I didn't. Oh my God."

"I know it's hard," I say. "Subtle and powerful manipulative bastards are the hardest manipulative bastards to deal with. But you're a damn good lawyer, and he's—"

"I have so much fucking work to do. I thought I was on top of everything. . . ."

Dizziness seizes my head and swings my brain side to side. I clamber onto the futon couch, facedown with my cheek against the pillow, the phone against my free ear.

"I'm sorry you've got to deal with this, Cynthia," I say.

We both go silent. After a good minute, I say, "Are you there?"

"I am," she says. "Better go. Thank you, Matt."

"I'll call you tonight. Take care. I love you."

"Oh, sailor," she says. "Love you too."

After we hang up, I keep still. I've got a bad headache and a constant urge to yawn, but lying here is not at all restful. Though we've signed emails to each other with "love," neither of us has ever said "I love you" before. This was probably the wrong time to make such a momentous declaration, yet every particular of this moment brought it out of me. Maybe what I really meant is that I am aching with pain for her and want to support her, that I'm trying my hardest to love her right now. I'm surprised and gratified that she used the word, too, though yes, without attaching her first-person pronoun to it. Maybe if I can solve this buzz and win St. Louis, she'll use her personal pronoun and we'll move to some downstate town together, commuting distance to St. Louis but also a semi-reasonable drive up to Chicago for days with Audrey—maybe I could even afford to keep this apartment—and make a new, good life. Everything may be in doubt, yet everything can still work.

On Tuesday, when I pick up Audrey, I'm all over her, father-wise. The trick to conversing with her, it turns out, is asking very specific dumb questions: *Did you make pictures of trains? Did anyone fly? Did you hear a story about penguins?* Nothing turns on her words faster than the chance to clear up my misconceptions.

After I finish bedtime reading, Audrey asks, "Is Steve going to be the boss of me?"

"Well, you have to obey him," I say. "Let's put it that way."

She considers this.

"Steve says Mama projects at me."

"Oh, sweetie, I don't know what that means. You're a good kid. You just concentrate on finishing first grade."

"Okay," she says.

. . .

During my Wednesday rounds at Golden Prairie, Richard seems reasonably hale. I range into some classical repertoire, which he seems to prefer to the folk tunes his daughter Erin first suggested. Once you get used to the oxygen tubes going in his nose, the occasional, brink-of-choking cough, and the purple patches on his scaly, thin forearms, he seems like a regular old guy who could cheer on the Cubbies for years to come.

Michael is sleeping when I poke my head in. Actually, he looks deceased. Until I'm within two feet of him, I'm not sure that his chest is still rising and falling. Once I see that it is, I think: *I'm glad he's alive; would it be better for him to be dead?; I'm glad I don't have to play; I'm sad I don't have to play; I feel guilty over my relief for not having to play.*

On my way out, Marcia nabs me to play for a woman who has been exclaiming "Help!" about every twenty seconds, mincing the nerves of all within earshot. When I play "Wouldn't It Be Nice," she smiles and stops crying out. Her addled nurse walks me to the front door, vowing to make me a lifetime supply of any baked good I might admit to liking.

In the evening, I meet Cynthia at a wine bar on Damen for a strategy-and-support session. We hash and rehash the politics of her situation. Now it's probably too late to go to the compliance committee. She really needs a confidant in the firm, but, ironically, Whitaker was her confidant and to some extent she picked up his enemies by association. There are also a few tough old birds, pre–Title 9 tough, on some distant floors of the firm, whom she met seven years ago when she was rotating through different practice areas as a summer associate. But it's a lot to dump on them after years of minimal contact. She doesn't know whom she can trust. She knows it looks horrible to get into trouble mere months before her partner decision.

"But didn't you have good reviews before this?" I ask.

"I thought I did," she says, "but I've been thinking about that. Whitaker is a real strengths-and-weaknesses kind of guy. He'd say stuff like 'Nobody's perfect,' like that's not the expectation, but then he'd go ahead and put your imperfections in your review. 'Let's make this real, let's grow'—he'd say shit like that. And you'd think, 'Wow, this guy is really authentic.' And now—voilà—there's negative stuff for him to work with."

"But there were strengths, too, right?"

"People ignore your strengths when you fuck up like this."

"You haven't fucked up."

"I did fuck up. I knew this would happen. I knew from the beginning being a lawyer was wrong for me."

"Come on, Cynthia. You've got a great mind for law."

"Thanks a lot."

"It's a compliment."

"It's a front."

"What's a front?"

"I don't know if I even want to *make* partner at this fucking place."

Cynthia flags down the waitress and orders yet another glass of merlot. She's ignoring me again, which puts an edge in my voice:

"Cynthia, for what? A front for what?"

"Oh, I don't know what I'm saying. I'm going out of my mind. I thought I was a normal person, but I can't function in this bullshit world."

"Sure, sometimes it can feel that way. But, hey—"

"Let's do something different this weekend," she says. "Maybe make a big dinner or something, have T.R. and Charles down."

Her eyes, which have been all over the place, swing onto mine and stay there.

"If that's what you need," I say, looking back at her.

"That's definitely what I need."

This would cash out the whole day, and what I'd really like to do is to keep my good practice momentum going. In these situations with Milena, I would usually decide in favor of practice time.

"All right," I say. "That sounds good."

21

~~~

PREPARATIONS FOR THE dinner take on mass and gravity and our lives fall into orbit. Time gets bent, foreshortened: Saturday night is everything, and what lies beyond Saturday night (St. Louis, Milena's nuptials, Audrey's therapy, Whitaker, intercourse of whatever fucked-up kind) falls into the category of what's outside the universe's edge.

Late Saturday morning, Audrey is lying on her bed watching *Monsters, Inc.* for the ten thousandth time when Cynthia pulls up in her Mini. Audrey and Cynthia have met just once before, on a snowy February day, when Cynthia came over on a Saturday afternoon and hung out until it was time to take Audrey up to her mother's—a trip we made as a threesome. Audrey was wary and quiet, and Cynthia, either out of savvy or disinterest, didn't pester Audrey with ingratiating questions. Audrey rewarded her by inviting Cynthia to the Lincoln Park Zoo with us sometime. Cynthia was charmed, but schedules have since conspired against this.

Now Cynthia comes to the door carrying her Martha Stewart cookbook and wearing a black camisole top and a flower-print skirt that comes to just past mid-bare-thigh. Her arms and legs are defined in a braided-rope sort of way. Maybe she spent those three weeks in Colorado on a cross-country ski machine. I'm glad she wants a big dinner; I need her to go easy on herself.

"Hey, girl, how are ya?" she calls to Audrey from the front door.

"Hi," Audrey says, smiling shyly.

"Ready to go shopping?"

"Okay," Audrey says, though I know she'd rather continue watching her movie. On another day, this would be tantrum-worthy material, but Audrey isn't pitching one today.

Cynthia thinks it's funny that we're putting on a dinner for two gay men with a menu out of a Martha Stewart cookbook: balsamic-marinated skirt steak; cucumber, string bean, and olive salad; grated potato pancake; and the kicker, Martha's Maypole Cake, which requires carpentry and pounds of cream-colored sprinkles and jellied citrus slices. Martha has been out of prison for over two years, but Cynthia has taken great delight in pointing out that her period of supervised release ended just two months ago. Apparently, one of her newly restored rights is the freedom to associate with known criminals, which Cynthia deems worth celebrating.

The menu's not too expensive until Cynthia buys four bottles of fancy red wine, an after-dinner brandy, and a six-pack of beer from a foreign land for yours truly. Then she insists on going to Crate & Barrel for a complete set of dinnerware for four. "This is on me," she says in the checkout line. "It's an audition gift," she explains, as if this were a Hallmark-approved occasion.

Having worked most Saturdays for years, Cynthia seems to relish playing hooky. Audrey's been day-cared into a tendency to bond with any semi-reasonable adult, and soon she's bounding around Cynthia like a puppy. Cynthia smiles at this, and, yes, I can't help but picture us as a family.

When we get back to the apartment, Cynthia runs up and down the back stairs to borrow things from T.R. With Audrey reabsorbed by the tube, Cynthia holds up potatoes to her eyes like binoculars, black olives to her breasts like nipples, stopping during our preparations to "feel me up," as she puts it. Her excitement makes me happy, yet there's also something over-the-top about it all, which puts a cloud in my blue sky.

At three forty-five I have to run Audrey up to Milena's place, while Cynthia stays and continues to prep.

When I pull up to Milena and Steve's house, Audrey says, "Can I ask you something?"

I brace myself. "Sure thing," I say.

"When you go to St. Louis, can you buy me a present from there?"

I laugh. "Definitely."

"Promise?"

"Oh, yeah, for sure."

"Thanks, Daddy!"

She jumps out of the car, runs up the steps, and through the door held open by Milena's hand.

As I return through the back door, Cynthia is scurrying down the stairs from T.R.'s. She says, "They agree: it's beautiful out, let's eat on T.R.'s deck."

I don't remember the proposal but say, "All right."

"Wonderful!" She rushes into the dining room and fetches the flowers—white, pink, and blue blooms she bought for the table—and carries them upstairs.

T.R.'s deck is on the level of his apartment, built on a platform that connects to the landing at the top of the back stairs. Cynthia sets the table while I follow the salad recipe, note for note.

"Anything I can do to help?" Charles says, entering the kitchen.

I'd really rather not put him to work or draw attention to the Martha Stewart cookbook on the counter, but the Maypole Cake recipe calls for the creation of eighty-four flower petals cut from jellied fruit slices, and with Cynthia flitting and gabbing, another hand would be good. So I give him the petal-shaped cutter Cynthia bought and the bags of jellied citrus and put him to work.

He's perfectly cooperative, which, of course, makes me attribute all the snarky things he says to his shtick. I'm pathetically vulnerable to his personality type: people who tease with an edge of meanness, so that when they're nice to someone he or she feels accepted in a special way.

"So, ready for your big audition?" he asks, taking great care with his citrus petals.

"Not quite."

"What are your chances?"

"Honestly, the odds are not good."

He drops a petal in the bowl. "Then why are you going?"

"It's my dream," I say.

"And you've done this before?"

"Many times," I say.

His silence presses me just enough.

"I've made audition finals with good orchestras twice," I add. I can get pretty wound up talking about my chances, but for some reason with Charles I can't resist. "In San Diego, I just blew it. It was my first finals, and I made a really dumb mistake in *Romeo and Juliet,* which is not a hard piece for me. I mean, I just sort of—unraveled."

"It happens." Charles shrugs.

"Then I got so prepared for Seattle it was scary."

"And?"

"It was weird. I didn't win."

"Why is that weird?" He smirks as he cuts another petal.

"Well, I don't know. But after they announced the winner, I ran into one of the judges—the retiring harpist, in fact. His name was Gottfried Barker, can you believe that?" Charles is unmoved. "Anyway, he's a big Salzedo guy—basically, he plays in a different style than I play, more ornate—and he said to me, 'Where was the joy?'"

"Ah, you were trying too hard," Charles says, finally looking up from his work.

"Well, you have to push hard," I say, trying not to sound defensive. "That's not really the point." The string beans are done steaming, and I start making a bowl of ice water to blanch them. The thought that I've been preparing for this dinner all day instead of practicing has not been good for my equilibrium, and this conversation isn't helping. "See, the Salzedo people are into how your arms look, and you've got to pluck the string a certain way. They're into *seeming* artful, basically."

"Mmm," Charles says.

"Actually, I was probably playing the best I've ever played back then. Right after Seattle I took fourth in the Israeli International Harp Competition—ten days in Tel Aviv. I know no one's ever heard of it, but it's basically the harp Olympics."

"That's all pretty impressive," Charles says. "I had you pegged as a pathetic loser."

I remember Seattle and Israel as the end of a stupefying two-year stretch in which I prepared like a madman to blot out the San Diego debacle. After it was over, Milena and I had gone into debt, and I was emotionally cracked—and then Milena decided that it was time we started a family.

"That was seven years ago," I say, and, as I put the warm beans into the ice water to chill, a wave of dizziness hits. I feel strange about lying down with Charles here and my dizziness spikes. The room pitches like a crazy-ass, funkadelic dance floor. I stagger to the bathroom, bouncing off doorjambs, and, just like that, I'm throwing up.

"Oh dear, was it something I said?" Charles calls from the hallway. Then, his voice pitched a different way: "I'm afraid I've made your boyfriend sick."

And I do feel better. It takes some explaining, but I manage to convince Charles and Cynthia that this is just audition nerves, two weeks early, nothing to be alarmed about. Charles accepts this diagnosis and prescribes many glasses of wine—or a twelve-pack of Old Style for people from Milwaukee. I lie down for about a half hour, just to get my bearings, but feel restless and find my way back to the kitchen, wondering if drinking may actually be the best way to let everything go for now.

Cynthia shoos away Charles and finishes decorating the Maypole Cake while I perform the manly tasks of broiling the meat and frying the latkes. Together we plate up the food. I find it important to arrange it as much like the picture as we can. Then we carry it up to the deck, where T.R. and Charles sit in early-evening sunshine.

"Lovely," T.R. says as I put a plate in front of him, and that's when I decide that this is going to be an extremely fun evening, all worries be damned.

T.R., Charles, and Cynthia drink a lot of wine. I go with beer, the odd man out. My head turns from a solid into something more cloud-like, any lingering wisps of anxiety-driven nausea recede, and light and air please me to no end. Cynthia chatters as if T.R. and Charles are her long-lost friends. She hasn't broken her happy stride all day. Charles has just landed an excellent job producing news segments at WGN, but he loves to tell stories about his demented ex-colleagues at the little vintage shop on Division where he used to work—a morass of substance abuse, cataclysmic relationships, and insider theft.

"Our little boy is all grown up," Cynthia says to T.R., and T.R. nods.

Cynthia is joking but I sense real happiness and pride in T.R.'s nod. I get the feeling that Charles arrived at "T.R.'s Home for Wayward Boys" a little mixed up himself.

This prompts me to ask about T.R.'s most recent attic crasher: "How's Max? I haven't seen him for a while."

"Max is in Galveston," T.R. says matter-of-factly, and I can't tell whether this is good or bad, so I decide not to press it.

Innuendo flies between Charles and Cynthia. She keeps using the expression "jump his bones" to refer to what Charles might do to a man who catches his eye, while I ask T.R. sober questions about his garden, his real estate, his philanthropy (he's active in all kinds of neighborhood initiatives throughout the city). Cynthia slaps her thigh and says, "Charles, stop it, you've become outrageous," as if she's imitating some character from a bad sitcom. I wince, but maybe Cynthia deserves to cut loose after what she's been through this week.

T.R. says, "This is actually quite good. What is it?"

"The meat?" I ask, drunk and stilted. "Skirt steak, I think."

"Skirt steak—what the hell is that?" Charles asks. "That's an oxymoron, isn't it?"

"I don't know," I say, not sure it's up to me to defend the cut of meat.

"But it kind of describes Cynthia, doesn't it?" Charles continues. "*Skirt steak*. Something girly with a manly edge."

"Come on, Charles," I say.

"Yeah, come on, Charles," Cynthia says teasingly, though not entirely displeased.

I try to catch her eye, but it's not quite catchable. I end up staring, feeling a bit lost, until Cynthia finally turns to me and smiles clownishly, with raised eyebrows, like a face you might see in a cartoon or a nightmare—she is quite drunk.

Then she abruptly turns away. "Time for dessert!" she says, getting up.

"Hear, hear!" I exclaim, and I rise as well.

"I've got it, sweetheart," Cynthia says. She gathers up the plates—I'm as proud as my mother would be that everyone has eaten every last bit—and heads down the stairs.

Charles turns to me and asks, "Did you just say 'Hear, hear'?"

My laugh turns into a full-body spasm that takes me beyond humor or any kind of pleasure. It feels strange to laugh so hard and then to regret laughing so quickly.

"T.R., what are we to do with him?"

"It does seem hopeless," T.R. muses, smiling warmly at me.

Cynthia brings her creation to the top of the stairs on a huge wooden cake server. It's just as Martha intended: A dowel painted white rises from the center of the cake. Eight green and yellow satin ribbons run from the top of this maypole, fasten to the edge of the platter, and dangle and flutter beyond that.

"These are the dancers," Cynthia says, smiling a crinkly-eyed smile, pointing her chin at the eight overflowing cupcakes encircling the cake. The dancers are capped with sprinkles and a flower—jellied citrus petals with a gumdrop in the center. Cynthia puts a small stack of plates on the edge of the table and then, with one straining arm, sets the platter in the center.

"Very nice," T.R. says.

"A perfect example of what straight people think is gay," Charles adds as he scratches his neck.

"Charles!" Cynthia says, as if she's really offended.

"Oh, stop," Charles says in a conciliatory voice. "It's perfectly hideous and I love it like a butch sister." He stands and holds out his hands. "Shall we?"

I look toward Cynthia and she smiles, and without another word, we rise and hold hands, though we can't quite close the circle. I'm holding T.R.'s big soft fingers, and he's holding Cynthia's hand, and she's holding Charles's hand, but there's a space between me and Charles, where, for an instant, I imagine Milena and Audrey standing. Charles leads us in a clockwise dance, skipping and laughing—and nearly tripping over chair legs.

"Maypole, maypole!" Cynthia cries.

"Phallic symbol, phallic symbol!" Charles mocks in return.

I'm sort of embarrassed, but I'm always sort of embarrassed. It seems like we're having a lot of fun.

Then we change direction and move counterclockwise, which sends me toward Charles, who lags enough to grab my hand, breaking his connection with Cynthia and putting himself at the head of the line again. I catch Cynthia's eye for a second—she is so pleased—but my eye can't hold her as she laughs. Finally, Charles says, "Fuck this. Let's eat." Peals of Cynthia's laughter ring out over the rooftops of Humboldt Park.

"Here's to the right to consort with known criminals!" she exclaims.

All in all, it's a pretty happy-go-lucky scene on T.R.'s deck. What's better than drunken friends and lovers, talking and dancing, sharing fine food and, now, huge slices of cake on a just-warm-enough May evening?

I fork up some cake and find myself thinking of Milena sinking into the arms of Steve, of him entering her with his no doubt large and firm husband-penis—and I almost lose my grip on my fork and the world.

But Cynthia is happy, and who can I be but hers in this little gathering?

Stuffed, we grow quiet, each of us taking a turn at gazing toward the horizon where the sun is disappearing. Charles has sated himself with two post-dinner cigarettes. Now the air is near chilly, and T.R. proposes that we go inside his apartment.

We settle in the living room, which is full of soft couches and chairs covered with afghans and pillows. There's a large-screen TV against the wall and a teen-style pleasure pit of cushions in front of it. On another wall there's an enormous square painting of what looks like Sigmund Freud sitting in a lawn chair on a beach near the water's edge.

Charles sits next to me and puts a space-invading arm on the back of the couch behind my head. I can smell cigarette smoke on him. The sun seems to have gone down the instant we left the deck. A few small lamps burn on end tables littered with magazines and books.

"Where'd you get that painting, T.R.?" I say into the air, though I don't see him in the room. No one answers. There are other paintings, I realize, including a possible real live Paul Klee on a wall I'm facing.

T.R. and Cynthia enter the living room, chatting with each other, and eventually I do get to ask T.R. about the painting, and, for the first time during the night, T.R. really takes the floor and talks about the Chicago art scene in the seventies (artists I'd never heard of called the Imagists), his days on LaSalle Street, and his nights in Boystown. He talks about how he hid his sexual orientation while he navigated a career in several testosterone-mad brokerages. He had to work hard and make the firm extra money and be discreet with the other closeted financial men he screwed. Charles pitches in a story of when T.R. was outed and had to leave a job.

We fall into silence as we absorb all this. Hoping to give things a more optimistic turn, I ask him how the same-sex marriage bill is progressing.

"Referred to the Rules Committee again," he says with a sigh. "Not looking good."

Cynthia sits quietly, her expression taking a turn for the morose. Possibly her wine buzz is wearing off; possibly the talk of homophobia and office politics is a downer. Suddenly, she sits forward. "The brandy!" she says. "I forgot about the brandy. I'll go down and get it. T.R., I don't think we have the right glasses. Do you have some?"

"Let me see what I have," he says. He sways to his feet and sets off unsteadily behind Cynthia, leaving Charles and me sitting together on the couch.

"No passing out, old man," Charles calls after T.R.

I'm also drunk and sleepy, and the burden of making small talk with Charles seems insurmountable. There's just the sound of music on the stereo—an old Eurythmics CD.

Charles slouches deeply in the soft cushions. Without turning to me, he says, "Cynthia says you play music for dying people. What's that like?"

His tone is quiet now, all sarcastic pretense suspended.

"I think I like it, but probably for the wrong reasons."

"Really?"

"It's depressing but it also makes me glad to be alive, sort of."

"Sort of?"

"Well, it's stupid, really. I'm not sure I feel the right things when I'm there."

Charles doesn't make any comment, and I find myself plunging on:

"Actually, it's affecting my audition prep. I've been imagining the dying people listening to me practice."

"Interesting. I'm starting to see a Lifetime movie here." He laughs.

"I'm playing a little differently—my tone is softening, maybe, or I'm more likely to bend a note." It occurs to me that I can say this sort of thing to Charles, but I would never think of saying it to Milena. I *could* say it to Cynthia, I bet; I just haven't. "One time I took a master class with this big-cheese harpist. Someone asked her how she decides what sound she goes for. And she talked about what the piece demands and predictable stuff like that, but she also said that at bottom every musician's sound is just an expression of her or his personality—and that absolutely scared the shit out of me."

"Because you're an uptight nerd and you don't want to sound like one?"

"Yeah. And something's sort of shifting now, but I don't know if it's my personality, or if I'm just in a different mood because of everything that's going on."

"So who do you play for at the hospice?" He shifts on the couch as he says this. We've been sitting side by side all this time, talking to the room in front of us, but now he's facing me, and I turn slightly to face him.

"One of them died," I say. "I never knew her, really—but now I've got two regulars plus some random people. One guy, a rich old guy—he's got something wrong with his lungs. COPD. And then, this other guy—" And I almost get completely hung up on how to say it, which of course Charles notices. "He's got AIDS," I finally say, and I try to look at Charles, but I can't quite connect with his eyes. "He's gay," I add, foolishly.

"Is that how you think of him?" Charles says. "As the gay AIDS man?"

I watched myself walk into this but I don't know how to step out of it. I look down at the couch and see a sliver of Charles's hairy ankle between his dark sock and the cuff of his jeans.

"What happened to him? Didn't he have access to the drugs?"

I don't know how much I can say. "It didn't work for him."

"Hmm," Charles says. "What's his name?"

"I don't think I can tell you. There's this patient confidentiality thing."

"Oh, you've got such integrity," he says facetiously. "What's his *first* name?"

"Michael."

"Oh, I know him! He's the gay one, with AIDS!" He laughs to himself. Then he sighs. "I've always wanted a man with integrity, just once, for the hell of it." He turns to put his back against the couch and leans toward me. "Preferably repressed." He flashes his eyes at me, scooches over, hooks his arm under mine and snuggles against me, resting his head on my shoulder. "You should put me in your audience sometime," he says in a quiet voice. "Serenade me. Haven't you always wanted to do that?"

He looks up at me from my own shoulder. Then his face rises up and over me, like a sun, and slowly sets toward mine. He kisses me and I sort of kiss him back, maybe just reflexively, my kissing instinct motion-activated by his face looming close, or just to avoid offending him. Or maybe my second face is finally asserting itself in this drunken instant because with the exception of Milena, I've barely functioned in bed with women; because after twenty-five years of dealing with the assumption my harp playing has created, I've never kissed a man—not even my father when I was a kid—and maybe I should, just to see. It would be worth everything to feel as if I were seeing my real self for the first time, to just *feel right,* unidiotic, to fit with the harp like a male harpist should and to acknowledge and complete my break with the average world, as if a kiss could reveal everything true, like in a fairy tale.

And it's not unpleasant to kiss him. Though his stubble scratches, his smoky breath is alcohol-clean. But his tongue gets too adventuresome, and I wonder if I do that to women. He moves his hand to my thigh and then onto my crotch, and I think of him, Charles, and his body and what he's like, and my will sets off with a message, swimming up to the surface of my face—I break the kiss and say, "Sorry, Charles. I can't do this."

"You are doing it," he says.

He grabs my hand and puts it on his jeans zipper, beneath which I can feel his hardness, and that's when I finally stand up. Charles looks at me from under his eyebrows, smirking, maybe pretending to be mad. "That's okay, sweetheart," he says. "It would have been fun, but you'd have just been a tourist. Honestly, *I* never thought you were gay." He puts just enough into the "I" that I wonder where Cynthia is.

I turn and walk through T.R.'s apartment, past the bedroom where I glimpse T.R.'s black sock-clad foot hanging off his bed. I stumble down the back stairs and into my apartment, which is completely dark.

"Cynthia?" I say. I see her silhouette in a front window. She's sitting on the edge of Audrey's bed. "What are you doing down here?"

"Resting," she says. Her shoulders are slumped in the exaggerated unconscious way kids sometimes let their shoulders slump.

"I thought you were getting the brandy," I say, and I sit next to her on the bed.

"I thought so, too." She looks away from me, out the window. The streetlight makes a sort of stage out of the far sidewalk, but no one is out there.

"Charles just made a pass at me."

"How'd it go?" she asks with a small smile.

She's not looking at me, but I can't help but watch her. I try to feel again the excitement and happiness from early in our relationship, when the sex, while not good, existed. I really want to love her but I don't know exactly how to be with her. My throat hurts with the perversity of this.

"Stop looking at me like that," she bursts out, glancing over. "You're always checking my face, or staring, or something—it's very creepy." This startles me so much that I keep looking at her, no doubt with a stupid and wounded look on my face. She turns away, exasperated. "You're the most unnatural person I've ever met!"

"I'm just paying attention," I say, though I know it's more than this.

"Well, don't. It's too much."

So I look ahead, to the space near the front door, where the stairs to the second floor used to start, and say what's been blooming in my mind: "Charles said something that made me think you put him up to it."

"It's just sex, Matt."

"What does that mean?"

"So you made out with a gay man, or you didn't, who cares? It doesn't affect us, it doesn't affect anything."

"Of course it does," I say.

She grinds a fist against her knee.

I put a hand on her shoulder. "Cynthia," I say.

"I don't love you," she says, twisting away. "I don't love you, Matt!"

My throat and my eyes close at the same time. This reaction is perfectly natural.

"Please, Cynthia," I manage to say. "I know how it's been. I don't blame you."

"Stop with that bullshit. It's not about you and your dick, for God's sake. Who cares? This just isn't working, isn't that obvious?"

"It's Anna, from law school?" I say. "You're still in love with Anna?"

"It's not Anna, you fucking idiot!" she says with bitter disgust. And then she starts crying, bringing her two small fists to her forehead in total anguish.

I've actually taken a huge breath to yell back at her, but her weeping stops me cold. The Barbie adventure van heads for the futon couch. Cynthia's chest heaves with sobs, and I feel as if I am also crying, though I'm not.

"Oh shit, Matt," she says, standing up. "I'm sorry."

She nearly trips over the van, catches herself on the harp column for an instant, then weaves her way out of my apartment.

22

~~~

VIKRAM DOES NOT chastise me for being twenty-two minutes late; in fact, he doesn't speak at all. I unfurl my whole
sarcastic repertoire, and I'm sure the brunchers would cheer
boisterously if they weren't so busy biting strawberries from
their stems or slathering their waffles with whipped butter.

I think of how Cynthia and I met as I play "Tiny Bubbles"
and "The Girl from Ipanema." I stir the embers of pain with
speculations: Is she just a closeted lesbian looking for a beard?
Possibly. More likely she's bi, or she's unoriented, or she's
straight, just sad and anxious. Is my erectile dysfunction with
her just a response to *her* ambivalence? I wish. Maybe I was
drawn to her anxiety, to her sense of being out of step with the
world; maybe I'm just in love with anxiety. I believe her when
she says she doesn't love me—that's all I really know.

"You're pushing your luck," Vikram says sternly at brunch's
end, as I wheel my harp to the door.

"Sorry, Vikram," I say. "Have a good week."

In the afternoon, I force myself to practice excerpts, and

after dinner I spiral into post-breakup grief, which keeps me awake and staring into the early morning until my thoughts turn to Milena.

I can't believe she really loves Steve. Otherwise, she wouldn't have cried on the phone on Mother's Day. And maybe I have to admit to myself, once and for all, that I can't function with a woman as intellectual and complicated as Cynthia, whatever that implies about me. There's really been only one woman I've been comfortable with.

Monday morning I call Milena at her office and say, "I really need to see you."

"Why?"

"Because I need to," I say. "I'm only going to do this once," I add.

The air on the phone is perfectly still for about twenty seconds.

"I can't see you," she says quietly. "I'm engaged."

"Okay, but then can we talk for a second?"

Her only answer is not hanging up.

"All right," I say, "I want you to be happy. And I'm not going to ask you whether you'll be happy with Steve—"

"Matt, don't do this," she says.

"Please just hear me out," I say. "Talking to you is the only thing worth doing right now, okay?"

This gets a tortured sigh, but she doesn't hang up.

"I'm thinking," I continue, absolutely clueless as to how to proceed. "What I'm thinking, just for my information, because we never got a chance to talk about it, I just want to know . . . if you think we made a mistake. Splitting up."

Her breath catches, and I realize how amazingly cruel I'm being. But before I can backpedal, she breathes out, "Sometimes."

"I think so, too," I say. "I really think—"

"But I just want a nice, simple life," she says. "You know?"

She sniffs. "Normal." She allows this word to hang between us. "I'm not like you," she says, and a sort of composure settles on her. "I don't need to be *someone*. I like who I already am." She pauses.

"And I don't want to feel guilty for holding you back," she adds.

"You never held me back," I say. "Never."

"If you think that, you're forgetting everything," she says quietly. "And that's why I can't go back to us."

A hot-cold feeling crawls up my neck. "I'm not talking about going back, Milena."

"Yes, you are."

"It would be different. It would have to be."

"I can't deal with the ups and downs, all the second-guessing and *worrying*. And Audrey can't, either. She needs, *we* need, something stable. We can't be jerked around anymore. And I love Steve. I can talk to him, and he's focused on being with me."

"But is he going to make you happy?" I ask.

"*You* didn't make me happy," she says fiercely.

"But I used to. Right? I loved you. I feel better with you than anyone else, ever, in my life." This is the truest thing I've ever said, and she might even believe it, but I'm afraid it sounds like a weirdly self-centered thing to say right now.

Silence.

"But I know why you didn't always feel it," I persist. "St. Louis is my last audition. I promise. It's my last best chance, and if I don't make it, I'm done."

"You are so full of shit," she says determinedly.

"I'm telling you, if I blow it in St. Louis, I'm getting a job. I'm sorry, I'm really sorry for what happened to us. Think about Au—"

"I think about Audrey *all the time*," she says.

It was stupid for me to bring up Audrey in this way—a bad,

old argumentative habit that doesn't take into account our new difficult reality with her.

"I told you not to do this to me," Milena hisses. "I told you I'm engaged!"

Then, without another word, we both hang up, quietly.

You know things are bad when you find yourself looking to dying people for some kind of lift. Maybe I'm getting used to the place. Lately, when the Alzheimer's woman honks at me, I honk back, which pleases her, and I look forward to talking with Michael. In any case, on Wednesday, after four hard-core hours of audition practice, I head out for my hospice rounds, stopping first at Richard's cottage. He's sitting in his recliner watching TV, but he clicks it off as soon as I intrude my smiling head.

"Hello, Richard," I say.

"Hello," he says in his breathless voice, no smile breaking his Muppet lips.

I set up, then launch into some classical stuff, and he takes this opportunity to unhook his oxygen tubes from his nose and from around his ears. He dabs the corners of his eyes with tissues and runs other tissues over the tubes, giving the nubs that sit in his nose the most attention. There's a deep red groove on his left cheek where the tube has been resting. He blows his nose several times. The man's beyond pretending the music does anything for him. After about ten minutes, he lifts his hand, and I stop playing.

"I need to use the restroom," he says. He gets out of his recliner, holding his oxygen tube in his hand, casually, like a cowboy with a rope, then he shuffles forward. He reaches the edge of his bed, and he bends over and puts his hands, one on top of the other, on the bedpost. His breathing has become labored:

with each in-breath he drops his jaw slightly and on the out-breath he purses his lips as if blowing through a straw. His right arm shakes.

I watch him and do nothing. This might be his typical resting spot on the way to the bathroom. Maybe because he carries some vestige of fatherly authority, I don't know how to enter his space. I'm only sure of what to do here as the harpist.

He looks about to keel over. I stand up and take a tentative step toward him.

"Could you get a nurse, for Christ's sake?" he says.

I do, and when I come back with her, he has sunk down right where he was standing, kneeling with his arms and face on the foot of the bed. The nurse speaks quietly to him and I see that he's wet himself. I carry the harp out and then I come back for my gear, my trips delaying the nurse's care for him. When I've finally gotten everything out in the hallway, the nurse closes the huge door behind me.

Nothing I can do but head on over to Michael's cottage. I run into Marcia, and she tells me he's been more lively.

"That's great," I say.

"Well," Marcia says, "sometimes you see a burst—right at the end."

Michael is awake, but, if it's possible, he's even more gaunt than the last time I saw him. He gazes at me too steadily, his head too still.

"Good to see you, Michael," I say.

"You don't look good," he says as I set up my harp, his voice even thinner than it's been. I'm stunned that he can see me at all, that he can still speak.

"Yeah," I say. "I just screwed something up."

He barely raises his eyebrows to invite more.

I tell him about Richard's accident, confessing my paralysis and how stupid it now seems.

"What's the matter with you?" he says with surprising harsh-
ness.

This catches me off guard, and I can't think of what to say.

"Kidding," he says weakly. "Didn't get along with my father,
either."

"What do you mean?"

"Wall," he says. At least that's what it sounds like. He raises
the fingers of his right hand an inch off the sheet.

"Wall?"

His eyes consider and then seem to cancel what he just said,
whatever it was. He seems about to speak again, then reconsid-
ers. Finally: "Too tired to say. Would kill me."

He smiles. His eyes flicker at me, then drift away. His arms on
the top sheet are as stiff as bed rails, inanimate, and I remember
Charles embracing my arm as he moved against me on T.R.'s
couch.

I am a father, I think and, strangely, it feels as if I'm realizing
it for the first time.

Michael looks away from me. "Didn't always treat people
right," he says, apparently following his own thoughts. Is he
confessing or complaining?

"Hey, Michael," I say softly, not sure he's speaking to me but
trying to formulate something supportive if he is, "sometimes
people—"

"Play something *you* want to hear," he says, suddenly turned
toward me, in a louder voice, as if I've asked him. "I don't care."
His expression doesn't match his words—it's too still—which is
eerie.

"I could do that," I say.

"Good," he says. "They live twenty minutes away. Schaumburg. You want their phone number?"

"Whose?" I ask. He's losing it. "Your parents'?"

"Schaumburg," he says, and he smiles broadly—the biggest

smile I've seen from him—and his eyes finally lock on mine. "Now leave. I have to rest up for my big day."

Thanks to my disastrous phone call to her earlier in the week, an extra layer of frosty awkwardness envelopes Milena and me as we sit with Audrey in the therapist's impeccably decorated Lincoln Park office for Audrey's first appointment. Dr. Oliver is a well-put-together woman in her fifties. She wears earrings that are surprisingly long and dangly, and they swing a fair amount when she speaks in her animated voice. The effect is hypnotizing and I wonder if her look is some way of distracting or taming her young clients.

After some brief chitchat, Dr. Oliver explains that therapy is going to be about helping Audrey develop some "practical skills" to handle "challenging situations." Audrey is solemn and attentive, utterly transfixed by her therapist.

"Everybody gets worried," Dr. Oliver says to Audrey. "Everybody gets upset. Everybody has to figure out what to do when that happens."

Her practical approach surprises me a bit. I'm used to thinking of psychological problems as mysterious and deep-seated, treatable, if at all, only through intense exploration and analysis.

Dr. Oliver asks Audrey if she's okay so far, and Audrey nods. Then she asks Audrey if she'd be okay with sitting in the waiting room while she talks with Mom and Dad. Audrey says, "Yes," and Dr. Oliver escorts her out. While they're gone, Milena and I sit in the most awkward silence I've ever experienced with her, each of us sitting perfectly still.

"Okay, let's talk process," Dr. Oliver says, breezing back into the room.

She will meet once a week with Audrey alone and there will also be some meetings with the three of us and possibly with

Milena and me separately. Audrey will have some leeway to say things that won't get back to us, but a lot will be shared with us.

"Divorce is hard on you and it's hard on Audrey—we can't get around that," Dr. Oliver says. "How you treat each other matters—a lot—but Audrey is her own person, with her own personality tendencies. She needs to cope with whatever her life brings her, and I'm going to help her develop the tools to do that."

Milena nods and coughs daintily. I glance at her but her eyes are trained on Dr. Oliver. Milena draws her bangs to the side with her middle finger. I don't understand why gestures like that make me want her as much as I do. What is the practical way for dealing with *that*?

"How does this sound, Matt?" Dr. Oliver asks, with an extra insistence in her voice. I must have missed something she said.

"Yes, sounds good," I say. "Thank you."

I listen to my excerpt compilation tape and look over scores, but I can't practice: not even someone as indulgent as T.R. can stand harp music at 4:00 a.m.

My stomach churns; my head feels unconnected to my neck; the sun rises and slowly finds its way through the window. I have a series of abject, intricate, and ultimately stupefying thoughts and feelings about blowing the audition, playing brunch at age seventy-five, lying erectionless with an anonymous woman who sits on the bed dealing out a hand of solitaire on a TV tray. It gets to the point where I *want* my head to explode, just to get it over with, to see if there's some relief on the other side. I remember what Dr. Oliver said about taking practical steps to deal with being upset, and with this in mind, I decide to deal with the buzz in the sixth-octave C string. Knowing it's unfixable ought to be the last straw, and then I can go ahead and completely lose it.

So as soon as the harp factory opens at 8:00 a.m., I take it in. Stanley is visiting a new wood supplier, but Carl is lounging around the showroom, looking bored. His gut and ponytail are especially droopy today. "Do you want to wait for it?" he asks, and I say, "Why not," because he seems eager to get down to business.

And sure enough, in an hour he's regulated the whole thing and tightened up some stuff—and again the buzz is entirely gone.

"Son of a gun," I say, playing some pristine licks. "I can't believe this."

"Well, your harp is probably still trying to settle down from when you dropped it. Maybe it's done, maybe this doesn't hold. Hard to say. When's your audition?"

"Starts a week from today."

"Hmm. Well, they'll have a tech on the premises, right?"

"They should."

"It's your call. You could talk to Stanley. If you'd left it today, he'd've probably gone ahead and broke it, for the insurance. He couldn't stop talking about what an idiot you were. But look at your karma." He gestures toward the instrument with both hands.

I ask if I can sit down at the new harp Stanley wants to sell to me. Playing the two side by side, I notice how the string spacings in the upper octaves are a little different. The tension is different, too. I wonder if that would screw me up at some crucial moment. I'd practically have to take out a loan even to rent this thing—that's how close I'm shaving it—unless I give up even my already embarrassingly nominal contribution to the Montessori tuition.

"Can we put this off a while longer?" I say.

"I'll tell Stanley you're still interested."

When I get home, I stand the harp in its spot, unshroud the same dirty cover. I look the harp square in the column and say out loud, "You're fucking with me, aren't you?"

23

~~~

On Saturday, after I drop off Audrey, I come home to a voicemail from Marcia, asking me to call the hospice as soon as I can. Maybe she wants to have a little talk about how I failed Richard on Wednesday, though that wouldn't account for the urgency.

"It's Michael," she says when I call. "He's very close. He asked for you this afternoon. He wants you to play for him. Matt, I know this is a big imposition, but I have to tell you, there's just no family here. No visitors lately. His parents don't get along with him or each other, and I've been trying for days to get in touch with his sister in Oregon, and she just called back. She'll never make it in time."

He could be dead by the time I get there, or it could be a long night. Just in case, I call Rhiannon, a harpist right out of grad school, who has subbed for me at the Marriott before, and she gladly takes my brunch, which will also help with audition practice time. I quickly pack a peanut butter sandwich, an apple, and a water bottle for supper in the car. I haul ass out to

Elmhurst with my 85P, all but choking on my sticky sandwich. The sun is low enough to make an oppressive glare as I drive toward it.

The hallways of Golden Prairie are relatively busy with people on their way out or chatting near the Great Room. They've put in a good chunk of time with their dying loved ones, and now they're probably thinking about an Olive Garden to overeat their stress away. I don't blame them. When they see the shrouded harp roll by, they look at me as if I'm bearing some arcane death-related instrument, which, I suppose, I am.

Michael is frozen-looking, with his glassy eyes half-closed. His lips are drawn together but open, as if he's about to blow a small bubble. All the muscle is gone from his bony arms. His forearms and his upper arms are the same thinness. There's no panic in his expression, but his hair is partly standing up and partly sticking to his forehead, as if he's been tossing and turning. The septum of his nose hangs prominently, and his jaw is even more narrow and tapered, like the snout of a wolf. A young nurse with a serious plump face is sitting on the edge of his bed.

"Knew it would come to this," Michael manages in a timbreless voice as I carry in my stool and my black shoulder bag. "Have to die to get a date."

The nurse tears up. She pats his arm and slips out.

"Hello, Michael," I say. "It's good to see you." This feels wrong to say, but I do mean it: it *is* good to be with him now.

He stares back at me, emptied out yet poised.

"What would you like to hear?" I ask. I sit down to the instrument and pull it back on my shoulder.

"'Amazing Grace,'" he says.

"Really?" I say.

He barely nods, no smile.

I start the song, and he closes his eyes. I know enough to speculate about what the lyrics mean to him, just as I tried to imagine my father's response to the meditation CD. I play it softly, to spare Michael's nerves, but that only makes it sound more sad.

I play some Britten—the Interlude from *Ceremony of Carols*—on a hunch he might like it, and he seems to lose consciousness. I remember Marcia telling me that otherwise-unresponsive patients can still hear, so I press on, playing the tunes I tried the first time I came to Michael's room.

Then, wallowing further in nostalgia and grief, I play "If" and "Green Is the Colour" by Pink Floyd, thinking of Milena, and "Do You Know Where You're Going To?" because my father once surprisingly let slip that he liked that song.

After a good hour and a half, I stop to shake out my hands. Michael has begun to take ragged breaths. Maybe this is it. I decide to play the entire audition sequence for St. Louis from memory, but very slowly, with spaces between the notes, so Michael's metabolism won't be affected. The room darkens as I play. The nurse comes in to check on him and turns on a lamp behind me.

Increasingly, his unresponsiveness helps me realize one of my twisted desires: to do my part in a relationship without having to suffer my partner's scrutiny, as if my partner is an unconscious instrument, a freedom I desire most during sex.

I keep expecting someone to show up, his parents, the resigned man I saw leaving his room weeks ago—someone. Maybe people didn't treat him right and vice versa, so this is how it ends.

I continue playing, with an almost absurd slowness. I finish the whole audition repertoire and start over. My right shoulder starts to throb. Then a sharp pain strikes above my shoulder blade, just downhill from my neck, forming a knot as hard as a stone. My left arm is getting heavy and twitchy, my bony ass is turning to concrete. In the huge spaces between notes, I can hear Michael's breathing, irregular, with long pauses.

I stop and stand and shake out my whole body and jump up

and down as quietly as I can. My muscles seem to fill with blood again. Everything loosens and aches. But it's like opening a fist that you've squeezed closed for a long time: you actually have to try to keep it from closing again on its own, so I sit down again, clenched over the harp, and enter a sort of drugged equilibrium in which I accept that this is the only thing I do.

It's almost 1:00 a.m. when the nurse comes in and takes Michael's pulse. Something makes her stay and stand there for a bit. A deep rattling, gurgling breath rises. "This is it," she says abruptly, almost excited, it seems. I play a fourth-octave G. She sits on the bed, exactly where she was when I came in, and watches Michael's face. A C-sharp and Michael breathes. Another note; another, softer, breath. A note and I listen. A note. A note. A note. A note. I stop playing.

"Second one tonight," the nurse says. She pats his hand where it lies on the sheet, picks it up, shakes it between her two hands—almost like shaking a dog's paw—then she sighs and leaves the room.

I lean the harp forward and rest my head against the sound box. I stand up, my aching torso stiff. I step awkwardly to Michael's bedside, watching myself try to do what the unscored moment demands. I should touch him somehow, I think, to say good-bye. Marcia once told me that dying people crave touch. I stand over him, staring at his face, hung up, like a child staring down from the lip of the high dive. I lean over, and kiss his warm forehead.

24

~~~

I<small>T'S A STRAIGHT</small> shot on I-55 to St. Louis. Sprouting green cornfields unzip under a wide, blue sky. I'm blasting my audition tape on the Volvo's old stereo as wind whips through the barely open backseat windows. The temperature and humidity have risen as I've plummeted downstate, but the car's air conditioner is feeble. I can't hear the tape with the front windows down, so I'm stuck venting out the worst of the heat through the back.

There's a sudden pop-*ping!* from the backseat. One of the harp's strings has broken—something in the second octave, by the sound of it. I'll have to retune that string more frequently once I replace it, and God help me if it starts to slide out of tune in the middle of the audition. This is why I left for St. Louis two days early, to give my harp a chance to acclimate.

Since my vigil with Michael, my concentration has been sharp and my immersion in audition prep has been total. I canceled my appointments with students for the week, and Marcia suggested I take a break from playing at the hospice. Besides my

Tuesday evening with Audrey, there's been nothing else in my life but audition repertoire.

Now, through the dashboard speaker, Slatkin conducts the St. Louis Symphony Orchestra doing *Ein Heldenleben,* and I listen intently, honing my feel for the dynamic of the whole ensemble (which of course I'll have to imagine when I audition). Suggesting the rest of the piece through your part alone is the sort of prestidigitation that wins auditions.

I couldn't find a recording of *EH* with Uchimura, the current SLSO maestro, though the scuttlebutt is that he is more about volume and articulation than setting speed records, so there's no fear his tempos will be unusually fast. Tatiana Zikorsky, on the harp, sounds colorful, moody, precise; she's finally retiring after thirty years and is a tough act to follow. I'm sure she'll be on the panel along with four or five other musicians elected by the orchestra—plus Uchimura will sit in most likely from the semis onward. And now I can't avoid thinking more about the great Salzedo-Grandjany feud, which is a destabilizing subtext at every harp audition. Even mild Salzedo partisans like Zikorsky care about how the arms look, especially the elbows, which must be well up and off the harp. Eddie (a Grandjany disciple) taught me to strive for a big clear sound even at quick tempos—it helps to have strong man hands!—which fits well with Uchimura's reputed outlook. Luckily, the prelims and the semis will be behind a screen, though the finals usually are not. Of course, Salzedo people claim they can *hear* the difference regardless. The bottom line is that some people think there's only one way to slice an apple, and if Zikorsky is partisan enough, I could be screwed before I've played a note.

The other big danger at an audition like this is that they've had a replacement in mind for years, someone the conductor has been drooling over, even openly wooing, while waiting for the aging prima donna to pack it in. Zikorsky could actually be irrelevant here, while Uchimura gets his pick. And this is one of the top ten U.S. orchestras. Stellar players are going to be coming from all over the world.

Just as I think myself into a downward spiral, on my right, past a stand of trees, I glimpse the St. Louis Arch, sticking up like a roller coaster over a distant amusement park. Soon I'm careening through the interchange and taking a huge black metal bridge over the Mighty Mississippi, tasting my destiny like river mud under my tongue.

St. Louis reminds me of Milwaukee, with its modest concentration of downtown office towers and the same low-rise mix of bungalows and two-flats and industrial remnants flanking the midtown freeway. Maybe this bodes well. I get off at Kingshighway and find my way over to the Best Western.

The street feels a bit deserted at four in the afternoon. A lot of the parking meters are unused and weedy grass creeps across the edges of the broken sidewalk. There's a twelve-story, old-fashioned stone apartment building down the street, the sort you'd see cheek by jowl with similar buildings in Manhattan or near the lake in Chicago, but here it stands alone.

The Best Western is a sixties-era motor lodge. Sweating, I enter the low-ceilinged lobby with my pulse beating as fast as a chipmunk's; in a sense, the audition begins now. Rolling my instrument down the third-floor hallway, I pass two doors behind which competitors play harp licks. I'd like to pause and evaluate their playing, but just hearing them is like an electric cattle prod to the kidney. I have to get set up and start practicing.

After making two more trips to get my luggage and all my gear, I replace the string without unpacking a single item or even taking a much-needed whiz, so the new string will have the maximum amount of time to settle down before I need it on Friday. The climate disparity between Chicago and St. Louis is serious: about ten degrees higher at around eighty and what feels like thirty more points of humidity. The air-conditioning is on. I can only hope the shift from hot car to cool room doesn't cost me more strings. There are two days of prelims, and I'm lucky to be slotted on the second day.

After finally using the bathroom, I determine that the best place for the harp is at the right foot of the king-sized bed, the spot where I've been camping for my dying clientele. There's a tall and fairly wide mirror on the wall between the bathroom and the short corridor leading to the door, and from this position I can see my full reflection.

My posture is beyond Frankensteinesque: the curtain rod of my spine seems to travel straight to the top of my skull, pitching my head slightly downward. My lips are thick, my mouth is too wide, and my furrowed brow seems strangely distended, suggesting my brain has herniated slightly from the strain of worrying. Suddenly I can't bear to see myself.

I've trained myself for all sorts of situations—distracting noises, darkness, no warm-up time, requests for radically different tempos. I've prided myself on my efforts to become unflappable, but right now I'm flapped. Telling myself there's no need to be prepared for mirrors onstage—it's likely no one will actually see me play unless I make the finals—I take practical steps: I try to turn the wall mirror around. But the mirror is well bolted, and the bath towel I drape over it keeps slipping. I'm on the brink of calling the front desk to have the thing removed, when I realize I can jab a few pens through the nap, pinning the towel between the top edge of the mirror and the wall.

Finally, I sit down and try to focus on the music.

After two days of productive practicing, Friday arrives. *Everything* is in my fingers, it seems. On my way to my prelim round, I spot my first nemesis in the Best Western lobby, a small-featured young woman with long flowing blonde-brown hair, wearing a floor-length black dress and accompanied by, I'm guessing, her heavyset mother in a black pantsuit. Their outfits seem coordinated, and I can picture the girl having to talk her mother out of being her page-turner. There's a brand-new brown padded polyester cover on her harp, which is being wheeled out the door by one of the bellhops. Her mother's carrying a clear plastic bag of bananas, which many harpists believe to have nerve-calming qualities. Then again I know several harpists who have such strong associations between bananas and audition jitters that whenever they encounter bananas, they experience stomach-twisting anxiety. I stop my harp at the restaurant end of the lobby, to give the pair a chance to clear out and avoid any contact or small talk.

Crossing the parking lot outside Powell Symphony Hall, the St. Louis Symphony's home, I see Gracie Hoffman walking with her longtime partner, Alicia. Gracie placed second at the USA International Harp Competition in Bloomington last year, a competition I was too divorce-wracked to enter. If gamblers cared about auditions, she'd be an odds-on favorite. She's wearing a blue tank top and a long, flowing colorful skirt with sandals. This could mean that Gracie had her prelim round yesterday, but my guess is that she's gotten a pass to the semis and is just swinging by to scare whoever might see her.

I wave and say, "Hi, Gracie."

Gracie does a double take from across the parking aisle. "Is that you, Matt?"

"It is."

"I didn't know you were still out there," she says, walking over with her odd hip-sprung stride.

"Can't stop believing," I say. "Hey, Alicia."

"Hey, Matt," Alicia says without quite making eye contact. She's wearing a black sundress with a swirling, flowers-and-paisley tattoo sleeving her upper right arm. She couldn't seem less interested in talking with me, but that actually relaxes me; I don't want to be seen.

"The field is incredible," Gracie says loudly. "Way better

than I expected." She stands with her hands turned on her hips so her elbows nearly point backwards. I've never been able to decide whether her idiosyncratic way of moving is a corollary of her dexterity as a harpist or a grandiose affectation. While Alicia repeatedly swings her arms to tap her fingers together, Gracie rattles off the names and most recent achievements of four or five harpists taking the audition.

"Those accomplished bastards," I say with a grin.

"Hey, are you thinking about the NIU job?" she asks.

"What NIU job?"

"You don't know Lynne LaBelle's retiring? They're doing a search in the fall."

For over twenty years Lynne's been teaching at Northern Illinois University in DeKalb, which is west of Chicago, maybe a forty-five-minute drive from my apartment. I've run into Lynne numerous times, but I'm not plugged into the academic scene. I remember hearing somewhere that DeKalb is where barbed wire was invented and first manufactured, and I wish I knew why this fact exerts a pull on me.

"I mean," Gracie adds, fighting off a smile, "if you don't win here."

"Are you thinking of it?" I ask.

"God, no! Plus you have to teach theory."

"Ah, probably not me, either," I say politely. "But thanks for letting me know."

"Yeah," she says. "Well, it's good seeing you. Good luck."

"Likewise," I say. "See you two."

The check-in table stands in the Grand Foyer of Powell Hall, which is decked out with gold fixtures and crimson carpets and shiny marble floors. Two-story cream pillars stand against a balcony and rise to a high arched ceiling with ornately painted moldings and double-decker crystal chandeliers. All the respect money can buy for music has been poured into this lobby, which is supposedly styled after Versailles.

An alarmingly attractive black-haired woman awaits in a chair behind the registration table.

"Hi, I'm Matt Grzbc?" I say, my hands clasped over my unreliable penis.

"Is that . . . ?"

"G-R-Z-B-C."

"All right," she says, checking me off. "Sorry about that. Okay, Candidate Thirty-Seven, you're at two-thirty, on the stage. You have dressing room C starting at one-thirty. Best way to get there is through the stage door. You know where that is?"

I shake my head. She directs me back outside and around the building.

As I head off, she says, "And here's the prelim repertoire. You'll want a copy of that." She laughs. "And official scores here, too," she says, gesturing to a spread at the end of the table. "And a list of things to see in St. Louis, if that interests you."

I give the repertoire sheet a quick look, but register nothing. My heart is pounding violently. It's useless to try to gather myself in front of her, so I murmur, "Thanks," pick up another sheet of paper and a packet of scores, and walk outside before I get dizzy.

What am I doing here? I think. I take a few deep breaths like a weight lifter before a clean and jerk, then hustle back across the parking lot to fetch the harp.

I roll my instrument to the stage door, where the proctor, Ty—a soft, slightly swollen man—hovers. With a finger to his lips, he leads me down a backstage corridor to a long row of guest-artist dressing rooms. I can hear someone auditioning on the stage. Sounds like Rimsky-Korsakov. Now my whole body seems to be beating as if I'm a walking heart. I sense the outlandishness of the backwash of my heart murmur. A sheet of legal paper with a "C" scribbled on it is taped to a door.

"I'll come by at two twenty-five sharp," he says.

"Thanks," I say, and I roll my instrument in. There's another huge mirror in this room, rimmed with Hollywood-dressing-room lightbulbs, above a sink and a counter in front of which is an old wooden chair with a heart-shaped back. Through the wall, I can hear someone else warming up with the Ravel. I see myself in the mirror and absently touch my cheek with ice-cold fingers. I destroyed my marriage for this fucking charade!

I finally look at the prelim sheet:

Solo of Choice	The committee will stop you.	
Tchaikovsky	*The Nutcracker: Waltz of the Flowers*	Intro. & Cadenza
Britten	*Young Person's Guide to the Orchestra*	Cadenza (Variation I)
Ravel	*Tzigane*	Cadenza ([4]-[5])
Rimsky-Korsakov	*Capriccio Espagnol*	Cadenza (4th movement)
Verdi	*La Forza del Destino Overture*	[G]-[H]; [M]

I know these pieces, I think, and I take the cover off the harp and tune. The new string is holding up. The buzz is still in abeyance. These facts calm me momentarily, and then I sit down to my solo, the Debussy "Danses." My pulse drops below 200.

Someone knocks. "Mr. Grzbc?" Ty's tone evokes the jailer-inmate relationship. He pronounces the "z," which reinforces my sense that I'm on no one's radar.

I've already put my harp on the dolly. Ty stuffs my sheaf of scores under his arm, grabs my music stand and my stool. We proceed down a poorly lit black-walled hallway to a wooden door wide enough to drive a car (or a piano) through. It's ajar and leaking whitish light. He pushes the door open, space blooms, and we're onstage, facing the towering tiers of red velvet seats. Adam's world and my world, too. They've got most of the lights on.

The judges are sitting fifth row center, behind a black, cloth-covered screen about eight feet high, which stands in the row in front of them. The screen plays right into my psyche's hands. As Ty points where to put my harp, he announces, "Candidate Thirty-Seven." I position everything, and he takes away my dolly.

My last stool adjustment makes a loud scrape on the wood floor, and I grin.

"You may begin your solo, Thirty-Seven," a female voice behind the screen announces.

I take a deep breath, then another from my toes, meditation-style, and on the exhale I imagine blowing all loathing and loathsomeness out of my body. There. I'm choosing confidence.

I play the first part of the Debussy just fine, and as soon as I pass through a well-known trouble spot, the female voice, probably Zikorsky, says, "Yes, thanks," and calls out the next piece, "The Nutcracker," which comes off nice and liquidy.

And it goes on like this.

The Verdi opera excerpt is last. After Zikorsky asks for it "as marked," which means the tempo on the official score, I flatten the page and lean the harp back. I played this for Michael at the hospice, I realize, both the first and last time I saw him. I don't tell myself to play it for him now but I sense him like he's in his bed onstage with me, right where he would be if I were in his room at Golden Prairie. The excerpt is fast and accompanies a clarinet solo. I hear the clarinet in my head, then my right hand darts into quick, flying airy eighths, while my left hand lobs bass notes that land like brief reminders of the heavy earth. I maintain the pulse through an awkward right-hand move, catching a G note that I'd put dollars to doughnuts some of my peers will edit out to keep pace. I finish rehearsal H, then pause and switch gears for rehearsal M, which minces dryly, then crescendos—I let emotion swell there—before ending short and precise.

I lean the harp forward.

"Thank you very much," the Zikorsky voice says.

As soon as I make it back to the motor lodge, I cross what I've already played off the main repertoire list and focus on the rest, trying to keep it together. I always prepare as much as I can for the next round, even before I know whether I'm moving on.

I've practiced well past dinnertime, when a call comes from Ty.

"Congratulations," he says. "Tomorrow, eleven a.m., onstage. You'll have dressing room C starting at ten."

"Thanks a lot," I say. I hang up the phone and hop up and down like a boxing kangaroo. "Fuck, yeah!" I say under my breath, working hard not to yell.

Just passing out of prelims sets my mind to fantasy and speculation. No one can laugh at me now. I'm one of ten semifinalists for St. Louis! Sure, the likes of Gracie are about to enter the fray, but I remind myself that the big competition winners are often oriented toward the solo repertoire. They sometimes don't have the best feel for orchestra teamwork, for how to fit in, which one learns quickly as the youngest of seven.

The front desk's advice on restaurants involves exploring nearby Euclid. The street's wine bars and indie bookstore and hip-looking restaurants remind me of Damen in Bucktown, where I last met Cynthia for drinks and strategy a few long weeks ago. But I try not to think about actually living here, because that makes me think of how things will be with Audrey if I win. I have to suspend all that to concentrate on the audition. I eat outside at a bistro, at a small square table against the side-

244

walk railing. A man walking by makes what seems to be extra eye contact. I toast him with a goofy smile. He smiles to himself as he walks on.

Making the semis temporarily banishes my more profound and irrational anxieties. I sleep like a brick and wake clearheaded. Dressing room C already feels familiar from the prelim round and that also calms me. My mantra is simple: *Think about music only.* It doesn't bother me to see myself in the mirror surrounded by the Hollywood bulbs.

A knock on my door. "Mr. Grzbc?" Ty asks. He sounds nicer now. He pronounces my name correctly.

This time they let me play the five pieces a little longer. This time Uchimura is behind the screen—there's no mistaking his maestro voice. He calls out tempo changes. He asks me to re-play something "more vibrantly." Once he says, "Don't forget what the horns are doing—play it again." I don't take these comments as criticisms. I tell myself they are just a test of how well he thinks he can work with me. And when I play it again with the horns better in my mind, this changes my playing just so, and I'm rewarded with a drawn-out "Thank you."

I leave the stage thinking, *Why not me?*

Ty says that after the rest of the semifinalists go, there's going to be a hiatus so the whole orchestra can use the stage to practice for a concert. I can leave my harp backstage pending the announcement of the finalists around four, but I don't want to break my spell with the instrument. I load up the harp, get a takeout sandwich, and head back to the Best Western. I cross out what I've already played from the repertoire list and look at the thirteen pieces they haven't called for yet, which include the Moncayo, *Ein Heldenleben,* and, of course, the pesky *Symphonie fantastique.* I open the curtains and take the towel off the mirror and I practice those pieces.

But in the middle of *Ein Heldenleben,* I start to pick up hints of the buzz in the sixth-octave C. It is definitely back. Maybe there was one venue change too many. I should have left the harp backstage and just relaxed!

There's a harp tech on call, but it seems presumptuous to get someone to work on my instrument when I don't know if I'm going to be in the finals—and I'm not sure I want a stranger messing with my harp right now. Then I realize this is not a confident line of thought. I don't have anyone's number at Powell, so I find the main number in the phone book. Of course, no one answers. It's the weekend. I leave a message. I could move my harp back to Powell and look for the tech, but another venue change so soon might cost me a string or make the buzz worse. With the whole orchestra getting ready to rehearse, backstage will be chaotic. After watching Carl work on the harp the last time, I bought my own set of Allen wrenches. I tighten a few things. The buzz improves slightly, but who knows how it will hold up if I change venues again to play in the finals. Stanley's words come back to me: "You can't rely on that instrument anymore."

"Shit," I say, and sweat bombs detonate from every pore.

I'm practicing work-arounds so feverishly that when the phone rings, I assume it's the harp tech.

"Mr. Grzbc," Ty says, "you're in the final round. If you have a pen, I can read you the repertoire."

I grab a Best Western pen and notepad.

"Are you there?" he asks.

"Yes," I say.

I scrawl the names of the pieces, but for each one my hand makes something like an EKG line right off the pad.

"Seven-thirty p.m. onstage," he says. "Dressing room E, starting at six-thirty."

"Can the tech meet me there fifteen minutes early? Six-fifteen? I've got a buzz."

"Oh. Certainly."

"Thank you so much, Ty."

I hang up the phone. I notice the circled "E" on the notepad. "Why E and not C?" I ask aloud. This should not be mind-deranging information, but the attack of dizziness is precipitous and I lie on the bed, the room merry-go-rounding wildly.

I try to breathe deeply but normally. It is impossible. I should practice but I can't. After setting the radio alarm for five-thirty in case I fall asleep, I lie down and try, again, to calm down. I turn my head to face an utterly blank gray matte wall. The wall is fine, and I am fine. I lie very still. Shadows lengthen. I know this even though my eyes are closed.

I arrive at six o'clock so I can tune before the tech comes, and luckily dressing room E is available. A padded pink slipcover, complete with a ruffled skirt, conceals the wooden, heart-backed chair. The mirror is the same. As I tune, I brace for the worsening of the buzz, and in fact the sixth-octave C does sound worse.

"Now, now," I say. My hand shakes as I pull the slip of Best Western stationery out of my pocket. I don't remember putting it in my pocket, so I'm very glad it's there. My handwriting is ridiculous but I can make out the six pieces: the Moncayo, *Romeo and Juliet* and *Swan Lake* from Tchaikovsky, *Ein Heldenleben*, Stravinsky's *Symphony in Three Movements*, and of course *Symphonie fantastique*.

The harp tech's arrival is still a few minutes away, so I sit down and launch into *Ein Heldenleben,* listening for the buzz, which is still there, and I have to admit getting even worse, note to note. I stay on course technically, but musically the harp is not cooperating. I come to the quick pedal changes at the start of rehearsal 33, and in the middle of ramming the C pedal all the way from flat into sharp, there's a muffled snap and a clinking within the pillar—no tension on the pedal, and six C strings go slack. I press the pedal the rest of the way into sharp position, but the disks in the neck don't move.

I spring up and open the door.

"Ty?" I call into the corridor. "Ty?"

Pat McCormick, a sparrow of a man with longish gray hair and a neat mustache, assesses my harp in five seconds. "Your C pedal rod broke," he says like a car mechanic announcing a bad fan belt.

"That's what I figured," I say.

I glance over at Ty.

"We can let you use an SLSO harp," he says. "It shouldn't be a problem at all."

"I'd really appreciate that," I say. "But what about my turn? Could I have a bit more time to warm up on it, or do I have to go on at seven-thirty?" My watch says it's already six-thirty.

Ty also looks at his watch. "Let me go ask. I don't know if I can get you anything past eight o'clock, though. You're the last finalist."

"Sure, if you can get that. I'll take anything."

"That should be fine. Pat, could you bring him the Lyon and Healy?" Then Ty strides out of the room with Pat in his wake.

I remember when I failed altogether with Cynthia on the futon couch. If I hadn't been so freaked out about that, I wouldn't have slept on the couch and I wouldn't have been late for brunch and I wouldn't have dropped my harp and my C rod wouldn't be broken right now. Someone is warming up *Ein Heldenleben* in the dressing room next door.

Then I hear the light rumble of dolly wheels coming down

the hall, and Pat stops at the door of the dressing room with a pristine Lyon & Healy covered in gold leaf from the top of the pillar to the front feet of the base.

"Matt," he says, "meet your new harp."

"Wow," I say. Then I hustle to move the injured harp into a far corner of the dressing room, which of course I should have already done.

"Should be fine," Pat says. "I regulated it on Thursday."

Ty pokes his head in. "Eight p.m. onstage, Mr. Grzbc. I'll see you at seven fifty-five. Good luck."

He leaves and raps smartly on the door to dressing room D. "Gracie," he says, "they're ready for you."

Gracie's door opens, and I hear her say, "And I'm ready for them."

"Good luck," Pat says. He slips out and pulls the door closed, and then I'm alone with one beautiful, seemingly flawless instrument.

I start to tune it. It's a little less tense than mine, which soon enough feels comfortable. But the string spacings are a tad closer in the upper octaves, which is probably fine for Tatiana's feminine hands, but not so good for mine. I finish tuning and go right at *SF*, in which the string spacing is going to matter most. I make two audition-killing mistakes in the contrary-motion sequence because my right-hand timing in the second octave is just a hair off. I start over and make a different pair of mistakes.

I pop out of my chair and start pacing the room. "Shit, shit, shit," I say. My heart rate is accelerating. I sit down again, but I pop right back up. My head sways as if it's on a spring. The voice from the meditation CD returns clearly in my head: *It's important to remember not to try too hard to relax; this will just create tension.* Gottfried Barker, back in Seattle, wants *joy*, Adam tells me to choose confidence, and Dr. Oliver tells me to *do* something. I swing over to the sink and splash cool water on my face, over and over. I'm afraid that when I stop and raise my eyes to the mirror, I'll see the world spin.

But at a certain point in the splashing, I wonder if I'm trying to drown myself, and I turn off the water. Without drying my face, I sit in the padded pink chair and rest my head on the counter.

"It's going nowhere," Claire Houghton said about her playing that day in the music room when I finally let her go. She eventually broke up with that handsome boyfriend. Married someone else I never met. Had two kids. Invents breakfast foods for General Mills. I don't think she plays much anymore.

Water slides down my face. I need to warm up on this instrument. I need to practice, but I can't sit at this harp. The padded pink chair smells like a mix of perfumes. I think I detect a scent Milena used to wear.

You need to practice, I tell myself. But I can't do that, either. I can't run toward the pain. I can't practice—this is suddenly crashingly obvious.

What I really want is just to *hear* some music, to listen to it for pleasure. That would be perfect right now. What you do for your audience you do for yourself—isn't that what Marcia said?

I stand and finally dry my face and hands. I sit down to the golden Lyon & Healy—just to play. Eddie always said that when a good musician plays you don't hear the musician, you hear music. I have to let my fingers—and all of myself—*play.*

And this new harp sounds great: better than the rattletrap I've been saddled with all these years. I've been sentimental and stubborn. Just like my father when he refused to trade in the old white Pontiac station wagon he had fixed so many times. Bart and George had to sneak it to the junkyard without him knowing.

I do nothing but play for over an hour, and when Ty comes back, he asks, "Are you ready?"

"Yes," I say. "I think so."

. . .

The screen is gone. And even though it was tiny relative to this concert hall, its absence markedly opens up the room. Fifth row center, Uchimura, Zikorsky, and four other SLSO members I don't recognize are eyeballing me. They know about having to switch instruments, which protects me somewhat. I bow to them and sit down to my new harp.

"Let's hear *Romeo and Juliet,* please," Uchimura says.

This is the easiest piece, technically. That I blew it in San Diego shouldn't matter. No doubt they want to hear the right emotion. There's little chance my fingers will trip up in the tight upper octaves. I play it as well as I can play it, and it sounds fantastic on this harp.

"*Symphonie fantastique,*" Uchimura says simply. There are no thank-yous or corrections or instructions. They, too, apparently just want to hear music.

I open the score, smooth the page though it doesn't need smoothing, lean the harp back, and start rehearsal 20 strong. My tone and articulation are crisp. I dampen the strings on the second beat at Rehearsal 22, observe a few measures of rest, and begin the first arpeggios with contrary motion. They go fine in the right hand while my left hand keeps the pulse with quarter-note chords. I reconfigure my right hand to grab a four-pack of ostinatos, during which I shift the E and B pedals from natural to sharp and back, then I start the second batch of contrary-motion arpeggios, higher in the scale. My right hand dances like a crazed spider—up, doubling back, then higher—until I have to jump five strings to the second-octave C. My thumb doesn't perfectly catch the string. I buzz that note badly, a godawful mistake.

There's no time to be a worm, or to panic. A professional would blow right on by a small mistake and play as if nothing has happened, but a confident performer in an audition where the judges know he's had to switch harps an hour and a half ago, where they can see he's a man playing on a harp built for a woman, where the mistake is not trivial—that's something else. I don't think any of this, not in the moment. I just stop and say in a level voice, "I'd like permission to do it again from the top."

Uchimura looks to either side of him. Several of the other judges nod.

"All right," Uchimura says.

I rebegin *Symphonie fantastique*.

25

THE FOUR OTHER finalists float among the wings or head for the lounge downstairs. Ty lets me hang out in dressing room E. I try not to think of how I played. I know that my impression of myself can be extremely unreliable during these waiting periods. The second time I played *Symphonie fantastique,* it felt perfect, and I can't remember any mistakes in the subsequent pieces. I lie on the thin carpet of the dressing room, letting the sweat under my armpits dry. My broken Aphrodite is mute in the corner. Time doesn't exist as it normally does, but it hasn't accelerated or slowed down. There's just the ringing pulse of an intense *now.*

A knock comes at the door. Ty pushes it open and waits until I get to my feet.

"Congratulations, Mr. Grzbc," Ty says, smiling a little crazily. "You're the new principal harpist of the St. Louis Symphony Orchestra."

He extends his hand. I shake his hand. My chest swells big enough to lift me off the floor like a hot-air balloon.

"Ha, ha, ha, ha, ha," I say.

I cup my hands over my eyes and look down. "I can't believe this," I say. "Oh, oh, I can't believe this." My own words rise into my face like an echo from a well. The realization blooms and blooms and blooms: *I won, I won, I won!*

"Maestro Uchimura would like to congratulate you," Ty says. "Please follow me."

I trail Ty through dark backstage halls, out a door, up a stairwell, down a marble corridor with a red carpet running down the center of it, right turn down another marble corridor. Along the way, I take ownership of every painting on the walls, every potted plant, every chandelier. *This is my place,* I think, *this is where I work.* And I'll be a full-time member of an ensemble again, something I haven't enjoyed since I used up my eligibility to play in the Civic Orchestra twelve years ago. There will be people I'll see regularly, whom I'll have something in common with. From such a position of normal stability and professional accomplishment, I might relax into an un-lonely, un-desperate life, with health insurance. Ty is striding quickly. Then he breaks to the side, almost sliding to a stop. Uchimura steps out of an open office door.

He beams at me, his eyebrows high and flaring, hand extended. "There's the old pro," he says. "Congratulations."

Uchimura takes Tatiana, Ty, and me out to dinner to celebrate. I'm able to convince myself that the audition is over and nothing I can say or do now will make them take back their offer. There's the formal contract to settle but that's not on tonight's agenda. When they start asking questions and giving advice about moving to St. Louis, I give brief answers and steer the conversation elsewhere. It only takes me a single question to Uchimura about the fall season to get him rolling on a track that doesn't end up passing near me. Tatiana tells us about a trip to India she's going to take by herself. Ty recounts the drama of my harp breaking, and as Tatiana and Uchimura listen, I see confirmed in their eyes that whatever they heard before the finals worked in my favor.

Back at the Best Western, I empty my pockets on the nightstand and sit down on the bed. I find the crumpled bit of motel stationery on which I wrote the repertoire for the finals, unfold it, and stare. The handwriting is so wild I can't decipher it now, even though I'll never forget what I played. I'm amazed I could read it when it mattered.

I check out and hit the road on Sunday morning, bound for Chicago. It's sunny and already hot and humid at ten in the morning as I merge onto Interstate 64 and float toward downtown St. Louis. My harp, its broken rod lying inside of it, sleeps in the back of the Volvo. I don't play my audition tape. I don't even listen to the radio. I put down all the windows and wind whips through the car, and I drive to that wild, air-tearing sound.

Yes, I've won, and this astounding fact is still gathering power. After calling my mother, and beating back the sadness that there was no one else critical to call, I lay awake last night remembering moments from the last twenty-five years: moments of hope, like when I made the Civic; moments in the drafty Rogers Park apartment when I soldiered on, sometimes just a few steps ahead of despair, sometimes overtaken by it; moments of crushing disappointment, like Seattle and San Diego. All harp moments, bad or good, are now vindicated. Divine providence, which I gave up on in my faithless mind, is suddenly looking plausible again. *This was all meant to be.*

Yet, even in the midst of this, a new and difficult thought has been fighting its way to the surface, and now, as southern Illinois scrolls by, it finally takes over my mind completely: *What about Audrey?*

Words from Ms. Grier's report come back to me: *He puts his own desires ahead of his daughter's emotional well-being. Serious demonstrable harm.*

I have listened to her report, and I have also fought against some of it. What will Dr. Oliver think about my commitment to Audrey's therapy, to giving her the support she needs, if I just skip town?

A street of motels and gas stations and fast-food joints materializes in the fields. Collinsville, Illinois. Before the audition, to suppress my Audrey guilt, I'd identified this as a plausible place to live if I won in St. Louis. About forty-five minutes to Powell Hall, at least in Saturday traffic. Roughly four and a half hours to Milena's tri-level bungalow on the Northwest Side. I can time that right now, since I need to pick up Audrey and replace the day I missed yesterday. Then I imagine her voice at the front door: *Daddy, what did you get me?*

I haven't gotten her anything. I've completely forgotten my promise.

I get off at the next exit. If I'm lucky, this Shell Mini-Mart will have something with a riverboat or a St. Louis Arch on it.

I pump thirty dollars of gas, then, inside, ask the guy behind the register, "Do you have any St. Louis souvenir stuff?"

He points across the counter to a tower of colored plastic lighters with the St. Louis Arch emblazoned on them.

"Is that it?" I ask. "Just the lighters?"

"That's it," he says.

And it serves me right, trying to take the easy way out. I'm almost glad that I need to go all the way back to St. Louis. I must prove that I'm capable of extravagant effort.

I get back in the Volvo and head south on I-55. One thing that makes the stupefying tedium of going backwards endurable is the knowledge that I have won, I have won, I have won. What isn't doable, what isn't endurable, for Audrey, for all of my loved ones, now that I've actually won? I'll live in Collinsville, keep my apartment at T.R.'s, and change my two days with Audrey into back-to-back days to make everything more workable.

Soon I see the Arch again, and then I'm cruising back over the Mississippi. I barely know the city, but I remember the sheet I got from the woman at the check-in table before the prelim round and the list of local attractions, including a zoo in Forest Park, not far from the motel. Cynthia and Audrey and I were going to go to the zoo. Zoo gift shops always sell stuffed animals. I imagine a bear wearing a "Meet Me in St. Louis" T-shirt.

I get off at Kingshighway and take a left on Lindell, then make the first turn I see into the park. It seems to be huge, and there are no signs on this curving road, which is flanked by open fields of grass and stands of trees and man-made ponds complete with ducks. Running on a bike path alongside the road is a woman, her black ponytail bouncing, wearing what Milena called a "jog bra." I could pull up beside her to ask for directions to the zoo, but this would probably creep her out. I find a sweaty old guy hitting golf balls on an open expanse of grass, and he points the way.

In the gift shop, most of the stuffed animals are zoo creatures—tigers and dolphins and elephants. None of these animals have St. Louis markings, but now it's clear to me that I'm the only one who would care about that.

I glance at my watch. I'm probably going to be late. The old impulse to make every effort to be on time with Milena, out of respect, is still there, but I see it from a distance now, like the distance from St. Louis to Chicago. It occurs to me that my commuting idea is somewhat delusional. On a low shelf stands a bright-eyed black-and-white husky. It's big. It's perfect. Audrey loves dogs.

Then I worry that her desire for a real dog may give this gift an edge of cruelty. I pick up a large dolphin. I pick up a husky. I hold them both. I am a dad who does what he can, who comes as close as he can—that's what the dog would say, that's what living in Collinsville would say. The stuffed dog would torture her. I put the dog down and step toward the counter with the dolphin. Maybe she has no interest in dolphins. Maybe this dolphin will come to represent to both of us everything I don't understand about her. I look back at the dog.

"Finding everything?" a chirpy, shelf-straightening clerk asks me.

"Yes, thanks," I say. I carry the dolphin to the register.

Then I'm cruising out of the park, back the way I came, back onto Kingshighway, back toward downtown St. Louis, and I fling myself over the Mississippi once again, going eighty-five, heading north. I sink into alternative realities: I hold on with Cynthia until after I've won the audition, and since I no longer look like such a loser to her, she gladly moves to St. Louis with me, escaping Whitaker in the process. We have the new start we always wanted. I don't freak in San Diego. I don't grind too hard in Seattle. I win *then,* and have everything. Safely in an orchestra, I pay more attention to Milena, to our children— yes, we have more than one. I have everything without choosing.

But eventually I remember Adam talking about how if you've got problems in your life, you'll still have them after you've had your moment onstage. Do I want to choose career success over my child? Has anybody who wasn't an asshole *ever* felt good about that choice?

I can try to keep two custody days a week in Chicago, but I know that distance and other practicalities will pressure those days, and eventually I'll drop them, I bet I will, holding on to them just long enough to cover a retreat back into my deep well of self-interest. And even if I keep my days, I won't be around for all the things that come up on non-custody days—the last night of swimming lessons or school events or taking her to the doctor when Steve and Milena are at work. I will fall further out of her life, no matter how hard I try to hold on. Can I knowingly be the selfish bastard who would let that happen? I've convinced myself that a lot of the world's problems happen after personal meltdowns, but doesn't unusual success also tempt the worst?

Then a surprising, multifaceted, hard-edged fact crystallizes: I've won, but I don't have to take the job. I don't have to leave a daughter who, after all, might have attempted suicide, just so I can play in an orchestra. Exactly why have I made playing in an orchestra the most important thing in my life? I've proven that my pursuit of the harp was not a huge folly. I'm a good player. Why not try for the gig at NIU and prove to Milena once and for all that I am a family man who is there for his daughter and also has a job like any other man?

The appeal of self-sacrifice is also there—so close and accessible and fundamentally effortless and yet wildly gratifying. Make doing nothing a virtue, make erasure feel like art. I can't believe in my mother's God, but maybe I can pay forward what she and my father did for me and for my many siblings and for all those bearers of broken appliances. I can live more for others and be better *and* happier. Escape from my wretched, inwardly twisted, insatiable self once and for all. The weightlessness of that. The freaking joy!

Bottom line: Can I bear to tell Audrey that I'm leaving town after I just told her in the hospital how much I need to know what's going on with her?

I get lunch at a Wendy's drive-thru in Normal, though I'm too excited to eat much. There's a danger that I will feel bitter down the road, of course. But wouldn't the pain of Audrey growing up troubled be worse? And, really, I can *still* have everything: the knowledge that I am good enough to win an audition; a crack at a good, stable job at NIU (though I would have to learn how to teach music theory or at least persuade them that I could—no small matter); a chance with Marcia, the soulful and intriguing hospice director, who might know a thing or two about renunciation herself; and, the kicker, time with Audrey as she stabilizes and grows up happier.

And so for the second time in eighteen hours, I am utterly astounded: I have won and I'm going to give back the prize.

I-55 finally meets up with I-94, my mother road, which I take north through just about the whole damn city of Chicago, all the way to Lawrence and the tri-level bungalow, only twenty minutes late. That no cop has dared to pull me over just affirms the righteousness of my reasoning and my resolve. I don't have the car seat, so we'll have to take our chances with Audrey riding without it.

I park on the street, and before I can get out of the Volvo, a dog comes around the side of the house and into the small front yard, chased by Audrey. It looks like a chocolate lab puppy. It gets ahead of her and then turns back and lets Audrey frisk with it and then it runs off again and comes back to her.

Steve comes around the corner, and he plays with the dog, too. He's in a Hawaiian shirt, cargo shorts, and bare feet. He notices me, but some form of politeness—or, who knows, disdain—keeps him from waving.

Audrey, too, must be aware of my car—just by the determined way she avoids looking at it even when the puppy's movements put me in her line of sight—but she is not coming to me. I know this doesn't mean as much as it looks like it means. She just doesn't want her intense puppy pleasure interrupted.

I toss the stuffed dolphin near the harp in the backseat, suddenly unsure of when to give it to her. I get out of the car. I walk across the sidewalk, put my foot on the first cement step, and rise toward their house.

I won. And there is no way not to have a profound source of unhappiness in my life because of this amazing fact.

Audrey finally turns toward me.

"We got a dog!" she cries.

She is so happy. Milena and Steve have done a brilliant pure good thing for her. They might have told me, but I'm not in their family. It's exactly what Audrey needs right now.

Yet the "we" feels bad. I wish she had at least said, "Daddy, we got a dog," as if I were somehow included.

I am up the steps and I stop there, right on the little section of walk before the last few steps to the front door. With each of the dog's excited movements and every degree of Audrey's delight, my grip on renunciation loosens.

"That's great," I say. "What's the dog's name?"

"Ralph!"

"Hey, Ralph," I say. At the sound of his name, Ralph comes over to sniff me. He puts paws on my jean legs. I am not comfortable with dogs, but I bend down to pet Ralph before he bounds away.

"Hey, how did it go?" Steve asks, hands on hips, friendly, confident.

Milena comes out the front door. She sweeps her hair back over her head, clearing it from her eyes for a second. She is in another short T-shirt and yoga pants. I can't look at her—she can't help herself.

"Steve's idea," she says, referring to the dog. The breadwinner strikes again. "So how'd it go?" she adds, smiling like the happy person she wants to be. She watches me closely.

"Well, I actually won," I say evenly, looking straight into her misaligned eyes. She has to know I won, even if I give it all up.

She delicately parts her bangs with her middle finger.

"You did?" she asks with a peculiar mix of skepticism, dismay, and even some abortive mockery.

"What's wrong with you two?" Steve exclaims. "That's fantastic! Congratulations, Matt!"

It's his hand reaching to shake mine that finally breaks the look between Milena and me.

26

~~~

"So, I SEE you're letting your hair grow out," I say. I've been noticing this for weeks and can't resist saying something about it today.

"I'm not going to be a tomboy anymore," Audrey says. "Just a regular girl."

"Not *just*," I say. But she doesn't seem to hear this. She's going to turn seven in a few weeks.

She holds the waning crescent of her burger upright in one hand and looks across the way to the penguin tank, where there are families at the railing. The long-awaited trip to the Lincoln Park Zoo is finally happening, but of course Cynthia isn't with us. More families surround us, sitting at white plastic tables or strolling by in loose formations. The wind gusts, and with her free hand Audrey claws at the hair blown across her face, drawing it clear of her cheek, her eye.

"And now you've got the rest of the summer to practice for second grade," I add. "That's going to be intense."

"I don't have to practice for second grade, Dad!" She laughs.

"Am I the only one who did? I have to practice for everything, it seems like."

There are more divorced-dad questions I could ask. *How's Ralph? Have you picked out your flower girl dress?* I could fish for revelations about how things are between Milena and Steve, though I wouldn't be as tempted to do that if this were just another custody day.

Instead, I run right at the pain: "T.R.'s going to let us stay up in the top of his house when I come back. It's kind of like an indoor tree house, except there's a bathroom up there and a new wall, so you can have a room and I can have a room."

T.R. is letting us crash there for a ridiculously low rent on my days back in Chicago, probably until some needier case comes along. For now, I still qualify as a wayward boy. My inquiries at NIU were inconclusive: the ability to teach theory is not primary but it matters somewhat; they encouraged me to apply. I would be auditioning all over again and for something I had never thought to want before. I have accepted the position in St. Louis.

Audrey dips her fries in her ketchup, but she is looking toward the penguin tank.

"How does that sound?" I ask.

"Like a sleepover," she says, chewing.

"Yeah, I guess. I guess it is kind of weird, having a sleepover at your dad's."

She shrugs. "That's what we used to do anyways."

"Sure, we did. Listen, Audrey, I love you so much, as much as I can love, my most love—" I stop, gather myself. "Okay, I know that, especially with everything that's happened, me going to St. Louis might feel bad, like I'm running away or something."

"Mama said it was very important to you."

I look down at my own half-eaten and cold burger. I've been back and forth to St. Louis and my Collinsville apartment half a dozen times since the audition, and even without missing any custody days I already feel the effects of living on different streets, under a different sky. I've hung one of my father's computer chip paintings on the wall in my new living room, in view of my harps but not next to them. Tomorrow I move for good.

"It is," I say, "and you're super important to me, and we're going to try to make this work, and see how it goes, all right? We'll be together almost as regularly as we used to, and maybe even more, sometimes, when my job in St. Louis is off-season. And you can come down there and stay with me for longer when you don't have school."

I don't tell her that I've got my eye on Chicagoland academic jobs at Roosevelt and Northwestern, where the harpists could retire within five years and theory seems not to be an issue. I don't want to mess with her hopes. Dr. Oliver has assured me that Audrey is catching on, doing better, but sometimes assurance still passes through me like a sieve.

"And I'll record songs for you," I add, "and send you CDs. Any songs you want. Like 'The Muppet Show Theme.' Or the Powerpuff Girls song."

"You can play that on your harp?"

"I can play anything, sweetie."

She considers this. "That's a good idea," she says.

I watch her as fully as I can, with the sort of intense look that freaked out Cynthia.

Audrey doesn't seem to notice. Her chest rises and falls—it seems she is about to hiccup. She swallows. Her eyes are dry. She looks at me. "I'll miss you," she says.

"And I'll miss you when I'm not with you, but I'll always be seeing you. I'll always be on my way to seeing you at some time coming up. All the time."

She keeps looking at my face.

"Okay?" I ask.

She nods and pushes away what's left of her food.

The pain in my chest feels like a piece of shrapnel too delicately placed to be removed yet not fatal if it stays where it is.

We stand up, and I remember that old urge to fold Audrey into my body, like a violin into its case, to take her with me, to protect her. Instead, I rest my hand on my daughter's head. She reaches up and pats my hand, alternating with each of her hands—pat, pat—and when she looks up to see my reaction, she's smiling. I smile, too.

I carry our tray to a trash barrel and slide everything through the orange door. I stack our tray on the other trays. Then we head for the penguin tank, to take our place along the railing.

Acknowledgments

~~~

A SPECIAL THANK-YOU TO my parents, Alfred and Elaine, for their constant love and support and also for the specific ways in which they enabled this book. My mother, a longtime nurse and hospice volunteer, sent me the image that inspired the novel: a newspaper clipping showing a harpist playing at a dying person's bedside. My father, an avid reader and book collector, gave me a library to learn from and an encouraging appreciation of the value of writing.

This novel grew up under the wise tutelage of Bonnie Jo Campbell, Lisa Lenzo, Mark Wisniewski, and Glenn Deutsch. This book also benefited from the feedback of Mike Stefaniak, Deborah Gang, Bruce Mills, Susanna Campbell, Josie Kearns, Sejal Sutaria, John Fraser, and Anne Marie Fadorsen. Representing my siblings, all of whom make me happy to be alive, two of my sisters, Elizabeth Senn and Catherine Bobbe, gave the book careful and useful readings. In Chicago, James Schatz, Michael Gillis, Barry Hamill, Mary Davidson Stanton, Stuart

Ross, and publicist extraordinaire Sheryl Johnston helped and inspired. Endless gratitude to all of you.

A number of harpists, harp makers and technicians, and orchestra people generously shared their experiences and expertise with me. Many thanks to David Ice, Lynn Williams, Barb Semmann, Saul Davis, A. W., Elizabeth Volpe-Bligh, Walt Krasicki, Pat Dougal, and Rip Prétat. Sarah Bullen's *Principal Harp: A Guidebook for the Orchestral Harpist* was a very valuable resource.

On the medical front, I'm grateful to my sister-in-law Amy Mozina, RN; my sister Margaret Hein, RN; Laura Latiolais, director of development at the Rose Arbor Hospice in Kalamazoo; Theresa Lynn, executive director, and Char Mohr, volunteer coordinator, at Wings of Hope Hospice in Allegan, MI. The CD quoted in chapter two is *Guided Mindfulness Meditation* by Jon Kabat-Zinn.

Thank you, Ryan Harbage and Christopher Hermelin, for your faith, sage advice, and miracle-working. Thank you, Laura Van der Veer, for understanding just what to question and for always making the book better.

Institutional-sized thanks to Kalamazoo College for generous sabbatical support and to Writers in the Heartland for the residency during which this book found its final form.

Finally, I want to thank my wife and favorite harpist of all, Lorraine Alberts, and our daughter, Madeleine. Much love, guys! See you around the house!

About the Author

~~~

ANDY MOZINA's first story collection, *The Women Were Leaving the Men,* won the Great Lakes Colleges Association New Writers Award. His second collection, *Quality Snacks,* was a finalist for the Flannery O'Connor Prize and other awards. Mozina's fiction has appeared in *Tin House, The Southern Review, The Missouri Review,* Small Chair (McSweeney's), and elsewhere. His work has received special citations in *Best American Short Stories, Pushcart Prize,* and *New Stories from the Midwest.* He is a professor of English at Kalamazoo College and lives in Kalamazoo with his wife, Lorri, and his daughter, Madeleine.

About the Type

‹‹‹

This book was set in Sabon, a typeface designed by the
well-known German typographer Jan Tschichold (1902–74).
Sabon's design is based upon the original letterforms of
sixteenth-century French type designer Claude Garamond and
was created specifically to be used for three sources: foundry
type for hand composition, Linotype, and Monotype.
Tschichold named his typeface for the famous Frankfurt
typefounder Jacques Sabon (c. 1520–80).